Animal

Barbara Meyers

Contents

Prologue

E merald Akira MacCallum woke early, Colin Lancaster's parting words still ringing in her head.

Twenty years ago, at the age of sixteen, she'd allowed Colin to seduce her. She'd only learned of his engagement and subsequent marriage into a refined, wealthy family well after the fact.

He'd continued to visit her in her Granny's shack, at the end of a long, twisted mud track in this secluded area of the Appalachians, fueling her belief that one day he'd realize she and only she was his true love.

He continued to charm her with each visit, showering her with trinkets, proving his devotion by taking her to bed each time, leaving her sated and sore.

She glimpsed his wife, Wynda, from time to time on her rare visits to the village. A pale wisp of a woman, hardly a match for a man like her hale and hearty Colin. Despite her youth, Emerald had become the most revered granny woman in the area, for her healing powers and potions, as well as her skill in midwifery. If Wynda was aware of his liaison with Emerald, she gave no indication. Emerald held her head high, in any case, not one to be cowed by such a weak rival.

Colin even had the nerve to call on her, begging her to aid his wife in the throes of birthing their fourth child. Emerald at first demurred, but eventually gave in to his pleas to save his unborn child. As much as she hated Wynda, Emerald found it impossible to deny Colin anything.

She arrived to find the babe turned the wrong way, Wynda exhausted and weak from hours of unproductive labor, the unborn child in distress. She issued orders to be carried out by a stream of nervous servants. Colin kept out of the way, watching from the corner, wringing his hands while she worked to save the child.

An hour later, his son's outraged cries rang out at the same moment Wynda drew her last breath. Emerald wrapped the babe and handed it to Colin, who cradled it close. Tears ran from his eyes as he gazed at the still form of his wife. Her parents, his parents, and his children soon crowded the room, pushing Emerald aside.

She left them to grieve, knowing Colin would not stay away from her for long.

He came to her two weeks later and continued to warm her bed for the year-long mourning period. She waited patiently for his proposal of marriage.

But instead, what he said to her yesterday was, "I'm leaving." He planned to move south to North Carolina, to marry the daughter of a tobacco plantation owner. A woman already pregnant with his child. Colin would help run the family business.

Emerald became very still. And her voice, when it came, was not her own.

"Damn you, Colin, I will make you pay in ways you never imagined for what you've done. I will curse you and all the males in your line for the animals you are and the ways you make women suffer. Each of you, in animal form, will witness the pain you inflict, and take it on as your own. You will all suffer as you make the women you touch suffer. Your sons and their sons will find love, but never joy. Once found, it will be snatched away. All of you will know only pain."

"My dear Em," Colin said, patronizing her for the last time. "I have so enjoyed our time together." He ran the tip of his finger under her chin and bent to kiss her frozen lips.

It was only after he left that she remembered the news she had not shared. Despite all the precautions she'd taken, she was with child. His child.

She'd honed her healing skills at the knee of her mother and her grandmother, revered granny women both. Emerald took her place in line, generously helping the mountain people with their injuries, illnesses, births, and deaths. Studying the local herbs, learning of their healing qualities.

But her treatment at Colin's hand led her to the darker side of her study. To make tinctures and potions created in ill will. To cause harm. The casting of spells and curses. She'd experimented, harmlessly, or so she'd thought. Until Wynda drew her last breath and Emerald learned the truth of the power she now possessed.

Emerald's grandmother had fiercely guarded many of the old texts, handed down from generations of her ancestors long before any had settled in these mountains. She'd forbidden her granddaughter access to these ancient writings, which were difficult to decipher in the old language. But Emerald had persisted in secret, shielding her growing knowledge from the perceptive eyes of her mother and grandmother. Until they were gone, and she no longer needed to hide.

Now up and dressed, she moved with deliberate purpose, gathering the things she needed, referring to the handwritten texts, silently rehearsing the incantations she'd use tonight when the moon was dark, and all was prepared.

Emerald chopped wood and laid it for a fire beneath the black cauldron behind the shack. She spent time in the woods replenishing her supply of jimsonweed and horsenettle, elderberry, comfrey, and holy basil. She'd learned that many of the plants used for healing, in the right combinations with the poisonous ones, could create devastating, deadly effects. With the correct proportions, and certain... additives, along with the exacting incantations, what Emerald had in mind for those males with Colin's lineage would be payment enough for his betrayal. They would know suffering far greater than hers. And they would be filled with regret and self-loathing during their lives, as well as at the moment of their deaths.

Next to the leaves, seeds, stems, and flowers she'd gathered, Emerald set a small, sealed jar. In it were strips of cloth she'd taken from Colin's clothes, hair he'd left on her pillow or in her bed, his seed, which she'd wiped away as it spilled out of her while he snored in contentment.

She needed to choose one more item, and the preparations would be complete.

Even the date tonight suited The Curse of Threes.

March 3, 1913.

As darkness fell, the time became right, the fire burned bright. The dark side of the moon showed no light.

She added the bits and pieces she'd collected for the brew. The words she'd memorized fell easily from her lips, murmurings in a language no one else would understand. The cold wind blew down the mountain upon her back as a wisp of smoke rose from the cauldron, twisting and turning gray in the blackness of the night, winding its way down the mountain trail toward the village.

Her voice grew louder as she called to the ancients, to the powers that came long before her, to aid her now. To grant her justice. Her words grew in strength as she felt her own strength grow, the life inside her feeding from it, growing strong and invincible.

She continued to stir until she became assured of vengeance and the contents of the pot were no more. The last of the smoke trailed away down the mountain, and only glowing embers remained of the fire. She ground the carved end of her thick casting stick into the object obscured by the ashes at the bottom of the pot, creating the mark, sealing the curse.

Emerald lifted her hands high and howled at the invisible moon.

Chapter One

The cloud cover that blocked the stars and the lack of a moon didn't concern Bree when she approached an especially dark stretch of the road. The forest seemed to press in closer, the already narrow shoulder even narrower here, but the flashlight cast an illuminated circular beam that bounced ahead as she ran.

She was more than a mile out of her own well-lit neighborhood, but this dead-end mountain lane saw little traffic, had few curves, and a manageable incline.

Something about this route gave her the feeling of being alone on the planet. Vehicles were nearly non-existent here, and only occasionally did she get a glimpse of a woodland creature or hear the rustle of one as it escaped her light.

Foolhardy on her part, perhaps, but she felt safe running along here alone at night. Still, instead of earbuds she used her phone's speaker to listen to her playlist so she could stay aware of her surroundings. Jenna would never forgive her if she didn't.

Bree sensed the rush of an approach from behind before she heard anything. The air changed, as if charged with an alien energy. She turned her head a split second before something knocked her to the ground. In that moment, she saw the shimmer of black fur and light reflected from a pair of amber eyes.

Her shoulder broke her fall as she skidded along the rough asphalt but didn't prevent her head from hitting the pavement. The flashlight died when it smacked the road. Next came the unmistakable crunch of glass and plastic, her armband providing little protection for her phone. But the music continued to play.

Her cry of surprised alarm mingled with her grunt of pain. Her attacker crouched on her chest, smelling of musk and growling near her ear. Its foul breath clouded the air and its teeth snapped with each snarl. She winced as the thing's sharp nails raked through her clothes and dug into her skin.

Even if she wasn't pinned down, her strength couldn't match this beast's. She tried to fight, but each time she wiggled an arm free the animal swatted at her, its claws ripping through her sleeves to her skin. Its weight immobilized her legs, hind claws piercing through her pants. A scream escaped her as a panicked whimper. No way could she reach the small can of pepper spray zipped into her pocket.

As she continued to struggle, her fingers brushed against fur, soft on the surface, but denser and coarser underneath. The points of the thing's sharp teeth grazed her but didn't sink into her flesh.

The flashlight still dangled by its wrist strap. She wrapped her fingers around the housing, managed to free her arm and brace it against the ground so she could direct all her energy into an upward thrust. She hit the beast as hard as she could with it.

The animal tilted sideways with a surprised grunt before it retreated to pace close by. She didn't know what it was. A mountain lion? Surely not a wolf or a bear. Something more...cat-like, she thought. She scrambled up and staggered as she tried to orient herself in case it knocked her down again. She righted the flashlight with shaking fingers and clicked the button, hoping by some miracle it might work. Nothing happened.

The armband had come off, and her phone lay face down on the pavement. She could see the glow from the screen and hear muted lyrics about the world floating to the dark side of the moon.

Bree thought the animal sighed, either in disappointment or resignation, before its footsteps rustled through the fallen leaves and the forest swallowed its retreat. She bent and picked up the phone, paused the playlist, and hoped like hell the flashlight app still worked. But strangely the world began to spin right before she crumpled to the ground.

Chapter Two

The animal lay in a bed of fallen leaves hidden by the dense brush, panting through indescribable pain. Its eyes squeezed shut in the erroneous belief that if it couldn't see what was happening, it wouldn't hurt as much. Its claws retracted to be replaced by fingers. Fur receded. Joints and ligaments, skin, hair, limbs, and fingernails, all transformed. Did it take hours or minutes? Time got lost during every transition.

That the hunt was over, this time, was slight consolation. Two more times it would happen this year. And then? *Never again.*

Finally, the transformation finished. Back in human form, he marveled at the effect of the dark magic, how he could be a predatory animal one moment and a man the next with no one the wiser. The miracle of returning to human form dressed as he had been before always came as a shock. Although occasionally a glitch in the system meant his boxers were on backward or his shoes on the wrong feet.

He lay there for several minutes while his mind and body settled, though the leaves didn't provide much of a cushion between him and the cold ground. Eventually, he rose, got his bearings, and made his way to his truck for a flashlight before he returned to the scene of the attack.

She should be gone by now. Whatever injuries he inflicted were never life-threatening. Like all of his prey, she could limp back to wherever she came from. Battered and a bit bloody, but ambulatory.

Much to his disappointment, she hadn't left. She startled at the flash of his light and froze like a deer in a hunting rifle's scope. He kept the light aimed low and strove for a somewhat friendly tone. "Do you need some help?"

"What are you doing out here?" He heard the tremble of fear in her voice.

"Checking my mail."

"Mail?"

He shone his light on the box, nearly hidden by an overgrown shrub to prove his point, glad he had a legitimate excuse.

"I didn't think anyone lived out here."

"Just me." He opened the box and stuffed the few pieces of mail in his pocket before he turned back to her. "Are you okay? What are you doing out here in the dark?"

"I—something attacked me."

"Attacked you?"

"Yes. I have a flashlight, but it broke. My phone..." She gestured to the ground near her feet. "I think I passed out. It should be here somewhere."

"Need me to find it for you?" he asked.

"Thank you." Her voice wobbled again. He approached in as non-threatening a manner as he could and kept the beam of light pointed down. "There's your phone." He shone it on the shattered case, and she bent to pick it up before he could.

"Whoa." It wasn't just her voice that wobbled this time. He put a hand out to steady her. Lightning flashed, illuminating them both for a second. A gust of wind chilled the already cool spring air.

"Come inside for a minute. Let me help you." He offered his hand, but she hesitated. Then she straightened as if her resolve had returned.

When she touched his hand, something sizzled under his skin the same way it had earlier, warning him of danger. Telling him she could wreck all his careful plans. She could destroy him. Destroy his legacy.

He couldn't let that happen. He *wouldn't* let it happen.

Once inside, he led her to the oversized sofa.

Now what?

He ran his hands through his hair, wincing as he touched the tender spot on the side of his head, and looked her over.

Sections of her shirt were shredded. There were long, bloody scratches on her torso, arms, and thighs, some deeper than others. She'd be bruised, too, there was no way around that. Given the weight on top of her while she struggled to fight the animal off? Bruises were inevitable.

Aside from the bump on his head she'd given him, his body mirrored the same damage as hers. He'd be uncomfortable for a few days, but he'd grown used to it by now.

What was more disturbing was that he recognized her. He'd encountered her briefly at Sanctuary a few weeks ago, though he hadn't spoken to or touched her. But still he remembered this visceral pull of attraction.

He never hunted this close to home. This random, unplanned attack was a mistake he already knew would come back to haunt him in ways he couldn't imagine. But only if he allowed it.

Absently, he explored the swelling above his ear. He hadn't expected her to fight back but found himself grudgingly proud of her desperate and ineffective effort.

But what really got to him was the music coming from her phone. *The world floating to the dark side of the moon.* It was like she *knew.* Like the universe had conspired to throw her into his path. Like it knew he hadn't prepared for tonight the way he usually did.

Fate had conspired against him—a meeting ran late, a jack-knifed semi blocked the state road—to keep him from his carefully selected hunting ground twenty miles west of here. The third new moon since his last transformation. He knew what would happen. It'd been happening since puberty. Going on twenty years now.

Sometimes the attacks were mentioned in the paper, but so far no one had connected them to each other or to him.

He lit the fire he'd built earlier, which cast gold and orange shadows around them. The only other light came from the kitchen. Like the animal he became on these nights, that was how he liked it.

She couldn't be too far from home. His was the only residence on this road, which meant she must have come from one of the townhouses in the planned community near the state highway. Once the danger of discovery had passed, he'd planned to follow at a discreet distance to make sure she got there okay.

If her flashlight hadn't broken, he wouldn't have been surprised if she'd tried to follow him. He smiled grimly at the thought. *Then* what would he have done? Turned tail and run? Part of him wished she'd carried a gun instead of a flashlight. Maybe he'd have stood his ground and let her put him out of his misery.

Chapter Three

Bree knew her wits were addled, but she also knew she was in a strange place. They walked through a normal enough door into a cave, or something closely approximating one. Primitive. Dim. He'd guided her to a sofa covered in something luxuriously soft, like suede, before he bent to light a fire in a stone fireplace. She'd never heard of a cave with a stone fireplace.

She blinked, but it didn't help. She couldn't see much of anything except a few masses that might be furniture. A long coffee table sat in front of the sofa.

Her head hurt. Her body ached. And several places on her skin felt prickly and uncomfortable. She wanted to stay strong, but she sank back into the cushions and squeezed her eyes shut. Moving *hurt.*

As she reached up to examine her pounding head, panic swelled inside her. The memory of the attack came back in full force. Her eyes opened to see her rescuer watching her. Had she been kidnapped? Was she a prisoner here in this cave-like dwelling?

She wouldn't be a victim again even if she had nothing with which to defend herself. She swore to herself she'd go down fighting if it came to that.

He approached, his body blocking out the firelight.

"I'll call 911, okay?"

Bree sucked in a breath at his voice. Low. Throaty. Sexy. Oh, God. She thought her kidnapper was sexy. *Insanity.*

She struggled to sit up straighter and back away, but she couldn't go any further once she reached the corner of the couch.

"Wait. Who—who are you?" She could barely get the words out of her dry throat.

He didn't answer her question, instead asking one of his own. "Do you know what happened?"

She'd been attacked. By *something.* Not a raccoon or opossum. Something big. She'd hit it with her flashlight, and it took off into the woods. Her flashlight broke, and she'd used it as a weapon. That's all she remembered.

"I had a flashlight."

"I think you'll need a new one." He sat on the table facing her and tapped the broken flashlight still attached to its wrist strap.

"Oh," she said. "I thought I lost it." She could barely make out the outline of him. Big frame, broad shoulders, too-long dark hair. But the firelight behind him left his face in shadow.

"I can't see you."

"Oh. Sorry." He reached past her to pull a chain, allowing a soft circle of light to encompass them both. She stared. She couldn't help it. His fierce features, hawkish nose, and harsh, angular face made her think of a primeval hunter. His eyes were so dark they were almost black, piercing beneath wing-like brows. His hair reminded her of midnight, thick, wavy, and disheveled.

He wore black flannel over a black thermal shirt and black jeans. She recognized him. She'd seen him before. But where?

"The dark side of the moon," she said softly. She didn't know where the thought came from or why she'd said it aloud. Except maybe, now she recalled, it was the last thing she'd heard playing on her phone before she blacked out.

He drew back as if she'd slapped him. "What did you say?"

"It's from an old song by 3 Doors Down called 'Kryptonite.' There's a line about the world floating to the dark side of the moon."

His penetrating gaze made her feel trapped, yet she wasn't afraid of him. Somewhere, though, in the back of her mind, she thought she *should* be afraid.

Absently, she scratched at the abrasion on the inside of her wrist while staring back at him, taking in his features, trying to fight the physical attraction she felt and failing.

The trauma of the attack must have affected her personality. She never behaved so boldly. Especially not with men. Never held a gaze this way when she'd just met someone. But she hadn't met him, she realized. She had seen him before, but she didn't know who he was, where she was, or what his intentions were.

"Could I have some water?"

Her simple question interrupted their contemplation of each other and made everything about this unusual situation seem less bizarre.

"Of course," he said.

The kitchen must be somewhere behind her because she heard him open a cabinet and then water going into a glass. She tried to take in more of her surroundings before he returned, although she couldn't make out many details because of the gloom.

A wall of rough-hewn stone shelves surrounded the fireplace. On the thick slab of wood which served as a mantel, she could see collectibles of some sort but couldn't tell what they were. She didn't see a television or an entertainment center anywhere.

Before she could note any more about the room, he returned and held out a thick glass tumbler. The cold, crisp water soon soothed her parched throat.

He was about to retake his seat on the table when she said, "Could you—?"

He paused, eyeing her, waiting for her question.

"Do you have anything for pain? I've got a massive headache." She unthinkingly tapped the side of her head and immediately regretted it. She sucked in a breath, wincing in surprise. More carefully, she probed the swollen area.

"What about 911? I could drive you to the ER."

"I don't think I need the ER, but something attacked me." she said.

"Something?"

"I don't know what. An animal. A big one. It came out of nowhere and knocked me down. That's when I hit my head."

"A bear?"

"No."

"Coyote? Wolf?"

"Wolves are rare in this area. But it wasn't a coyote, either. More like a big black cat, judging from its claws."

"I thought panthers were extinct around here, but that would explain what happened to your clothes," he said.

"My clothes?" She examined the rips in her shirt with one hand, as well as the scratches on her skin which were causing a prickly feeling.

"These scratches don't look bad enough to warrant a trip to the ER, do they?"

He held up his hands to indicate his lack of knowledge. "I'm no doctor, but I can get you something for the pain."

As he left, Bree took a closer look at her shirt and skin. Her arms and torso bore the hashtags of scratch marks. There was an especially large gouge across her midriff, but that was the worst of them, and fortunately none of them were too deep. Her favorite pair of capri-length running pants were ruined, as was her shirt, but her sports bra remained intact. She could see bruises darkening beneath the torn skin. Her arms weren't as bad, but there were several scratches there. And what looked like bite marks not deep enough to draw much blood. The underside of her wrist bore an odd, abraded area. The skin wasn't broken but the outer layer had been effectively removed.

She found the entire incident puzzling. What kind of animal attacked the way this one did and then gave up after a clunk to the head? Or bites but doesn't sink its teeth in? When she'd hit the beast, she hadn't been thinking beyond that fight or flight response. But given everything she knew about animals, especially wild animals, this behavior was very much out of the norm.

She set the broken flashlight on the coffee table as she heard the wide floor planks creak slightly. He retook his seat and handed her two white capsules. She examined them.

"What are these?"

"Generic acetaminophen. It's all I have."

She stared at him for a moment. He didn't blink. When she hesitated, he said, "Do you want to see the bottle?"

Yes. "No." If he'd wanted to drug her, he'd had plenty of opportunity. If he wanted to hold her prisoner, she'd be no match for his strength. He could lock her up, throw away the key, and no one would ever find her. She knew she should be afraid. Why wasn't she?

"I've seen you before. But I can't remember where."

"I met with Carter Hayes at Sanctuary a few weeks ago. We ran into each other there."

Bree frowned. After Carter had retired from teaching agriculture at the nearby college, he'd taken on the job of Sanctuary's groundskeeper.

"You probably don't remember, but we nearly collided in the lobby. You dropped a couple of file folders—"

"Which you helped me pick up." It came back to her now. "But I don't know who you are," she said.

"I don't know who you are either."

"Bree."

"Just Bree?"

"Bree Mason. Maybree Anna Mason. I'm the executive director of Sanctuary."

"I'm Griff."

"Just Griff?"

"Griffin."

Bree waited.

Finally, he said, "Lancaster. Griffin Lancaster."

"What? No middle name?"

Again, with the piercing gaze. Maybe he thought it made him look intimidating.

"Henry."

"Griffin Henry Lancaster. That's a very strong name."

He shrugged. "If you say so."

"You don't like it?"

"I had no choice in the matter."

"Me either." She swallowed the pills and set the glass on the end table before she continued. "My father wanted to name me May after his grandmother. My mother wanted to name me Breeanna." She lifted a hand and let it fall.

"Bree's better. It suits you." He waited a beat before he said, "Look, if you're not going to the ER is there someone you should call? To pick you up? Someone who will be worried about you?"

She checked her phone. The casing was cracked, and the screen had shattered, but the phone seemed to be operational. She thought about his question for a moment. "No. There's only Pete, and he'll be fast asleep by now. He won't miss me."

Griff frowned. "Guess you'll need a new flashlight." He picked it up and examined it.

She took it from him. The battery housing had come apart, the casing was broken, and the lens and bulb were crushed. The batteries were new, though, so she plucked them out before handing it back. "You can throw it away."

He started to get up when something on the broken light caught her eye. "Wait!"

He froze. She took the flashlight back and examined the base of the battery housing. She thought she saw some hair and maybe something else on the outside of the case from where she'd hit the beast. "Do you have a plastic bag I can put this in?"

He waited so long to answer she thought he was going to refuse. Finally, he said, "Yes."

He moved to the kitchen and returned with a clear, resealable plastic bag. She carefully placed the flashlight into it and sealed it shut.

She brought her cell phone to life and gasped. "It's almost nine. I got held up at work earlier, but I had no idea it was this late."

"It's not that late."

"I should go." She swung her feet to the floor and cocked her head. "What's that sound?"

He gave her a quizzical look, as if he didn't understand the question. Then comprehension dawned. "Rain."

"Great."

She pushed herself reluctantly off the sofa, but as soon as she got to her feet, she swayed. The room spun and she reached out to make it stop. Her hand connected with his chest. It was like using the trunk of a hundred-year-old tree to hold herself up.

He caught her and held her elbows before lowering her back to the sofa. Something odd passed between them, leaving her confused and disoriented. The places where she'd been scratched throbbed and burned, especially the one on her wrist. She rubbed her forehead. "Wow. That was weird." She shot him an accusing look. "You sure those were acetaminophen?"

"Swear," he said with a smirk.

Her suspicion grew. "What did you give me?" she asked, panicked now.

"Generic non-aspirin pain relievers. When's the last time you ate?"

She frowned. She didn't like to run on a full stomach. She'd planned to eat when she got back home. "Lunch?"

"Whatever you're thinking, I didn't drug you. I can take you home right now if you want. I can also make us something to eat, and you can leave as soon as you feel up to it. If you'd rather, you can call someone to come pick you up. Your choice."

Chapter Four

Bree'd never thought of herself as someone prone to low blood sugar, but she knew she was in no shape to go anywhere right now, even if it was only a mile or so up the road to her house. She was disoriented and shaky in a way she'd never been before. Was it him? This place? The attack? Maybe a combination of all three.

He'd given her more choices than she could deal with. No, that wasn't true, even if she couldn't explain her reluctance to head home in pouring rain. She simply didn't want to leave her rescuer's nice warm... lair.

He'd offered food. Maybe she'd feel a bit steadier if she ate something. Maybe she'd be able to gather her wits and figure out why she wanted to reject most of the options he'd suggested.

"If it's not too much trouble, I might feel better if I ate something."

"Okay. Any food allergies I should know about? Lactose intolerance? You're not vegan, are you?"

She wasn't sure if he was teasing her or not, but the earnest way he asked made her smile.

"Whatever's easiest. A snack is all I need."

"It'll be more than a snack," he assured her.

"So, how well do you know Carter?"

"Not that well. We've had a couple of discussions about some Sanctuary landscaping projects."

"If I call him, will he vouch for you?" she belatedly thought to ask. "A girl can't be too careful these days." She wanted to roll her eyes at the irony of that statement.

"He may not know me well enough for that. But like I said, I'll take you home. Just say the word."

She watched him leave as she snuggled back against the soft cushions. "I should call him anyway."

Animal magnetism. She'd heard the term before, but she wasn't sure she'd ever met a man she'd describe as having it. He reminded her of a panther with all the black he wore. Patient. Quiet. If he had a tail, it would surely be twitching. But he also made her think of a buck. Solid. Strong. Wild. In fact, she could probably name ten more wild animals he brought to mind. A grizzly bear because of his height and solid frame. His intense gaze made her think of a wolf.

She thumbed through the contact list on her phone until she found Carter's number. Carter was surprised to hear from her, but once she explained the situation, he said almost exactly what her host had told her. They didn't know each other well, but Griff was well-known and well-regarded in the business community. She'd used the term accident rather than attack in her explanation. No reason for him to have the details, but Bree acknowledged the comfort that having someone else know where she was gave her.

She closed her eyes against the firelight and thought how warm and safe she felt in a place that reminded her of an animal's den.

Her wits must be addled. She dealt with men daily. At work. Socially. But the last time she'd been so viscerally attracted to someone the way she was to Griff? There was no last time. Attraction to a man, yes. But this allure, this pull she felt, had never happened.

She made her way to the kitchen where the under-cabinet lighting only added to the cave-like ambience. Most of the kitchen hugged two walls to form an L with an island that looked over the living room. The counters were smooth stone, but nothing Bree had ever seen before.

The cabinets and shelves looked like they'd been hewn and carved from the same massive pine as the coffee table.

Griff's back was to her. "Can I help?" Bree said from the far side of the island.

"It's fine."

She noticed that all the walls here were curved. There were no harsh angles anywhere. Even the cabinets were rounded and fit perfectly into the walls.

She turned around and stared at the front room, the fireplace, the door. No wonder she'd thought she was in a cave. Heavy drapes hung on either side of the front door. The low lighting only added to the shadows. There were no windows, she realized. No view. No doors leading to a deck. Only darkened hallways leading off in two directions.

She felt a moment of panic. "Is this... are we in a cave?"

Griff turned, wiping his hands. "Sort of. Not really. More like underground."

"Underground?"

"It's an experimental design. Energy-saving, eco-friendly. The hills and mountains are here, anyway. Why not live inside of them, instead of on top of them?"

"You mean we're inside a mountain?"

"More like a foothill, but yeah."

"That's why the walls are curved?"

"The idea is to disturb the earth as little as possible."

"How long have you lived here?"

"Three years." More prolonged eye contact before Griff said, "I'll give you a tour sometime if you'd like, but right now? We should eat."

Bree realized she was gripping the island's countertop with both hands because her legs were trembling. "Okay. Bathroom?"

"This way."

She followed Griff into one of the hallways where their presence triggered some recessed lighting. He flicked on a light inside a doorway and gestured for Bree to enter. "There are towels in the cabinet beneath the sink," he said. "There's a tube of ointment in the medicine chest. Might take the sting out of those scratches."

She closed the door and used the facilities. The bathroom was like a little cave within a cave. The shower was the same smooth stone as the counter tops. The sloping walls seemed to hug her and once again she felt that sense of safety. No outside force could penetrate this underground fortress.

She frowned at herself in the mirror. She looked done in. Strands of hair from her loosened ponytail straggled around her face. Dirt streaked her torn shirt. Not much she could do about that. She cleaned herself up as best she could, doctored her wounds, looped the hair band around her wrist, and finger combed her hair. Before she closed the medicine cabinet, she noticed a small plastic bottle with a drugstore label. She opened the child safety cap and shook a couple of capsules into her hand. They looked exactly like the ones Griff had given her.

After she got settled back on the sofa, Griff set a tray in her lap. There was a big soup mug filled with what looked like beef stew. She could make out chunks of beef, potatoes, and carrots in a thick broth. On a plate next to it was a sandwich stuffed with cheese, lettuce, tomato, and she wasn't sure what else. Her stomach growled.

Griff once again made himself comfortable on the coffee table, picked up his own mug, and dug in. She did the same.

The stew was homemade, with bits of onion and fat green peas. The sandwich? Like something out of a high-end bistro. The light, crisp texture of the roll and the added spread brought out the flavors of the cheeses.

"You should open your own cafe," she said after a few bites. "Did you make the stew? Bake the bread? Age the cheese?"

She liked the warm, rumbly sound of Griff's chuckle. Like it came from somewhere deep inside. His eyes softened. The intensity ramped down. "I've mastered the crockpot, so I'll cop to the stew. I leave the bread and cheese to the experts."

"You're an expert at putting it together, though. Everything's delicious."

She couldn't tell if the compliment pleased him or not. They ate the rest of the meal in silence. She could hear the rain pounding outside and resisted the thought of leaving, even though she knew that's what she should do. What any sane woman finding herself in these circumstances should do.

After Griff piled the empty dishes on the tray, she made herself say, "I should leave."

He regarded her with curiosity.

She smiled sheepishly. "I don't know why, but I really don't want to."

He waited.

"Is it too weird?" she asked, still trying to figure it out herself. "I just met you. I don't know why I feel so comfortable here."

"You were attacked. It's raining. I don't make a habit of bringing strangers into my house and letting them sleep on my couch...but under the circumstances, it might be prudent." After a beat of silence he added, "I can take you home first thing in the morning. I'm usually up by five."

"Yikes."

"It's settled then." He picked up the tray and went to the kitchen.

"I can help with the dishes," she called after him.

"No need."

He came back after a few minutes with a pillow and blanket. "There's a throw there, too, if you need it." He gestured to the back of the sofa before he held out something else to her. "It's one of my shirts, if you want to change."

She took it. "Thank you."

It was the same dark thermal cotton as he wore underneath his flannel. It'd be miles too big for her, but it took everything she had not to rub it against her cheek.

"Get some sleep, okay? My room's down the hall from the bathroom if you need anything."

"Okay. Thanks."

He put a screen in front of the fireplace. The fire had burned itself down to glowing coals, but she could still feel their heat.

She listened to him tinkering in the kitchen, loading the dishwasher, and storing the leftovers. After he turned off the lights and left, she removed her torn shirt and let Griff's fall over her head. She pushed her arms through the sleeves and shoved the cuffs up over her wrists. If she stood, the hem of the shirt would probably reach mid-thigh. She didn't care about the fit. It was warm and soft. She wrapped it around herself, settled under the blankets, and closed her eyes.

Chapter Five

She dreamed of the attack. Not the one from earlier, but one like it. In this dream, she was being pursued. She didn't know what chased her, but she was terrified. She ran through a forest in the rain, slipping and sliding in the mud and the foliage and tripping over fallen logs. The thing, whatever it was, matched her breath for panting breath. She thought it was a part of her, or she was part of it.

Then she couldn't run anymore. She came up against a smooth stone wall, any rough surface it might have once had was long since worn away. She turned to face the beast. It would kill her now, she knew it. It would maul her, play with her perhaps, as if she were a toy, tossing her near lifeless body from side to side and into the air where she'd fall and hit the ground again and again.

She could feel it. Waiting. Watching. She searched the edge of the woods for it. She could sense its presence. She was almost paralyzed with fear because she knew she couldn't escape. Trees trembled. She heard rustling from the dense undergrowth. She stared and listened. But the thing that stepped forward wasn't a thing at all. It wasn't an animal. Not a beast intent on killing her.

It was Griff.

Griff went through his normal pre-bedtime routine. Showering. Brushing his teeth. Doing his best to ignore the towel and washcloth Bree had used and hung neatly back on the towel rack.

Weariness swamped him, as it always did after a transformation. He needed sleep, but it wouldn't come easily. How had he allowed a woman to spend the night in his home? And not just any woman. *Her.*

He tossed and turned, wishing the restlessness would leave him because he needed to relax. He closed his eyes and forced himself to concentrate on the sound of his breathing. To empty his mind. But images of her played across his consciousness whenever he began to relax. His sense of good fortune to find a victim close at hand when he'd expected a much longer hunt. The heady sense of power he always felt when his prey was at his mercy, when he drew their blood as he fed on their terror.

His body spasmed involuntarily as it relived the blow to his head from her flashlight. He smiled as he finally drifted off, remembering those brief touches, his hands bracing her, her hand on his chest.

The dream returned. The same one he'd been having for years. More vivid and revealing on the nights after he transformed.

A woman's long black hair and lush body. Luminescent green eyes. A weather-beaten cottage surrounded by mountains. The indistinct features of a man she looked at first with love and then with contempt. With *hate*.

A cauldron over an open flame. Murmurings in a language he couldn't understand. A thin plume of smoke twirling its way down the mountainside. The woman's smug expression as she watched it travel.

The smoke wrapped itself in coils around the faceless man until he turned into Griff. He fought to free himself, but he was bound by the poisoned smoke.

He couldn't escape his fate.

Bree woke up but didn't open her eyes. She was too warm, too comfortable, too drowsy. Behind her, in the dimly lit kitchen, she heard someone trying to be quiet. Water ran, then stopped. Something beeped. Footsteps.

"I'm awake," she said.

"Good," Griff replied. "Coffee will be ready in a couple of minutes."

She sat up, no longer disoriented. She remembered where she was and who she was with. The events of last night came crashing in on her. Her headache was mostly gone, but with each movement she made, the rest of her body reminded her she'd been in a fight.

She shuffled off the sofa and into the kitchen, smothering a yawn with one hand and pushing her hair over her shoulder with the other. "Time is it?" she asked.

Griff looked at her as if he'd seen an apparition.

"Based on the way you're staring I must look quite fetching this morning. Or a complete disaster."

He relaxed slightly. "Sorry. It's just after five. How'd you sleep?"

"Rock solid. But I'm never up this early."

"You want some coffee?"

"I'd love some." They regarded each other. She said, "I can't believe I spent the night here. Talk about overstaying my welcome."

He turned to the coffeemaker and poured some of the brew into a travel mug. "I wasn't too keen on dragging both of us out into the rain."

She gave him a rueful smile before she started down the hall to the bathroom. "I'll be right out."

The mirror reflected crazy hair and circles under her eyes. Not to mention his big, baggy shirt falling off one shoulder and draping to mid-thigh. She looked like something a cat had dragged in, albeit a very large cat.

Well, he'd already seen her, and she figured this was about as bad as she'd ever looked. There wasn't much she could do about it, anyway. She splashed her face with cold water, hoping it would revive her. She gathered her hair up and wound a band around it. It flopped at the top of her head into a messy bun.

Griff, on the other hand, looked as divinely sexy as he did the night before. He hadn't shaved and the extra whiskers made him look even darker and more danger-ous. Again, he wore black.

When she returned to the kitchen, he handed her a travel mug of coffee. "Need cream or sugar?"

"No, I like your black."

He quirked an eyebrow.

"It. I like *it* black."

She took a sip and studied him over the rim of the mug, daring him to call her on her slip of the tongue.

"I have to get going," he said.

"Sure." She put her shoes on and wrapped her torn shirt around her phone and the plastic bag covering her broken flashlight and followed him out. The air was cool and crisp and fresh from the rain.

Griff locked the door, a thick wood portal curved at the top. As she followed him to his truck, she took in her surroundings. The house was barely visible, but the parts she could see reminded her of a hobbit house, though for a very large hobbit.

His big, double cab, black truck sported a logo on the door. Lancaster Landscape Design, as well as a phone number and web address. He opened the passenger door for her. She didn't know if that was because he was a gentleman, or her hands were full, or because the door was nearest to the path they'd taken from the house.

Once he got in, the truck roared to life. They reached the road and turned left. She realized why she'd never noticed the access path. The unpaved driveway curved sharply behind a line of trees. The foliage almost completely buried his black mailbox. Must be hell to find for any new mail carrier taking over the route.

"Where to?" he asked.

"Just up the road. I'm in Halloway Hollow," she said.

He drove in silence on the wet pavement, the truck's headlights sweeping aside the pre-dawn gray.

"Take a right here," she said, and pointed to her town-home. "This is me." He pulled up in front.

"Thank you—" she began.

"I'm sorry," he said at the same time.

"Sorry?"

"About the attack."

"It's not your fault."

He looked at her but didn't say anything else.

"Thanks for rescuing me. Oh, you want to hang on a minute? I'll change out of your shirt."

"Keep it. I have others."

"Oh. Okay." She didn't want to get out of the truck but couldn't think of any way to delay. She opened the door and got out. He continued to watch her.

"Here's your mug back." She held the travel mug toward him, although she'd barely taken a sip from it.

"You can have it. I've got a hundred of them."

"Really?"

"Literally." He gestured at the mug. "They're part of my advertising budget."

She hadn't noticed before, but the mug sported the same logo, phone number, and web address as the door of his truck.

"Ah."

She didn't close the door. He had that intense look in his eyes again, studying her, as if trying to figure something out, and if he looked at her long enough, she'd provide the answers.

"Anything else?" he said eventually.

"I can't think of anything." She wished her scrambled brain could come up with something, though. Some way to keep him here, keep him talking. She didn't want him to leave. She rubbed at the tender flesh on the inside of her wrist.

"I've got to get going. You're okay, right?"

"Yes. Sure." Bree nodded. "Bye then."

She closed the door. He drove away and left her there wearing his shirt and clutching the coffee mug in her hand.

Chapter Six

Griff drove out of the cluster of townhouses and didn't look back, though he wanted to. Badly. He prided himself on never letting things go too far with a woman. He didn't let himself get attached, and if he ever sensed they were, he broke it off. He knew all too well how it would end if he didn't.

The curse his family had lived under for five generations would end with him.

But dammit. This one. Bree. He might have been the one who'd attacked her, but she'd somehow sunk her claws into him as well. A set of more delicate claws perhaps, but their touch sizzled beneath his skin.

Was it the music? The damn song playing on her phone? What were the chances of him being forced to find a random victim and she just happened to be listening to a song which almost perfectly described his plight? *The dark side of the moon...*

Everyone knew Kryptonite made Superman weak. Griff had an uncomfortable feeling that Bree Mason could be his own personal Kryptonite.

Just as well he hadn't encouraged her. He hadn't even been friendly, just courteous. Once he'd left her neighborhood behind and took the highway heading into Asheville, he could admit the truth. He hadn't wanted her to leave last night. He'd liked the idea of her being there, that he could keep her safe. Still, he'd revealed little of himself. Hadn't led her on by saying anything ambiguous like, "See you around."

He allowed himself to feel a little disappointment, knowing he wouldn't see her again. He got on with his day and tried, unsuccessfully, not to think about her.

The moment Bree unlocked her door, Pete ambled toward her. "Hey, baby." She bent to rub his grizzled head while he gazed up at her with cloudy, adoring eyes. She clipped on his leash and took him outside. He did his business quickly on the small front lawn.

Back inside, she hid his arthritis medication in a chunk of cheese, fed him, and refilled his water bowl. She recapped the bottle of pills, wondering if they'd help her currently aching body. Whatever she'd taken last night had long worn off.

Walking slower than Pete, she went to the bathroom and got the shower going. While she waited for hot water, she undressed and examined herself in the vanity mirror. Her upper body and arms were covered in bruises and sported a variety of long, thin scratches. The one across her abdomen was by far the deepest. Along her thighs were lines of torn skin, not serious enough to warrant medical attention, although she could see heavy bruising as well. How much had that thing weighed? It'd felt like a ton when it had been on top of her. It could have easily inflicted much more damage. *Why didn't it?*

The place on the inside of her wrist she'd noticed before wasn't a scratch, but the skin had puckered into an odd hexagon-shaped pattern. She'd never seen anything like it before. If it weren't for the physical evidence left behind, she'd almost think she'd dreamt the entire episode.

She stood under the spray of hot water, letting it pummel her muscles and soothe her aches. If the animal had wanted to kill her, she'd be dead. When she'd fought back, it retreated instead of becoming more aggressive. The attack made no sense.

After her shower, she dabbed antibiotic ointment on her wounds and took some more over-the-counter tablets for the pain. Her reflection showed little improvement from her earlier examination, but makeup could work wonders after a rough night.

She dressed in a loose, long-sleeved top and slacks, told Pete goodbye, and drove to Sanctuary. As she arrived, she felt not only a burst of pride at what she'd built, but a sense of homecoming. Although the changes to her grandparents' legacy were significant, the land itself was filled with childhood memories.

The farmhouse where she'd grown up had been converted into a veterinary practice run by her best friend, Jenna Scott. Next door were the Sanctuary administrative offices. The outbuildings and barn housed the rescue animals. Everything from dogs to goats to horses, as well as a lone llama. Bree had put a ton of blood, sweat, and tears into creating a top tier non-profit animal sanctuary, rehab, and adoption center. It mostly ran on volunteers, donations, and grants. Hungry land developers always seemed to be circling the property, looking for a way to take a bite out of the remaining parcels of undeveloped land. Bree often had her hands full keeping them at bay.

She was way early this morning. The only other car in the lot was Jenna's, which suited her intent perfectly. She let herself into the vet facility and called out as she closed the door.

Jenna turned from her desk, her bright blue eyes alert as always, brunette curls bound up into a fetching topknot. "Hey, what's up? You're here early."

"Can you take a look at this?" Bree asked her.

Jenna held the plastic bag up to the light. "Sure. What is it?"

"It's what's left of my flashlight. I think there might be some hair on it. Maybe some other matter as well."

Jenna moved from her desk to a microscope on the counter. "So... what am I looking for?"

"I don't know exactly," Bree said. "If there's hair on it, can you tell what kind of animal it's from?"

Jenna carefully extracted the contents of the bag with a pair of tweezers and set the pieces on a glass plate. She turned her attention back to Bree. "Why is it in pieces?" She frowned. "Wait, what happened to you?" She reached for Bree's hand and examined it. She grabbed Bree's other hand. Then she pushed up the sleeves of Bree's sweater. "What the hell, Bree?"

"I was attacked."

"Attacked? Where? How?"

"I was running," Bree began.

"After dark," Jenna said with a frown.

"Yes," Bree admitted. She and Jenna had a long-standing agreement. Jenna could disapprove of Bree's choices but wasn't allowed to criticize. The reverse was also true. She explained about the attack as best she could.

"You're telling me this thing just ran off? And you have no idea what it was?"

"No. My flashlight stopped working when I fell, and it broke after I hit him—it. I was hoping maybe there was hair or some kind of evidence on it that would indicate what kind of animal it was."

Jenna turned back to the microscope and slid the glass plate under the lens. She adjusted the scope once and then again.

"Is there anything on there?"

"Yes. There's hair." She picked up a pair of tweezers and another instrument and maneuvered them beneath the scope. Carefully, she lifted a bit of the flashlight away and set it aside, along with the instruments, before she peered into the scope. She stared for so long Bree became nervous.

Jenna finally sat back and made Bree go over everything again. "You're *sure* it was an animal that attacked you?"

"It had to have been. Yes."

"But you never saw it."

"No. Not really. I mean, what else could it have been? An alien?" Bree's attempt to lighten the mood fell flat.

"It could have been human."

"No. Definitely not. There was fur and claws and growling. It was an animal. It had to be."

"Well, then I don't know what to tell you because *this* hair? I'm ninety-nine-point nine percent sure it's from a human."

"That's just not possible."

Jenna said nothing.

"I mean, the thing that attacked me. It wasn't human."

"Is it possible this hair isn't from whatever attacked you?"

Bree chewed her lip. "I suppose... I assumed because it was stuck in the flashlight, it would have to be the attacker's hair. But you're right. Could it be mine?"

"Not unless you're hiding some black hair on your head," Jenna said.

"It must belong to the guy who rescued me."

"Wait? What? You were rescued? You didn't tell me that."

"I haven't had a chance." The phone in the front office rang. Bree picked up the extension from Jenna's desk. "Sanctuary. Bree Mason." She listened before she put the caller on hold. "I have to take this. We'll talk later."

"You bet we will," Jenna said.

All morning, Bree's thoughts drifted back to last night. Her tired mind kept isolating bits and pieces of the incident from the moment she'd been knocked to the ground until she'd arrived home this morning.

Should she have asked Griff to call 911 when no real emergency existed? She wasn't incapacitated and could have walked into an emergency room on her own. Perhaps the hospital would have been compelled to file a report with the sheriff's office or the state park service. It wasn't too late for her to do so now. She still had her torn clothes and scratches on her body to prove she'd been attacked. Someone from the sheriff's office would probably want to question Griff because he'd found her.

They'd want to know if he'd seen or heard anything. He'd already told her he hadn't.

She knew what Jenna would say. *Of course,* she should have gone to the emergency room last night. But there'd been no need.

I'm fine, Bree assured herself, *except*... Except she felt invaded. By Griff. She didn't know if it was her own imagination doing this to her, or if he'd gotten under her skin somehow and planted tiny magnets that drew her to him.

She was being dumb. He was a good-looking guy, that's all. Tall. Dark. Handsome. Mysterious. The stuff romance novel cover models were made of. He'd rescued her. Swept her up in his arms (so she imagined) and carried her to his lair, where he'd nursed her back to health (two generic acetaminophen tablets and a bowl of stew). Then he'd delivered her safe and sound back home and ridden off into the sunset... er, sunrise.

Honestly, the way thoughts of him kept creeping into her mind when she should be concentrating on more important things like the upcoming donor appreciation fundraising event, it was like she was a teenager mooning over the bad boy in study hall.

"Stop it," she hissed to herself. She stared at the guest list on her computer screen. Several names need to be added to the gold and silver sponsor levels and thank-you notes, which she liked to handwrite, thanking them for their support.

The multi-colored logo of her web browser in the corner of her monitor drew her attention, almost taunting her. *Wouldn't you like to know*? She ignored it, but her eye drifted back.

"Dammit." She clicked on it and typed in search terms. A list of possibilities presented themselves. She clicked on the second one, and there it was. Lancaster Landscape Design. She searched the site for a photo of Griff, but there wasn't one, although he was listed as the owner. There was contact information and numerous pictures of his company's breathtakingly beautiful work. Golf courses and residential developments. Commercial properties. High-end homes.

Jenna tapped on the partially open door of Bree's office and stuck her head in. "We still on for lunch today?"

Translation: "I want to hear about this guy who rescued you."

Bree planned to tell Jenna about him anyway. She might as well do it over a plate of nachos at Dante's.

"Sounds great. I've got some calls and a stop to make first, though. I'll meet you there. Twelve-thirty?"

"Cool."

Bree guiltily clicked off Griff's website and picked up her phone to call her contact at the North Carolina Division of Parks and Recreation.

Chapter Seven

"So, spill."

Bree and Jenna were ensconced in their preferred booth in their favorite haunt, skinny virgin margaritas, a basket of tortilla chips, and a bowl of salsa on the table between them. Bree's arm ached from the rabies injection, but she'd be damned if she'd whine about it to Jenna. It would just give her more ammunition to fire at Bree's foolhardiness.

"There's not much to spill," Bree said. "I told you most of it."

"You told me about the attack. You didn't tell me about the rescue. By the way, did you call the clinic? You need to get a rabies shot today."

"Already done." Bree picked up a chip, dipped it in the salsa and munched, stalling for time. She didn't want to talk about Griff because Jenna would put her own spin on it, make it sound twisted and creepy instead of Gothically romantic.

She wiped her fingers on a napkin and took a sip of her drink.

"Some guy rescued you," Jenna prompted. Bree knew that tone. It meant, *tell me everything, and I'll tell you what's wrong with the picture.* Bree loved Jenna. And even though Jenna was forbidden to lecture or scold, she still somehow managed to sit in judgment on Bree's life choices. Usually, Bree ignored her and let it slide, but she didn't think she'd be able to if Jenna started to put her own unflattering spin on Griff's behavior and intentions.

"I was still shaky when he found me. I didn't know it, but his house was right there." Bree wondered how to edit the details to keep Jenna from prying. "It was dark inside and he lit a fire. At first, I thought I was in a cave." She laughed. Jenna frowned. They sipped their drinks. Jenna picked up a chip and broke it in half. She always watched her calories and believed if she ate small bites, she'd eat less.

"Good thing he was there," Bree added.

"Who is he?"

"His name's Griff."

"Just Griff?"

"Isn't that enough?" Evasive tactics, Bree reminded herself.

"Did he call the cops? After he found you?"

"Um. No."

"Why the hell not? Doesn't he have a phone?"

A few heads swiveled in their direction. "Would you keep it down?" Bree said irritably. "I told him not to."

"You *what*?" Jenna hissed, leaning across the table. "Seriously, Bree, sometimes I wonder what's wrong with you."

"Absolutely nothing," Bree said, sitting up straighter and pulling her dignity around her like an invisible cloak. "I told him not to. You sometimes forget, Jenna, that I'm an adult perfectly capable of looking out for my own welfare."

Jenna sagged back in her seat. "I'm sorry. I know I big sister you and I know you hate it. But I can't help it."

"I was conscious, and I wasn't hurt that badly. Whatever attacked me was long gone. He did offer to call 911 or take me to the ER."

"And you declined."

"I was shaken up, but I honestly don't know what the ER would have done for a few scratches and a bump on the head. Make me spend half the night there and send me a bill for a few thousand dollars, I suspect."

Jenna tilted her head, conceding the point.

"Then it started pouring rain and—"

"Tell me you did not spend the night with a perfect stranger," Jenna interrupted.

"He said he'd take me home whenever I felt up to it."

Jenna sagged once again, this time in relief.

"I did spend the night, though," Bree said with a satisfied smirk. She reached for another chip and more salsa.

"You spent the night with him?" Jenna asked. "You probably need more than a rabies shot, then."

"Not *with* him. On his couch."

"And nothing happened?"

"He gave me a bowl of beef stew and a sandwich. And something for the headache."

Jenna ate half a chip. "Uh-huh."

"Oh! And he gave me one of his shirts to wear. And an extra blanket."

Jenna took a drink before she said, "You spent the night on his couch, and what happened this morning?"

"He got up early and made coffee."

"Go on."

"He brought me home."

"And?"

"End of story."

"Seriously? He didn't say he'd call you or anything?"

"It wasn't a date, Jenna. It was an accident."

"It was an *attack*. Which should be reported."

"Fine. An attack. From which he just happened to rescue me. And I did report it. I talked to Darryl at the parks division. He'll post an alert about the incident, but without more detail, that's all he can do."

"At least that's something."

"Did I mention I'd seen Griff at Sanctuary a couple of weeks ago? We weren't introduced then, but Carter knows him."

"No. You didn't mention that."

"I called Carter. He vouched for him."

"What does he look like?"

"Who? Carter?" Bree grinned and Jenna threw a chip at her. "Tall. Dark. Handsome. Like he should be on the cover of a romance novel. Brooding. Intense."

"And you've been thinking about him all day, huh?" Jenna added knowingly.

"Hard not to. I don't get rescued by romance cover models every day, you know."

"True." Jenna broke another chip in half and nibbled on it. "You don't get attacked by some random animal every day, either."

Two hours after they returned from lunch, Jenna tapped on Bree's office door again. This time, a female sheriff's deputy was right behind her.

Bree's first thought was there'd been an incident on Sanctuary property. But if that were the case, she'd have been notified immediately. "What's going on? What's happened?"

"This is Deputy Gardner. She's going to take your statement about what happened to you last night and file a report."

Bree glared at Jenna. "I *told* you I didn't want to do that. Dr. Jaffrey's office will file a report with Animal Control anyway. Deputy, I'm sorry, my associate here has wasted your time."

"Well, ma'am, I'm here," Deputy Gardner said. "I'd be here anyway once I got the alert from parks division. If you let me take a statement, you won't have wasted my time. Might not be anything we can do about it, but from what Dr. Scott here told me, whatever attacked you might be the same thing that's gone after some other women."

Bree turned her attention to the deputy. "Really? There have been other attacks like this?"

"Can't say for sure until I take your statement. May I?" Deputy Gardner indicated the two visitors' chairs.

Resigned, Bree nodded. "Thanks for interfering, Jenna. You can go now."

Jenna was not the slightest bit perturbed. She turned and left.

Bree waited until the veterinary clinic staff left and Jenna was alone in her office doing paperwork. She'd locked up the Sanctuary offices earlier, and a peek at the parking lot told her everyone had left except her and her best friend.

Bree didn't knock on the partially opened door. She knew Jenna knew she was there and waited until she looked up.

"I'd like to know where you get off," Bree began, "calling the sheriff's department after I specifically told you there was no reason to file a report."

"I know you think I overstepped—"

"I *think* you overstepped? We both know you did. You expressly went against my wishes, and frankly, Jenna, I resent it."

Jenna didn't say anything. She appeared to be thinking.

"What the hell, Jenna?" Bree exploded.

"Look," Jenna said in a reasonable tone. "I'm a vet. I deal with animals every day. Whatever attacked you, there's something off about it."

"So what? That doesn't give you the right—"

Jenna ignored the interruption and kept on in that reasonable tone of hers. "This thing, this animal, whatever it was, this was an unprovoked attack, right? Animals in the wild don't normally attack unless they're threatened in some way. They avoid confrontation with people unless they're starving or protecting their young. Or, of course, if they're rabid."

When Bree refused to admit what she already knew, Jenna went on. "Not only did this animal attack you, but it doesn't seem to be for any of those reasons. Animals don't attack and then walk away. They fight to the end, *especially* if their victim puts up a fight."

"I told you I hit it in the head with my flashlight."

"Sure. Maybe you stunned it for a minute, but that should have made it angrier. It should have torn you to pieces after you fought back. But from what you said, it didn't. It slunk away, back to the woods, right?"

"Right."

"And this guy, this Griff, finds you out by the side of the road. Bree, whatever attacked you could have, *should have* come back and finished you off. It shouldn't have retreated in the first place. It doesn't make any sense."

"What doesn't make any sense is you going against my wishes and calling the sheriff's office. That deputy practically forced me to file a report," Bree said.

"Look, Bree, I talked to Darryl after you did." She held up a hand to hold off more of Bree's tirade. "I wanted his take on it. He told me of Deputy Gardner's interest in these types of attacks. He said she's been investigating them in an unofficial capacity. I got in touch with her because I knew you wouldn't."

"You had no right. After what happened last year, I thought we made an agreement about overstepping boundaries with each other. But since you can't abide by it, until you admit you were wrong, I don't want to be around you."

Bree slammed the door behind her and strode down the hall to the exit. Everything inside her felt jumbled. She knew she should appreciate Jenna's concern, but all she felt was resentment. This morning she'd wanted Jenna's help. But Jenna simply didn't know when to stop helping.

Bree also didn't like the ring of truth in Jenna's assessment because Bree herself had thought there was something abnormal about the animal's behavior. It could have easily mauled her to death, yet all she had were a few scratches and bruises.

On the drive home her thoughts drifted to the last time Jenna's behavior had strained their friendship. She'd been suspicious of the guy Bree'd been dating. It wasn't the first time, either. But it was the first time Jenna's snooping had turned up anything concerning. During a dinner with friends, she'd confronted Shawn about the fact that he wasn't quite divorced. Bree knew Shawn's ex had been dragging her feet over the financial settlement, but she'd allowed Jenna to believe he was legally out of the marriage. Because she didn't want to deal with Jenna's thoughts on her choices. The two of them had it out with each other and Bree honestly thought Jenna could stop interfering. Especially after Shawn broke things off, citing Jenna's behavior as one of the reasons.

But Bree saw now, that hard as Jenna might try, she couldn't hold back when it came to what she saw as being best for Bree.

Absently, she scratched at the weird abrasion on her wrist, while she tried to stamp out that tiny part of her that believed her best friend's suspicions might, on occasion, have merit.

Chapter Eight

Griff waited anxiously as the auditorium began to fill. He'd arrived early so he'd have his pick of seats. Third row on the aisle. He'd have to endure others crawling over him for the middle seats, but it was a small price to pay. He wanted to hear every word Dr. Madeline Stark had to say about Appalachian history, folklore, myths, and legends. According to the Buncombe County Historical Society newsletter, she was the foremost authority on those subjects. He didn't know if she took on private clients, but if anyone could help him, it would be her.

The auditorium on the campus of Appalachian University seated maybe a couple of hundred. He didn't know whether to be surprised at the number of seats already taken five minutes before the start of the program. How many others besides him were interested in the subject matter? Of course, a lot of them appeared to be students. Maybe the lecture was a course requirement.

Eventually, a guy in a tweed jacket complete with elbow patches walked out onto the stage and took his place behind the lectern. The lights over the audience dimmed. He adjusted the microphone and made a few opening remarks before he began his introduction of the featured speaker. Griff tuned the professor out. He knew Dr. Stark's credentials, and he'd read the slim volume she'd written on Appalachian folklore. He wanted to hear about the stuff that wasn't included in her book and learn whether it would be worth his time to approach her and ask for a private consultation.

He'd left his research materials in the truck. The last thing he wanted was to lose them or have some random lay person find them. God only knew how it could be used against him. Things were bad enough in his life. He didn't need to take unnecessary risks.

He kept thinking about Bree Mason even though she represented nothing but danger for him. After carefully avoiding connections to anyone who could become important to him, especially a woman, the last thing he needed was to make such a connection *now*, right when he was close to ending this curse for good. He told himself he was strong enough, disciplined enough, hell-bent enough to finish what he'd started. Nothing and no one would stand in his way.

Lost in thought, he tuned back in when Dr. Stark came on stage. She shook hands with the professor and thanked him for the kind introduction before she repeated his adjustment of the microphone and fussed with some papers on the lectern. She was a good deal shorter than the previous speaker. Griff guessed her age at around fifty. She dressed conservatively in a black pantsuit and wore minimal makeup. A few grays streaked her dark hair, which she wore in a bun at the nape of her neck.

He hung on her every word, even though much of it might not be relevant to his situation. As her lecture progressed, he became convinced she might be the one person who could help him. Assuming there was help to be had.

She began by mentioning how her interest in Appalachian history had started when she'd traced her own family tree, and how she'd discovered her great-grandmother, one of the granny women of the time, had been not only a revered healer, but one who had learned the ancient Scottish traditions for not only medicinal potions, but spells and incantations as well. Dr. Stark had intensely studied and translated some of the ancient texts brought from the old country in order to understand why her ancestor had been labeled a witch, and not always a good witch.

Polite applause followed the conclusion of her talk. Her books were for sale at a table set up in front of the stage. A student appeared to oversee the money while Dr. Stark chatted to anyone who wanted a word with her or to purchase a book.

Griff hung back. He should have brought his copy with him and asked her to autograph it. It would have been a great way to break the ice before he segued into asking for a private consultation. But his social skills were so rusty as to be non-existent. He normally only needed them in a business setting. But this was business, he reminded himself. Serious business. Personal business where his life was at stake.

Griff kept reshuffling himself to the back of the line until he was the only one left. Dr. Stark regarded him with a faint smile. Something in her dark eyes flickered. A moment of recognition, or something else? They'd never met before, as far as he knew.

"Dr. Stark," he began. "I enjoyed your presentation." He saw the student aide looking at him and summoned a smile. "Actually, I already have your book. I didn't think to bring it for an autograph."

"You can go, Katie," Dr. Stark said. "Thank you for your help."

Dr. Stark began to box up the few remaining books. She set the cash box and a cell phone on top, along with her lecture notes before she looked at Griff expectantly.

"I could carry that for you if you like," he offered.

She nodded and her gaze turned direct and curious. "Have we met?"

"No. We haven't." Griff hoisted the box and followed her toward the exit. "I was hoping to consult with you. Perhaps you'd give me the benefit of your expertise. I'd pay you, of course."

She pushed open the door to the parking lot. "What kind of expertise are you looking for?"

She pointed out her vehicle and unlocked the trunk with the key fob. Griff set the box inside. She took her cell phone out and closed the trunk. Only a few cars were left in the lot, a few people still chatting nearby. A cool breeze carried the scent of pine. A half-moon on a blanket of stars lit the sky.

"My name is Griffin Lancaster," he said. "I've been doing some research on my family history, and I've run up against something I'd like to understand better."

"Your family is from Appalachia?"

"My ancestors, yes. I can share everything I have about my ancestry. If you're willing to take me on as a client, of course."

Her shrewd eyes assessed him. "This seems important to you."

"It is. Very important. I'd go so far as to say you might be the only person who can help me."

"Well now, I *am* intrigued," she said with a ghost of a smile. "Give me your contact information. I'll check my schedule and get back to you. After the initial consultation, I'll decide whether I can assist you or not and we can go from there."

"How long?" Griff asked, not caring if his desperation showed. "Before I hear from you, I mean?" He took his wallet from his back pocket and removed a business card.

"Some time this week." She held the card so she could read it beneath the parking lot's light. "Oh, you're in Chandler," she said.

"Just outside it, actually."

"Me too. Might be easier for you to come to my home." She opened her car door. "In any event, you'll most likely hear from me in a few days. Pleasure to meet you, Mr. Lancaster."

Before Griff could reply, she slid into the car and started the engine. He watched her drive away. A tiny sprig of hope, something he never allowed himself to feel before, took up residence inside him. He couldn't help thinking, *what if Dr. Stark came up with a solution?*

Chapter Nine

Instead of running, Bree walked her usual route. There were no streetlights on this road because there weren't any houses nearby. Instead, the land had been left to the woods and water, a dense bit of forest in its natural state. Although until two nights ago, Bree had never considered the area particularly threatening, it was especially dark. She paid more attention to her surroundings this time, sweeping the beam of her new flashlight across the road and turning around periodically to check behind her.

In her other hand, she clutched the can of pepper spray with her finger on the button. She'd secured her new phone in a sturdy wristband, where she could see it easily and use it if necessary.

She puzzled over the attack and fumed about Jenna's interference. A tiny part of Bree conceded that making the report and documenting her injuries could prove helpful to the authorities since there had been similar attacks before. When Jenna apologized, Bree would forgive her. She always did. But for now, Bree wanted to stew in resentment of Jenna's highhandedness.

She thought about what Jenna had said about the attack. How it wasn't at all normal. The animal, whatever it was, had not wanted to kill her. Harm her? Yes. End her life? No. He (why did she think it was male?) seemed intent on exerting his superior strength over her, digging his claws into her, and terrifying her. But the blow to his head with her flashlight hadn't enraged him. If anything, he'd seem *offended* when she fought back. And he'd retreated as if... he'd already done whatever it was he set out to do. She didn't want to admit it, but Jenna was right. None of this was normal animal behavior.

The whole event was so crazy, she couldn't conceive of it happening again. But if it did, she was better prepared. She turned around where the road dead ended. A single security light shone above an old state park maintenance shed. The rusty gate wouldn't be much of a deterrent to anyone intent on getting access.

She was still feeling bruised, and her energy level was low, but she kept up a brisk pace on the way back until she reached what she now knew to be Griff's driveway.

She turned the flashlight off as she approached his mail-box. She was just curious, she told herself. It was only natural considering the circumstances under which they'd met. Not like she was stalking him or anything.

She crept up the circular driveway, gravel crunching under the soles of her running shoes, until she could see the hulk of his truck in the dim light. She studied the house, though there was little to see. Only a few solar-powered landscape lights broke the darkness.

No light penetrated the windows; he'd have those heavy curtains drawn over them. She thought of him, alone in there.

Maybe he's not alone.

She didn't know where that thought came from, but she didn't like it. She'd seen no signs of a woman's presence, but she hadn't exactly had a chance to look. Bree refused to entertain the thought that he had a girlfriend, but why wouldn't he? By all accounts he was good-looking and successful. Not overly friendly, sure. And he didn't exactly smile much. Maybe he had no sense of humor. All the magazine surveys she'd seen said a sense of humor was high on the list of what women found attractive in men.

Bree wasn't afraid of competition, but she'd prefer to start without any. She didn't want to have to oust a woman who'd already established herself in Griff's life.

Where were these thoughts coming from? She'd never felt possessive about a man like this before. Even during the few relationships she'd had she'd never felt threatened or jealous. When those liaisons ended, she hadn't been devastated. Had, in fact, been ready to move on. Because there hadn't been a man in her life yet who'd made her care enough, one she thought she couldn't live without.

But Griff? One odd meeting and she was already obsessing about him. It was all she could do not to march up to his door right now and demand he let her in. The pull she felt was that strong. Only the thought of how foolish she'd feel if he rejected her, of how inappropriate it was to just show up and expect to be invited in stopped her.

She forced herself back to the road, turned her flashlight back on and kept walking until she was safely back in her townhouse.

As she prepared for bed, she thought up ways she could get herself invited into his house without appearing to have an ulterior motive. The only one that seemed reasonable was to show up with something… as a thank you for rescuing her.

How could he turn her down without being rude? He wouldn't, she decided. If she showed up with homemade cookies, for instance, he'd accept them and say thank you. And if he didn't invite her in right away, she'd keep him talking until he did. And if that didn't work, she'd remind him he'd offered her a tour of his house.

She made a list of the ingredients she'd need to make cookies. If she started baking as soon as she got home tomorrow, she could be at his house with a plate of them by seven or seven-thirty. She wouldn't be interrupting his dinner. He wouldn't feel like he had to offer her a glass of wine or anything. Although, if he did, she wouldn't turn it down.

Maybe, she thought happily, after she pulled off her perfect plan, he'd suggest they get together again.

Hanging on the hook on the back of the bathroom door was the shirt Griff had given her. He'd said she could keep it, although probably she should wash it and give it back to him. But she really didn't want to return it.

She picked it up on her way to bed. She buried her face in it, hoping for a trace of his scent, but all she smelled was her own scent, layered with whatever detergent he used in his washing machine. Or maybe it was fabric softener. Still... it was his shirt.

Dumb, she thought. *You are being so dumb.* She yanked her pajama top off and pulled the thermal shirt over her head. She smiled as she turned off the light and snuggled under the covers. There was no one here to see her silliness. She liked wearing the shirt. Because it was his.

Chapter Ten

Griff was in his home office reviewing the figures he'd put together for a golf course renovation. The bid was due by midnight tomorrow, and he'd been swamped with recent work and hadn't gone over it as thoroughly as he normally would. After tonight he wouldn't get another chance to make sure his numbers were where they needed to be in case he landed the contract.

He heard what sounded like a knock on his front door and ignored it. Visitors were rare, and the indistinct tapping barely registered. But a minute later he heard it again, more insistent this time, and he looked up from his laptop and frowned. Perhaps he could ignore it and whoever was there would go away. He couldn't think of anyone he wanted to see, least of all a salesman or a religious zealot looking to convert him.

He went back to his labor calculations, running them once more through his head and deciding he'd allowed enough for overruns.

More knocking. Non-stop now. Knock. Knock. Knock. Whoever was out there wasn't going away. Not unless he got rid of them.

He shoved his rolling desk chair back and strode through the semi-dark house. God, he loved this place. Loved the way it made him feel like he could hide from the world, and nobody would ever find him or his secrets. Loved the darkness of it, the way it blended into the hillside, so it was almost invisible.

Except somebody knew he was here.

He threw the deadbolt and yanked the door open. "*What?*"

It was her, damn it. He should have known. He hadn't been able to stop thinking about her since he'd dropped her off at her townhouse the other morning. Visions of her constantly distracted him. He'd thought of tracking her down. He knew where she lived. Where she worked. But he'd refused to do so. Such a thing could only end in tragedy. He made himself ignore the pull he felt whenever he drove by her neighborhood. Refused to allow his truck to turn into the entrance and stop at her place to see if she was home.

No. No. No.

He couldn't invite anyone into his life. He'd made a promise to himself, and he'd kept it for almost thirty-three years. And her showing up on his doorstep wasn't going to change that.

"Hi," she said. She smiled. "I didn't see a doorbell, and I wasn't sure if you could hear me knock."

"I heard." He stayed where he was blocking the entrance, even though every instinct told him to step back and invite her in.

No. No. No. He wouldn't do that to her. Not now. Not ever. It was bad enough that life had been so unfair to him. He wouldn't inflict that on her.

"How are you?"

He crossed his arms and did his best to act annoyed. "Is this a social call?"

"Yes. Well. Sort of. I made you some cookies." She held up a plate.

"Why?"

"To thank you. For the other night. For—for rescuing me. And taking care of me. Letting me stay the night."

"You already thanked me."

"I'm thanking you again. And this time I brought cookies. See?" She held the plate a bit higher.

"You didn't have to." He used a stern tone. "You shouldn't have."

"But I did. And I'm here. And I have cookies." She lifted the aluminum foil to show him, and the scents of chocolate and vanilla wafted his way. "They're still a little warm. I just baked them."

Griff could feel himself weaken. He couldn't remember the last time anyone had baked him cookies. Not since his mother had died, he supposed.

No. He had to stay strong. For her. For himself. He had to send her away. He wouldn't ruin her life. "I'm working."

"Really? It's kind of late."

"I have a lot of work."

"You should take a break. Have some tea. Or coffee. Or hot chocolate. And a cookie. Or two."

She wasn't going to leave unless he accepted her offering. Except if he let the cookies in, she'd expect to come with them. "Fine." He held out a hand for the plate. "Anything else?"

She held on to the plate. "Well, you *did* say you'd give me a guided tour of your house, and I have to say, I'm extremely curious. I'd love to see it."

And he desperately wanted to show it to her. He looked her over again. She wore a long dark green sweater over gray leggings. Her hair flowed over her shoulders. She'd never be called pretty, he decided. But she was striking. Interesting. Intriguing.

He knew he was making a mistake before the words even left his mouth. "Fine. Come on in." He stepped aside.

She grinned as she brushed by him. "Thank you."

She went directly to the kitchen and set the plate on the counter. "Do you have any tea? Or should we have coffee?"

"I thought you wanted a tour?"

"I do. But I wouldn't turn down a drink first."

He sighed in defeat and filled a kettle with water. "You're awfully forward."

"I know. I'm not usually like this. It's just—just…"

He turned the fire up under the kettle. "Just what?"

"I wanted to see you again."

He didn't know what to say. He couldn't admit that he felt the same way. The weird mark on his wrist began to tingle. She was different. She was the one. He'd destroy her if he let her get too close the same way his father had destroyed his mother.

No. No. No. Griff wouldn't fall into the same trap. He'd keep his distance. Have some tea. Eat one of her damn cookies. Give her the guided tour and send her on her way.

He retrieved mugs and tea bags. When the kettle whistled, he poured. He was acutely aware of her watching him the whole time. Probably waiting for some kind of response to her last statement. The fact that he hadn't offered one probably stung.

See? He reminded himself. Inviting her in was a mistake. Five minutes and you've already hurt her. And that's all he'd ever do. Hurt her. He didn't want to. But it was the only way to make her keep her distance. He might have to be cruel to be kind.

He'd start by being kind, he decided. Let her down gently, make it clear that nothing would happen between them. A smart woman like her? She'd get the message.

He slid one of the mugs over to her. She lifted the foil covering off the cookies and pushed the plate closer to him.

"Those look good," he said. He picked one up and took a bite. "Delicious."

She beamed like he'd named her Miss America and lifted her mug in a silent toast. Her smile transformed her features and took his breath away.

He'd have to be careful. Very careful.

"Ready for the tour?"

He showed her his office and pointed to the paperwork spread across the desk. "See? I really was working."

She nudged him gently with her elbow. "Admit it. You were dying for a break. You're glad I showed up."

He didn't take the bait but instead moved down the hallway. "Spare bedroom. Bathroom. Laundry room."

"Where does that door lead?" she asked.

"Outside." He opened the door to reveal a set of stairs leading up.

"There's another entrance?"

"Uh, huh. At the top of the hill next to the greenhouse. There's a path leading down to the driveway. We incorporated a water collection system and solar panels. About as eco-friendly as you can get."

"Wow. This is all so cool."

"You've already seen the other bathroom," he said as they retraced their steps to the kitchen.

"What else is down that hallway?"

"Nothing, except my bedroom."

"I didn't see that."

"It's just a bedroom."

Their gazes locked, and Griff reminded himself he wasn't going to go there. She didn't need to see his bedroom. If she did, he wasn't a hundred percent sure she wouldn't try to maneuver him into the bed and have her way with him. And if he allowed her to do that, he'd be lost. And so would she. It would be a mistake of such magnitude he'd go to his grave haunted by it.

Not. Going. To. Happen.

He breathed a sigh of relief when she finally backed down.

"Fine. I guess you should have some secrets."

If she only knew. "Look, I need to get back to work," he said. He set his mug on the counter. "I've got a bid due, and the deadline is tomorrow."

She surprised him by taking the hint. "Oh, all right. Thanks for the tour. Enjoy the cookies."

He walked her to the door. "Thanks for stopping by."

He closed it and leaned heavily against it. He hoped he'd hit the right note. Polite but not encouraging. Because if she showed up here again, he didn't know what

he'd do. But he was pretty sure she'd get to see the bedroom she was so curious about.

Chapter Eleven

The next evening, there was another knock at his door. If it was Bree Mason again, Griff decided there'd be no more Mr. Nice Guy. He'd tell her to get lost and leave him alone in no uncertain terms because she obviously couldn't take a hint.

He yanked the door open and froze when he saw a sheriff's deputy, her hand raised to knock again. Behind her was a county-issued SUV with the sheriff's logo and insignia all over it and red and blue lights mounted on top.

"Mr. Lancaster? Griffin Lancaster?" the deputy asked.

He refocused on the female deputy.

"Yes."

"I'm Deputy Gardner. Wonder if I could ask you a few questions about the incident the other night?"

"Incident?"

"There was an attack on a young woman." She glanced down at the metal clipboard she held. "Maybree Mason. She claims you were involved."

"Is that what she claims?"

"Well, she says that you found her on the road and brought her here to your residence. Mind if I come in for a few minutes?"

"I'm in the middle of a project. This isn't a convenient time."

"When would be a convenient time, Mr. Lancaster? I can come back."

Great. This deputy was as stubborn as Bree. She'd be as hard to get rid of, too. Griff stepped out and closed the door behind him, forcing the deputy to step back. The air held a chill, and he wouldn't have minded a jacket, but he wasn't going back inside for one. "What is it you want to know, Deputy?"

"You found Ms. Mason disoriented on the road in front of your house, correct?"

"Yes."

"What time was that?"

"I don't know. Probably close to eight."

"And how did you come to find her?"

"What do you mean?"

"I mean, were you driving home? Were you out for a walk? How is it that you saw her?"

Good question. "I walked out to check my mailbox. It was dark, but I thought I saw something on the other side of the road. Turned out to be Ms. Mason."

"And you didn't think to call nine-one-one?"

"Didn't have my phone with me. Didn't want to leave her there. I'm not a doctor, but she didn't look to be badly hurt. I offered to call an ambulance. She declined."

The deputy scribbled down his answers. "Have you had any encounters with wild animals around your property?"

"Raccoons. Opossums. Squirrels and rabbits. Birds. Occasionally, I've seen deer."

"No bears or big cats?"

"No."

"Wild boars? Feral dogs?"

"No."

"Any idea what attacked Ms. Mason?"

"None."

The deputy looked behind Griff. "Nice place you've got here. Pretty isolated."

Griff said nothing. The deputy was not his friend. He didn't want to give her any reason to nose around further.

"Thanks for your time." The deputy tipped her hat and Griff watched her get into her cruiser. He waited until she turned onto the road before he went back inside.

Griff stared at his laptop, at the blueprints and site plans spread out over every flat surface in his office, but he saw none of it. In his mind's eye, he saw himself as a hunted animal. Sheriff's deputies with guns and bloodhounds combing the hills for him. Only they didn't know what kind of animal they were looking for. They didn't know what kind of animal they were dealing with.

They could hound him—no pun intended, he thought grimly—all they wanted. Unless they caught him in his animal state, they couldn't prove anything. His worst nightmare, and he'd had a lot of bad ones, was being captured while in his animal state *before* an attack. Because he couldn't change back to his human state until after he'd hunted down and hurt a female. After he'd drawn blood.

Where would they put him if they caught him like that? *Sanctuary*? Oh, God, an added bonus to his nightmare if he were captured and *she* was there, standing outside his cage, studying him. How would she look at him? With pity? Curiosity? Would she approach? Try to pet him? Probably not. She'd been around animals her entire life. She knew better than to put her hand inside the cage of a wild animal.

The thought of her looking at him with pity in her eyes would be more than he could bear.

What if he ended up in a lab? Poked and prodded and clinically studied? He saw himself, trapped, caged, pacing back and forth, looking for a way out. What would they do with him? Take him to some remote facility for further study? What would they feed him? Raw meat? Dog food? His stomach clenched at the thought. He'd have to be more careful. Maybe cross the state line into Tennessee next time.

He scrubbed his hands over his face, his concentration shot. He glanced at the calendar above his desk. He'd transform twice more before his birthday. Then none of this would matter anymore.

Chapter Twelve

As he sipped his morning coffee, Griff stared at the empty plate he'd been staring at every morning for nearly a week. There was nothing special about it. It was plain, white, ceramic, and square. It didn't belong here in his house. Not in his cabinet with his round matte black plates and not on his kitchen counter.

Every morning, its presence confounded him. He didn't know what to do with it. He'd long since finished off Bree's cookies. He'd scraped up the crumbs with his finger and ate those too. He'd washed the plate. Dried it. Set it on the counter. Where it had stayed for days.

He knew where she lived. He didn't have a good reason not to return it to her. No reason except it meant he'd see her again. That was probably her intent to begin with, a ploy to force him to have more interaction with her. A conversation, a brief one at least. Knowing what little he knew about her, she'd invite him in. Into her home. She'd offer him a drink or coffee or tea. Tell him to make himself comfortable. It would be hard to say no. He wouldn't want to say no. He'd want to say, yes, thank you. And once he walked into her house, he probably wouldn't want to leave.

The plate's presence insured that he'd be greeted with thoughts of her every morning. He'd never felt this kind of attraction, this pull toward a woman before. He knew what it meant, and he knew he had to fight it.

He looked away from the plate and refilled his travel mug with coffee. He'd put the plate in his truck. Perhaps bury it under the clutter of site plans, receipts, and invoices that resided there. Maybe he'd sneak by her townhouse one day on his way to work or on his way home and leave the plate on her doorstep. He didn't have to ring the bell. He didn't have to see her. He could do a plate-and-run. A drive-by drop-off.

Coward, he inwardly hissed at himself. For chrissakes, couldn't he be a man? Couldn't he control himself? Surely, he could. He'd been controlling himself for years now, except for the nights he couldn't. He'd learned to accept those things that were beyond his control. His attraction to Bree Mason didn't have to be one of them.

He gathered up his tablet, a couple of rolled up plans, his enclosed metal clipboard which he used to make notes and drawings, and a few other items and put them into a soft-sided black leather carrier along with his tablet. He stuffed the plate into a side pocket, picked up his coffee, and left.

By nightfall, Griff had convinced himself that he was man enough to return Bree's plate to her without the risk of any further involvement. He'd rehearsed the dialogue between them in his head as he drove between his home, his office, and his various job sites. He'd decided it would go something like this:

I'm returning your plate.

Thank you. Would you like to come in?

No. I have to go. Thank you again for the cookies. Bye.

At which point he'd turn around and walk away. He drove into her neighborhood and parked in front of her unit. He grabbed the plate, marched to her door, and knocked.

Perhaps Pete, the guy she'd mentioned that first night, would answer the door. If Pete was her boyfriend, Griff would want to deck him. What kind of man let his woman spend the night away from him without knowing where she was or who she was with? How could the guy fall asleep knowing Bree was out running alone after dark? Anything could happen to her. Something *had* happened. Did Pete even know? Did he care? And if he didn't, why was Bree still with him?

The thought of this faceless man in her life annoyed Griff. She should have someone who at least appreciated her, who would worry about her and come looking for her if she went missing. If Pete was so great, why did she show up at Griff's place with cookies, wanting to see him again? He glowered at the door.

It was dusk now and growing darker by the minute. An overhead light lit the small, recessed area near her front door, and a few solar landscape lights glowed along the walk.

Griff waited a minute. When nothing happened, he pressed the doorbell. He heard a generic chime inside, but no footsteps. No one was home. Perfect, he decided, refusing to acknowledge his disappointment. It was best this way. He could leave the plate near her door. She'd find it when she came home.

He bent to set it in the corner near the frosted glass side panel and noticed the space was already occupied by a nearly dead potted plant on a small metal stand. He picked the pot up and set the plate down in its place. He took a couple of steps back to study the plant in better light.

It was a Christmas cactus. Technically a member of the Schlumbergera family. It wasn't doing very well and no wonder. He could see the soil was dry. Bright red foil wrapped around the cheap plastic pot. She'd probably acquired a green, healthy, and blooming the plant over the holidays, but it hadn't had proper care since.

He fingered one of the shoots. There was still hope. With a bit of care, some water, better soil, a bigger pot, this cactus could make it. He took it with him back to his truck. He doubted Bree would miss it because she obviously didn't know how to take care of it.

He was already home before he realized what he'd done. Instead of severing his connection to Bree Mason, he'd merely changed the format. Because once he revived the cactus, he'd feel obliged to return it to her, along with some instructions on how to care for it.

Idiot.

Chapter Thirteen

As he turned into Dr. Stark's driveway, Griff couldn't recall the last time he'd been this nervous. He was about to reveal things about his family, about himself, that no other living person knew. Information that could destroy his life. Assuming she even believed him.

But he had no choice. Dr. Stark was his last chance, his *only* chance, to find the answers he sought. Once at the door, he took a deep breath and knocked.

She answered, and it might have been his imagination, but he thought she looked genuinely glad to see him. For some reason he felt a brief spark of kinship with her as he stepped inside. He'd brought his binders and his fat files of documentation with him. He'd gone as far as he could with the research he'd amassed. He needed her expertise. He'd lain awake at night, praying that she'd be able to help him.

"How are you, Mr. Lancaster? Please come in."

"You can call me Griff."

"And I'm Madeline."

He followed her to a spacious home office, where she offered him a comfortable seat in front of her desk. Feminine touches such as white bookshelves and floral cushions abounded. Shelves in front of the windows contained potted plants. Mostly herbs, from what he could tell. Parsley. Dill. Lavender, mint, oregano, and rosemary. He sniffed, taking in the mix of aromas.

He saw Madeline smiling at him. "I suppose you're one of the few visitors who would know what they all are."

"Medicinals?"

"Very good. Most people assume they're only for cooking. I make tinctures from time to time. For special clients or friends."

"It's quite a collection. You take good care of them."

She relaxed back into her chair. "I did some research on you, Griff, before I decided to meet with you again. I hope you don't mind."

Since he was about to tell her everything anyway, Griff didn't see why he would.

"I looked into your family history as well," she said.

He raised an eyebrow. This was a step on her part he hadn't anticipated, but perhaps he should have.

"Would it surprise you to know that we have connecting branches on our family tree?"

Griff frowned. He had his family tree in one of the files he'd brought with him. But he'd only ever traced his own ancestry. Or rather, his father had before he died. But he'd only been interested in the male descendants of Colin Lancaster.

"Does the name Emerald MacCallum mean anything to you?"

He didn't try to hide his astonishment. "Yes."

"She was my great-grandmother."

"But she never married into the Lancaster family." Of this, Griff was certain.

Madeline smiled. "You don't have to be married to bear a child."

"A child of one of my ancestors."

"Colin Lancaster."

"How do you know? I mean, how can you be sure?"

"As I said in my talk, I've researched my ancestry. I found the old texts along with writings Emerald left behind. I also had my grandmother as a resource."

"Emerald's daughter."

"Correct. Mirren learned plenty about how she came to be. Emerald's bitterness toward the man who seduced and abandoned her never abated. She went to her grave cursing him and all his descendants."

"But that would have included her own child," Griff pointed out.

Madeline's smile turned sad. "True. And while I've not found evidence that was her intention, I can say the Mac-Callum women have had their share of bad luck. Would you like some tea?" she asked abruptly. She stood and said, "I'll be right back," before Griff could reply.

While she was gone, Griff tried to work out what relation he and Madeline were to each other. The best he could come up with was distant cousins, several times removed. He didn't see what difference it made. Except, perhaps, Madeline would have more insight into someone from her own family. He knew now he'd made the right choice in coming to her.

She returned after a moment to find him looking over the books on her shelves. She set a tea tray down on a small corner table. "Cream? Sugar? Lemon?"

"Black's fine." Griff went back to his seat and accepted the dainty, gold-trimmed mug she handed him. She prepared her own tea and sat behind the desk.

The tea's aromatics mixed with those of her plants created a heady, spell-binding fragrance. Griff took a careful sip, tasting ginger and orange and oolong.

"You were saying your branch of the family has had its own share of misfortune?"

"It would appear, from the research I've done, that since Emerald's time, we bear only female children."

"That doesn't sound like a bad thing."

"It's not. In fact, we're survivors of misfortune, just as Emerald was. She lived well into her nineties, yet she never married and had only one child."

"Your grandmother."

"Correct. My grandmother married and had one child. My mother. Her husband died young."

Griff tensed. "How old was he?"

"In his early thirties."

"Thirty-three by chance?"

She raised an eyebrow. "Yes."

"And your mother?"

"The same. One child. My father died and I know he was thirty-three. It was right after his birthday."

Griff's shoulders slumped in defeat. Had Emerald inadvertently cursed her own branch of the family tree at the same time she cursed Colin's? "And you?" He watched Madeline carefully.

"The same. One daughter. One husband. They died in a car accident when he was thirty-three."

"Your daughter didn't survive?"

"She survived the accident. In fact, initially, the doctors thought she would recover completely. But her internal injuries caused her to hemorrhage. They couldn't save her."

"I'm sorry."

"It was a long time ago now."

"How did your father die?"

"A blood clot or more accurately, a pulmonary embolism after Achilles tendon surgery. Fairly rare, but not unheard of."

"And your grandfather?"

"Gunshot during a bar fight. By all accounts, he was a wild one with a hot temper."

"Your mother and grandmother didn't remarry?"

"No."

"Nor did you? Never had more children?"

Madeline gave him another sad smile. "Never met anyone who interested me enough. And losing a child does something to you. Or to me, anyway. Even if I'd found another partner, I'm not sure I'd have had it in me to try for a family."

"It sounds like Emerald put a curse on her own family."

"Based on everything I've learned about her, Emerald suffered greatly. She wanted more than anything for others to suffer as much as she did."

"If that's what it is, it will end with you then, won't it?"

Madeline gave him a bitter smile. "Definitely. There's no one else to carry on such an evil legacy. Now let's talk about you."

Chapter Fourteen

*E*xactly *what I want for myself. I want to leave a legacy, but not the one perpetrated by Emerald Mac-Callum. No son of mine will be touched by her.* "Are you aware of the curse Emerald cast on the man who would have been your great-grandfather?"

"Colin Lancaster. Of course. There were still whispers about him, even when I was a child. There were many things I didn't know about the women who came before me. From Emerald on down, they were great healers. Traditional granny women in those mountains were the midwives, the doctors, the nurses, the paramedics. They knew every plant, every herb, and the healing or poisonous properties of each.

"I remember my grandmother's kitchen, lined with bottles and jars with crude labels. I used to watch her and my mother create tinctures and potions for the locals. They'd come to her with an ailment or an injury, and she would make a poultice with a combination of those things in the jars, handed out in a tiny bottle with verbal instructions."

Griff could see it. He'd dreamt of that kitchen, which must have once been Emerald's and her mother's and grandmother's before her. Crude shelves, a worn wooden worktop, a hand pump for water. Hard-packed dirt floors, a minimum of furniture. A cookstove in the corner. Women in faded flour-sack dresses, messy braids down their backs, tending boiling pots, creating medicines, delivering babies, setting broken bones.

"You said you studied the old texts that were handed down through your family, correct?"

"As much as I can. The pages are delicate, as you might imagine, and I had to find help for translation."

"What I want to know. What I *need* to know is if there is any way to break the curse Emerald put on Colin's descendants. Because like you, I'm the last of that line."

They eyed each other across the desk, as if sizing up an opponent, or possibly an ally. Determining if the other was up to the challenge they knew was coming.

"My answer is I don't know. I don't know the exact nature of the curse. Only that it involves imbuing the male line with an animal's nature." She paused, her eyes seeming to pierce through his skin, as if she could look into his soul. "But I will tell you this. Based on what I know, for every spell or curse someone like my great-grandmother cast, there is a way to break it. To end it."

She must have seen the expression of hope on Griff's face, because her tone became more foreboding. "From what I've learned, however, the cure might be worse than the curse. Whatever spell you're under, Griff, I guarantee the solution will be beyond unpleasant."

His gaze locked on hers. "I'm going to die, like all the men who married into your family. Like all the men born into mine." The bald statement of fact landed between them with a heavy thud. "I'm going to die without ever really getting to live. This curse either dies with me, or you can help me end it. You're my only chance."

Now Madeline's shoulders slumped. "I don't know if I can. You might be wasting your time."

"I don't have much of it left, but I want to die knowing I did everything I could to find another way."

Griff could see Madeline struggle to control her distress before she asked, "When's your birthday?"

"The end of November."

"That doesn't give us much time."

"I know. I've brought you copies of all the research I have. My father compiled most of it before he died." He handed the file to her.

"You're the last of your line?"

"Yes." Griff hesitated. "I had a twin brother. Gregory." Madeline waited.

"He killed himself."

"Because of the curse?"

"Yes." Due to a bizarre set of circumstances Greg had attacked one of his classmates and had come close to being caught. Griff didn't share the details with Madeline for it wouldn't change the outcome. After the incident, Greg sunk into a deep depression and eventually took his own life.

"I'm sorry."

"Will you help me?" Griff didn't like the pleading sound in his voice, but what choice did he have but to throw himself on this woman's mercy?

Madeline sat up straight and placed her hands flat on the files. "I don't know if I can help you, but I will try. Let me look over what you have here. We can meet again."

"When?"

"A few weeks, perhaps."

"Fine." It wasn't, but what choice did he have?

She followed him to the door. "I'll do my best," she said, "but I feel I should warn you not to expect too much. From what I have learned, Emerald was a powerful woman."

"If anyone can help me, it's you. There isn't anyone else."

"I'll do my best," she repeated, though regret swept across her expression. "I'll be in touch."

On the drive home, Griff swung between hope and disappointment. He'd had numerous debates with himself over the years about ending his life the way Greg did. His brother's death at nineteen devastated what was left of the family. Their mother, already crushed by losing their father, never recovered. Griff did everything he could to give her a reason to hang on, but she'd faded away, with one mysterious ailment after another, until she passed from what the coroner termed "unknown causes."

Griff's vow to end the curse had never wavered. For years he'd been on a quest to find a way to end it that didn't require his own death. There must be an antidote to the poison Emerald had infected his family with, even if—as Madeline had suggested—the cure was worse than the affliction.

He could never knowingly pass this curse to a son of his own.

Not. Going. To. Happen.

He'd considered a vasectomy, but he'd read about unsuccessful reversals of such a procedure. The curse kept him from seeking a partner, but what kept him going was finding the cure and having a family. He put the responsibility for those thoughts squarely on the head of that tiny seed of hope lodged somewhere deep inside of him. There had to be a way out.

And if there wasn't?

Back at his house, he settled in his office and unrolled a set of plans, indulging in one of his pastimes—reviewing the project he wanted to create. A way to leave his own legacy. One that had nothing to do with Emerald Mac-Callum's wickedness.

The Lancaster Family Botanical Garden. He'd perfected the plans over the past few years. He had a vision. He had the funding. All he needed was a sizable plot of donated land. This was the mark he needed to make to ensure his family was never forgotten, even if it all ended with him.

Chapter Fifteen

Two weeks went by, and Bree heard nothing from Griff. She didn't see him either, even though she'd resumed her nightly runs on the route that led past his house. She refused to give in to the urge to take a detour up his driveway and knock on his door. He hadn't exactly wanted to invite her in the first time. She could only guess how he'd react if she showed up again uninvited.

Nope. Not going to happen. She'd resigned herself to spending time with Griff only in her fantasies. They were wonderful fantasies, though. She daydreamed about him. At night she dreamed about him too. She had a crush of epic proportions on him, far worse than any she'd had in adolescence. But a whole lot of nothing fueled her feelings. Chances were good she'd never see him again unless he purposely arranged it.

These thoughts wandered through her head as she walked the path from the barn at Sanctuary to the administrative offices. The cool April air made her hug her thin cardigan around herself and glance at the sky where dark clouds were gathering. She'd heard rain mentioned in the forecast for this evening. She turned the corner of the building and saw a black truck parked near the entrance. Her steps slowed as the driver got out.

After two weeks of thinking about Griff non-stop, he had shown up right in front of her. It was like the slowest summoning spell ever. Not like she'd put a spell on him or anything. More like he'd put a spell on her to make her think of nothing but him.

"Hello," she said as she met him on the sidewalk leading to the double doors.

He seemed taken aback. "Hello." He looked around as if some explanation for her presence would present itself.

"Are you... here to see me?"

"No." His definitive response caused a hard pinch to her heart. "I'm meeting with Carter Hayes."

Mentioning his name seemed to conjure the man himself, because one of the office doors opened and Carter came toward them. He extended his hand.

"Griff. Thanks for stopping by again. You've met our director, Bree Mason."

Griff's gaze flickered toward Bree. "Yes. We've met."

"I've got another meeting scheduled shortly, so if you don't mind, we should get started," Carter said. "Bree, if you'll excuse us."

"Would you mind if I tagged along? I'd like to hear what Mr. Lancaster has to say."

Griff looked from her to Carter and back. Carter was a bit flustered by her request. "Oh, well, no, of course not."

"I promise to behave myself," she said to Griff. "I know you're *terribly* busy."

"Thanks," Griff deadpanned. "I appreciate it."

As good as her word, Bree trailed behind the two men and listened. She knew that Carter had asked for several landscape designers to meet with him to discuss Sanctuary's needs. She let much of their conversation wash over her. She wanted only to be near Griff.

The temperature dropped as more clouds gathered overhead, and Bree rubbed her upper arms. She should have made the men wait while she'd gone to her office for her jacket. But she hadn't wanted to inconvenience them since they weren't too keen on her tagging along. Especially Griff.

"Are you cold?" Griff asked. "Here." Before she could answer, he pulled off his black flannel button-up and draped it over her shoulders. Apparently, he was comfortable enough in the thermal shirt he wore underneath.

She smiled at him as the warmth from his shirt and the touch of his fingers seeped into her. "Thanks."

His gaze locked with hers for the briefest, tiniest moment. But she thought she saw something there. Longing. Sadness. Wistfulness. Absently, she rubbed her wrist. Her other injuries from the attack had healed, but the place on her wrist, although not as inflamed as it had been, remained. It never scabbed over. Somehow the animal had managed to leave its imprint on her, like a brand. It didn't bother her. She thought of it as a badge of courage.

He turned back to Carter, and the moment was gone. She crossed her arms and clutched the edges of the shirt, pulling it snugly around her. Maybe he'd let her keep this shirt, too. She smiled to herself as she envisioned being decked out in a whole set of Griff's clothes. The black jeans. The boots. She'd look ridiculous. But she'd be warm. Comfortable. Safe.

Ridiculous.

She stopped trying to pretend she wasn't there to concentrate on Griff. He and Carter were in a deep discussion of how to best showcase the entrance to the barn and the white rail fence surrounding the pasture.

The thermal shirt Griff still wore outlined the strength of his upper body and hung over his belt buckle. He'd pushed the sleeves up to his elbows. Bree couldn't stop thinking about what lay beneath his clothes. She watched him talk and gesture, tuned into the rhythm of his words and the tone of his voice. She wished she could run her fingers through his hair, gaze into his eyes, kiss his mouth.

She yearned for him. That was a good word for how she felt. She *yearned* for him. She didn't know how or why or what exactly had happened to her to make her so fascinated, so obsessed with this man who acted like he wanted nothing to do with her.

Unfortunately, she couldn't help herself. He was here and she tried to be discreet. But she drank in every detail she could about Griff.

Griff took photos and made notes on his tablet while he and Carter talked. Every now and again, he rubbed at his left wrist, even though he wore a watch with a wide leather band. Bree wondered if that was a nervous tic or if his wrist itched the way hers did.

As they were concluding their discussion, Carter's phone rang. He glanced at it and said, "I'm sorry, I need to take this. I'll be in touch." He shook hands with Griff and nodded at Bree before he headed back to the administration building, phone to his ear.

"This is quite a set-up you have here."

"The property belonged to my grandparents," Bree said as they paused near the corral. "When times got tough, the only way they could hang onto it was to convert some of it to a land trust for a non-profit." Two of the horses in the pen ambled toward them. "The outbuildings were already here. An animal sanctuary seemed the logical choice." When the horses were close enough, Bree rubbed their noses. "Sorry, guys, I didn't bring any treats for you."

"These are rescues?" Griff asked.

"Yes. All the animals here are. Want to see the baby goats? They're adorable."

Griff hesitated. He reached a hand out toward the horse nearest him, a black mare with a white star on her forehead. She rolled her eyes and shifted away from his touch, nudging the horse next to her, an aging paint, who snorted in annoyance. Griff dropped his hand. "Maybe another time."

"Not an animal lover?"

He watched her carefully. "It's obvious you are."

"I grew up here. There were always cats with litters of kittens in the barn. Always a couple of dogs. Cows. Pigs. Goats. If it had four feet, my grandparents took a shot at raising it. They had llamas for a time. Donkeys. Miniature horses. Down by the pond, there were ducks and geese. My grandmother kept chickens and sold the eggs." She slanted a look up at him. "So yeah. I love animals. Okay, guys. Gotta go." She patted each horse in turn and started back toward her office.

"Running a place like this as a non-profit must be a lot of work."

"It is, but we offer several programs to defray the costs. We also have a lot of volunteers, and we offer internships. We do events in conjunction with the school system, even the county, when they need to place individuals for community service hours."

"It seems like you have a lot of land you're not utilizing, though."

"Some," Bree agreed. "I've thought of some additions I'd like to make, other programs we could offer to the community."

"Such as?"

Bree stopped and looked up at him. "A community garden, for example. I think it's a great idea... in theory." She turned and gazed out over the property. "My grandmother raised all her own vegetables. She had flower gardens everywhere. I, however, did not inherit her green thumb." Beyond the pasture, a quarter mile away, stood an old apple orchard.

Griff's gaze followed hers. He pointed. "Northeast of your office, there's a fairly flat plot of land. There's a stream running through there, right?"

"Yes. A very small one."

"Which could be used for irrigation."

"I guess. I'd have to see if we'd need permits or clearance from the county."

"I can help you with that. I don't think they'd require much since you already have the sanctuary. The way your parking lot curves around the side of the building, all you'd need is an access path of some sort."

"We'd need the land prepped. A fence, probably. It's not in the budget."

"You might be able to get it donated."

She caught his gaze. "From you?"

"In part. I can use the tax deductions, and part of my company's mission statement involves supporting the community. Plus, it's good advertising. *Free* advertising. If we can't get everything donated, I've got some contacts that would probably do some of the work, like the fence and gravel for a path, at cost."

"That would be wonderful."

"Carter sent me a site analysis and survey a while back. It's in my truck."

Two spaces from his vehicle Madeline Stark was getting out of her car. Apparently, she and Griff were acquainted for the two exchanged greetings. Bree had her own wrong-footed history with the woman, who'd volunteered at Sanctuary almost from the beginning. As director, Bree recognized Madeline's value and the two maintained a civil, if not exactly friendly, relationship when they crossed paths. They offered each other the briefest of hellos before Madeline took the walkway to the barn.

Griff retrieved the documents as the wind began to pick up. He followed Bree to the office building, reaching ahead to open the door.

Near the front desk, a cluster made up of mostly middle-aged women listened attentively to a younger woman wearing a Sanctuary t-shirt and jeans. They were either on a guided tour or were a new batch of volunteers here for orientation, Griff decided. The young woman caught Bree's eye and held up her hand to indicate five minutes and Bree inclined her head in acknowledgment.

He followed Bree to her office, where a large orange cat lounged in her desk chair. "Hello, Pumpkin." She picked the cat up and kissed the top of his head. He appeared unmoved by her affection, staring at Griff with his pale green eyes as if to say, "See what I have to put up with?"

The cat's ears were too short and stubby for its face. When Griff looked closer, he saw they were scarred and had been cut off at the top. He was also missing a line of fur along one jaw, and a jagged bald spot ran across his nose. "What happened to him?"

"We don't know," Bree said. She shifted Pumpkin so he could peer over her shoulder while she stroked his back. "Most likely a run-in with another animal. He was pretty mangled when we got him, but he survived. Didn't you, Pumpkin?" she said, scratching his head. "He's our office mascot now and has the run of the place." The cat squirmed, and she bent to release him. Pumpkin landed heavily on his feet and strutted out into the corridor attempting to maintain his dignity. Based on the cat's physique, Griff decided 'Pumpkin' suited him.

Bree took off his flannel shirt and didn't seem to notice the liberal sprinkling of pumpkin-colored cat hair clinging to it before she handed it back to him. "Thanks for the loan."

She cleared off the center of her desk and he anchored the site survey on it, pointing out the spot he wanted her to consider.

The young woman who'd signaled Bree earlier rapped on the open door of Bree's office. "Sorry to interrupt," she said, her gaze filled with undisguised curiosity. "But we're ready for you."

"I'll be right there, Faith," Bree said, then turned to Griff. "Can you give me five minutes? I have to give the 'Welcome-and-thanks-for-volunteering-at-Sanctuary' speech to the group."

"Not a problem."

"Can I get you water or coffee or anything?"

"I'm fine."

"I'll be right back."

Chapter Sixteen

Griff took the time to study his surroundings. Bree's standard office desk connected to an L-shaped workspace and credenza. Above were cabinets and shelves. Some of the items she had moved aside for the map were framed photographs. He picked up the nearest one out of curiosity. Bree and a dark-haired woman in a white lab coat grinned in front of the Sanctuary entrance sign.

He set the photo back and picked up a smaller one. The faded snapshot showed a group of teenagers in an outdoor setting. It looked like it had been taken at one of the nearby national parks based on what he could see of the sign in the background. He picked out a much younger Bree, her hair pulled back, dressed in hiking boots and jeans, as were the others. A young man draped an arm casually over her shoulders. A soon-to-be boyfriend, perhaps, based on their body language.

He sensed Bree's return before she came around the desk. He set the photo back where he'd found it. "You like to hike?" he asked, indicating the picture.

Bree hesitated. A shadow crossed her face, an unpleasant reaction to an old memory, perhaps. "I do. I don't go as often as I used to, though." She gave him a forced smile. "Now, where were we?"

"Clearing the land, prepping the garden, and putting up a fence," Griff said briskly. "Think you could get some of your volunteers to help?"

"I know I can," Bree said. "In fact, a community garden would probably generate a whole new set of volunteers."

"Have you considered doing some work on the orchard?"

"I *consider* lots of things. But there's only so much money to go around. In this economy, even with the generous support we have, and I have to allocate assets where they're needed. First and foremost, we're an animal sanctuary. That's our focus."

"Sure. I understand. But an apple orchard could also generate income."

"But to get it to that point would take time. Effort. Money. Are you going to donate that as well?"

Griff shrugged. "Let me make some calls and put together some numbers for the garden and the orchard and get back to you."

"Thank you."

"No problem. I'm betting we can get some plants donated for the garden. I'll check with a couple of the wholesale nurseries. Maybe you'd consider letting me start an experimental project with the orchard."

"Experimental project?"

"There's some interesting research on hybrid plants, organic fertilizers, that sort of thing going on in-state. Carter and I discussed it during our first meeting."

"I'd be willing to consider it if I had more details. But those decisions are made by the board."

"Of course. Another question." He pointed to a blank area of the map, marked Conservation. "All of this acreage here? You're conserving it? For what?"

Bree folded her arms. "Mainly to keep it out of the hands of developers." She pulled her chair out and sat, then looked at Griff expectantly until he took one of the visitor seats. "I was always involved in Sanctuary because of my grandparents. All during high school and college. They set it up, but it was never a money-making proposition. When I took it over, it was fast sinking into the red, and developers were at the door making offers. This place is all I have left of them. Do you understand?"

She could have no inkling of exactly how well Griff understood the desire to have and to preserve a family legacy. She waited until he said, "Yes," before continuing.

"I fundraised like nobody's business. You name it, I did it, well me and the volunteers we had at the time. I begged and borrowed and groveled until things started to turn around. I recruited board members with enough influence to raise more money. But we can only do so much. Those developers are still out there. Some of them would be willing to settle for half the land instead of all of it."

"The part you're conserving."

"Exactly. It's been with the state's land trust alliance for five years."

"You never thought of another purpose for it?"

"Like what?"

"A botanical garden."

"I'll admit that's not something I ever considered. I'm not even sure I know what a botanical garden is, exactly."

Griff almost smiled. "But I do."

"You'll have to explain it to me."

"I will."

"Over dinner?"

Griff's jaw clamped shut. They engaged in a brief stare down before Griff said, "When does the alliance agreement come up for renewal?"

"I'd have to check," Bree said. "This summer, I think."

Griff rolled up the map and put the rubber band back around it. He put his shirt back on. "Don't make plans for renewing it. Not yet. I'll get back to you in a couple of days." He noticed her business card holder and took one of the cards. "Should I go through you or Carter?"

"I'll tell him we talked, but I'll need more information before I commit to anything. But like I said, the board would make the final decision."

"All right."

"Do you have a card you can leave with me?"

"Sure." Griff reached into his back pocket, withdrew a wallet, and handed her a card. Once again, their fingertips touched. Something sizzled in the air between them. "I should be going. I'll be in touch."

Chapter Seventeen

B ack in her office, Bree returned everything to its place except the photo Griff had been looking at. The one of her and Jeremy.

Her mind transported her back to that day.

She could not believe her luck as she panted and climbed the trail, using Jeremy Taylor's backside as an incentive to keep going, even when her muscles screamed, and her lungs begged for relief.

She'd had a crush on Jeremy since eighth grade and finally, miraculously, near the end of her sophomore year, he'd noticed her. Maybe because her long-awaited figure was starting to take shape. She'd grown taller, leaving her adolescent chubbiness behind, and her body had filled out in new and interesting ways. Maybe it was because she sat in front of Jeremy in World History, and he could hardly miss her. Maybe because her best friend Jenna Scott was dating his best friend, Ryan Welsh.

Bree didn't know and didn't care. Jeremy had called her a couple of times. He'd chatted her up before the bell rang in history class and walked with her down the hall afterward. He'd invited her to hike Smokestack Mountain with him and a few of his friends. They were mostly juniors, and Bree didn't know them very well, but they were friendly enough. They were all jocks, the guys and girls alike, and they were all in better physical shape than she was. But Bree didn't care. Jeremy didn't seem to mind that his friends had passed them, and he and Bree were virtually alone on the trail. He kept up a running commentary between panting breaths, tossing his words back over his shoulder.

She laughed at his jokes and agreed that the recent spring rains made the trail more slippery than usual in some areas and exposed even more rock in others.

"We should take a break," Jeremy said when they reached a small flat area where the trail widened a bit. He turned and offered his hand as she climbed the last few feet. His warm fingers clasped hers. Something fluttered in her chest.

"Look at this," he kept hold of her hand and swept his arm out over the vista.

"Wow." They were far above the gorge. Beyond were mountains and pines and other trees beginning to leaf. Below them only a few hearty trees and bushes clung to the unforgiving granite. A long way down the river churned and rushed, swollen from melted snow and the recent spring rain. "It's beautiful."

She had an image of her and Jeremy, ten years into the future, out of college, married, of course, hiking this same trail and standing hand in hand, remembering their first visit here. She enjoyed romantic daydreams, and Jeremy Taylor had figured strongly in them for three years.

Some of the mud at the edge of the trail fell away. Bree stepped back to firmer ground, tugging Jeremy's hand. She knew how dangerous some of the trails could be, especially after a lot of rain. How easy it was to slip on exposed rock or slide or lose your footing because of accumulated leaves and mud. A fall could result in a devastating injury, or death. That's why there were warning signs at every trailhead.

"I'm glad you came today," Jeremy said.

She smiled at him. "Me too." The wind whipped his chestnut hair around his head, and his brown eyes regarded her warmly. "But I'll need to join the track team or something next year so I can keep up with you guys."

He looked her over. "That's a good idea. You're built for running."

"Maybe a year from now, we can race to the top."

"I'll give you a head start."

"I won't need it."

"Mmm. Confident. I like that."

Bree laughed. Jeremy leaned closer and kissed her. He didn't linger, just pressed his lips against hers.

"What was that for?" she asked.

"I like you."

"I like you, too." Wow, this was easy, Bree thought. Where was the subterfuge, the push-pull, the he-loves-me-he-loves-me-not angst most girls went through with guys?

"Want to go to prom with me?" Jeremy asked, still holding her hand.

"Really?"

"Yes, really." He swung her hand. "A bunch of us are going in together for a limo. I'll rent a tux. You get a dress. We'll eat, drink, and be merry."

"And dance," Bree added. "You do know how to dance, don't you?"

"Of course. Allow me to give you a small demonstration." Jeremy kept hold of her hand and began to improvise some intricate steps.

"Careful," Bree warned, remembering the mud she'd stepped back from earlier.

Jeremy gave her a spin under his arm. "You will be amazed by my—"

Jeremy yanked so hard on her hand Bree was on the ground before she realized what had happened. Jeremy had slipped, or the ground at the edge of the trail had given way. He was pulling her with him, his weight nearly wrenching her shoulder from its socket.

"Jeremy!" she screamed, her voice absorbed by the woods, the mountain, the rushing water far below. She could only see his arm and the top of his head.

His fingers were white where they were wrapped around hers. "Bree! Help!"

Bree slid a couple more inches toward the edge. With her free arm, she grabbed onto the trunk of a small pine. She wondered how deep its roots were. She had a brief terrifying image of yanking it up and going over the edge with Jeremy.

She saw his free hand grasping for purchase on some-thing, but there was nothing to hang onto. Mud and debris and bits of rock crumbled away each time he tried.

"Bree," he pleaded.

"*Help*!" she screamed. Her mind went blind with panic. She couldn't remember any of the names of Jeremy's friends. The trees and terrain bounced sound around. Could they even hear her?

"*Help*!" Jeremy hollered. Their cries echoed off the gorge and drowned in the rushing water below.

"Pull me back up," Jeremy pleaded.

Bree tried. If she could get him up far enough to grab the tree, he could make it the rest of the way.

"Give me your other hand."

Bree froze in terror. Jeremy outweighed her by what? Fifty pounds? He was taller and athletically built. If she let go of the tree, she might go over the edge.

"Jeremy," she pleaded.

With his free hand, he reached up and grasped her wrist. "Help me! Please!"

She tried to pull him back up, but his weight and des-peration defeated her efforts as more of the ground fell away beneath them. Bree could feel it crumble below her elbows. She could picture herself falling headfirst down the wall of granite and into the river beneath, crashing into the rocks below.

But that's what would happen to Jeremy if she didn't do something.

"Hold on."

"Bree, I can't." Jeremy's grip began to slip. She heard footsteps rushing down the trail from above.

"Help!" she screamed again. She let go of the trunk and reached for Jeremy at the same moment someone grabbed her from behind and Jeremy lost his hold on her wrist.

She watched in horror as he disappeared with a long anguished "ahhhhh" before crashing into the water below.

In her office, Bree stared at herself and Jeremy in the photo, his arm draped across her shoulder, and wished yet again she'd have done something different that day. Wished she'd been able to save Jeremy, been strong enough or brave enough. But she'd been too afraid of going over the edge with him.

Jenna thought Bree ghoulish for keeping the photo where she'd see it every day. But she kept it there to remind herself how short life was, that she had to take risks, live in the moment, be brave even when she was terrified. That was Jeremy's legacy to her, and to do anything different would be to dishonor the memory of the first boy she'd loved.

I can help you with that. Let me make some calls and put together some numbers.

The words he'd spoken reverberated in his head as he accelerated on the highway. Griff banged the heel of his hand against the steering wheel in frustration. What the hell was wrong with him? Why hadn't he kept his mouth shut? Sure, he'd already studied the site map, and the community garden idea was a good one. There was plenty of space for it, and it fell in line with what Sanctuary was all about. Serving the community. It'd be a great project for service clubs, families, and anyone who wanted to garden but didn't have the space.

But when he'd arrived for his meeting today, *especially* after he saw Bree and she decided to tag along, he'd warned himself not to encourage her or spend any more time with her than necessary. Evidently his warnings to himself flew right out of his brain because it seemed like the most natural thing in the world to engage her and listen to her ideas.

When she invited him into her office, it was all he could do not to reach out and touch her hair or see if he could smell her perfume. No, he chided himself now, she probably didn't wear perfume to work. Or it had worn off by now. He hadn't picked up on any specific scent, but still he'd been drawn to her. Which is exactly what he shouldn't be.

Even though he'd ignored her dinner suggestion he'd opened a line of communication, and if he knew one thing about her, if he didn't follow up, she would.

He could refuse to share a meal with her, but he didn't see how he could take back the offer he'd made to help with the community garden without looking completely unprofessional, not to mention foolish.

But if he could get the Sanctuary land out of the conservation trust, if he could get her to agree to donating it for the botanical garden instead, whatever torture he had to go through would be worth it. Even if he couldn't complete the project before he died, he'd have everything in place and assign the right people to see it through after he was gone. The Lancaster Family Botanical Garden would be the legacy he'd always hoped for.

He caught a whiff of something and turned his head to make sure no one was in his blind spot before he passed a semi. He lifted the collar of his shirt and sniffed. Maybe it wasn't perfume. He didn't know what it was, but something about it reminded him of Bree. The same clean, fresh, wholesome scent he'd noticed the first night during the attack. Pure. Untainted, he'd thought then, and he'd hated himself for bringing her down, forcing her to struggle against him in the dirt and weeds. Making her bleed.

He'd have to steel himself, he decided, to keep his distance from her in the future. No matter how much he wanted to do the exact opposite. It would help if he thought of her well-being instead of his own desire.

Chapter Eighteen

Bree dressed with extra care and took a little more time than she usually did applying her makeup. A meeting had been scheduled with Griff, Carter Hayes, Sanctuary's board of directors, and a couple of senior volunteer staff to discuss the community garden project, Griff's experimental use of the orchard, his proposal to create a botanical garden, and to go over the numbers for each.

Bree hadn't seen Griff since they'd reviewed the plans in her office a month ago, but she'd spoken to him on the phone a few times. He'd been business-like on each occasion, almost to the point of brusqueness. She hadn't been able to steer the conversation to anything personal. But maybe today, after the meeting, he'd... what? Ask her out? Suggest they grab lunch?

She set the lip gloss back in her makeup drawer and steeled herself to face the truth the same way she faced herself in the mirror.

Griff was not going to ask her out. Even though she sensed he wanted to. She'd felt that charge in the air between them from the very first. She couldn't believe he didn't feel the same pull she did. The chemistry. Something held him back, but what?

It would be best if she stopped fantasizing about something happening between them. She promised herself she would. Instead, she would make sure he knew what he was missing out on. She adjusted the sleeves of the silk sweater set. She loved the soft shade of peach paired with a gray pencil skirt and gray pumps.

She smiled at her reflection. "Eat your heart out."

Griff was already in the conference room talking with Carter Hayes and one of the volunteers when Bree arrived. She greeted those who were gathered around the conference table before she went to the counter where coffee urns were set up.

"Good morning," Carter said to her, stepping aside so she could reach the cups.

"Good morning, gentlemen." She flashed them a smile, refusing to single Griff out with his own greeting before she turned back to the table to pour her coffee.

"This shouldn't take long, should it, Bree?" Carter asked. "Griff's got a couple of projects going and needs to be out of here by ten-thirty."

"Oh, believe me, I'm well aware of how busy Mr. Lancaster is." She gave Griff her most brilliant smile. "And to answer your question, no, I don't think the meeting will take long. We sent everyone the agenda well ahead of time and they've got the proposals for the garden and the orchard as well as the botanical garden. Mostly, this is a Q and A before we vote. We'll have you out of here in no time, don't you worry." This last line she directed at Griff, looking directly into his eyes.

He looked amused and bemused at the same time. "I appreciate it."

He wore all black again, but this time it was a black dress shirt, black tie, and black slacks. Could a signature color be taken too far? Bree didn't think so. Not for someone like Griff, anyway. His hair looked shorter than the last time she'd seen him. No beard stubble either. He looked good. Damn him.

"Excuse me." She strode to the head of the confer-ence table, trying not to spill her coffee on the way. He didn't have to do anything except look at her and she lost it. He unsettled her, and no matter how hard she tried to squelch her sense of excitement and anticipation every time she saw him, she couldn't. Electricity buzzed through her whenever she got close to him. How could he not feel it? Absently she rubbed at her wrist, feeling a tingle around the weirdly shaped mark that refused to heal. Her earlier cocky attitude deserted her.

"Let's go ahead and get started. I think everyone is here." She waited a few minutes while those attending found their seats and quieted. "We have Griffin Lancaster of Lancaster Landscape Design with us today to answer any questions we may have about his proposals. In order not to take up too much of his time, let's start with that and we'll conduct any other business afterward. Who'd like to start?" Bree nodded to Mark Collins, one of the board members who'd raised his hand, to begin.

Forty-five minutes later, as the meeting wound down, another board member, Shawn Lanniker, said, "And Carter, you'll liaison with Mr. Lancaster here on behalf of Sanctuary until the work is complete?"

Carter nodded. "Yes."

"I think all of these ideas are excellent," Shawn pronounced, glancing around at the others who nodded in agreement. "Especially with the amount of donated goods and services. If all our questions have been answered, perhaps we should let Mr. Lancaster take his leave?" Shawn looked at Bree.

"Of course," she said and stood. "Thank you for taking time out of your busy schedule to be with us this morning, Mr. Lancaster."

Griff offered her another of those amused smiles. "Miss Mason." He tilted his head. "Ladies. Gentlemen. Thank you for your time."

Carter pushed back from the table. "I'll walk you out, Griff. Excuse me."

The volunteers followed Carter and Griff leaving Bree and the board members. After a bit more discussion, they voted to approve all the proposals unanimously.

Bree walked across the lobby with Shawn and Mark, still chatting about the future of Sanctuary. They seemed almost as excited by the possibilities as she was. She stepped outside and bid them goodbye, but something stopped her before she went back in.

Griff hadn't left. His black truck was parked near the end of the lot, facing away from her. He and Madeline

Stark seemed to be deep in conversation. It didn't appear to Bree to be a discussion between mere acquaintances. Something about their body language and their focus on each other spoke of a more significant relationship.

They were too far away for Bree to hear what they were saying, and they wouldn't notice her watching them. Madeline put her hand on Griff's arm in what looked like a reassuring way. He nodded at her and left, leaving Bree to contemplate what she'd seen.

It wasn't a surprise that the two knew each other. Their paths could have crossed in any number of ways in the relatively small community of Chandler. Except that Griff was practically a hermit as far as she could tell.

She knew that Carter and Madeline were meeting to-day because he had stopped by Bree's office yesterday to tell her. "We have time to offer a few classes in basic gardening skills and she's happy to teach them with me," he told her. "I have Charlotte Young from the farm extension service on board as well. I'm not sure how much interest there will be, but since we'll be starting late in the planting season this year, I think we owe some kind of education so participants can get the most out of their gardening experience."

"Of course." Bree rejoiced that her presence at the meeting would not be needed.

"We'll be finalizing the schedule and agendas. I'll send it to you so you can add it to the website, and we can get some flyers printed."

"Perfect." Bree smiled. "Anything else?"

"No, that's it for now. I think this is going to be big, Bree. Really big."

"Me too."

When Madeline began unloading supplies from her car, Bree went back to her office, where she planned to stay until she was sure the woman had left.

Chapter Nineteen

ree's stomach knotted up, the way it had for years every time she crossed paths with Madeline Stark. Madeline's husband and daughter had both been killed in an automobile accident years ago. Some said the reclusive Madeline was a healer. She had a way with living things, especially plants and animals. Supposedly she had even revived her eight-year-old daughter for a brief time as she lay in the emergency room, but her powers weren't strong enough, or so Bree imagined at the time, for the girl died anyway.

Madeline was a college professor and she'd published several books on mountain lore, mythology and one about the various uses for plants indigenous to the area.

As a child, Bree had believed the rumors about Mrs. Stark's ability to heal sick and dying animals and bring dead plants back to life. To learn more about Madeline's secret powers, Bree had done something stupid and humiliating and she tried to avoid the woman ever since.

Madeline Stark had lived down the road from her grandparents for as long as Bree could remember. She rode her bike past the Stark place often, slowing as she passed, her curiosity about the woman who now lived there alone never quite satisfied.

Bree had only been a baby when Madeline Stark's husband and daughter had died, but the woman had become the stuff of local legend.

Mrs. Stark was a fascinating enigma to Bree's fanciful mind. She wanted to know her secrets. How did she heal the sick and bring dead plants back to life?

She'd overheard her grandmother's friend, Mrs. Banks, telling how Madeline had saved two of her orchids. Another local woman swore Madeline had healed her daughter of her drug addiction after several "sessions" of her unique brand of therapy.

Bree wanted to believe the stories were true, that there was a good witch living right down the road and that if she ever needed someone with magic powers, Madeline Stark could help her.

One summer day when she was ten, Bree rode on past the Stark place on the way to the crossroad, where her grandmother had firmly instructed her to turn around. At the corner, she stopped to look both ways and saw something horrible. A raccoon lay motionless by the side of the road.

On foot Bree approached the animal slowly, stopping when a couple of cars whizzed by. It was easy to understand how an animal could get hit and left for dead. Bree squatted next to it to get a closer look. The raccoon didn't move and didn't appear to be breathing but...

She'd seen an old movie recently about a little girl whose beloved cat had been hit by a truck. The girl thought the cat was dead and arranged a funeral. But when a local woman who everyone thought was a witch appeared, the children scattered in fear, leaving the cat behind. The woman discovered the cat was still alive and took it home and nursed it back to health. It turned out the woman wasn't a witch at all, just someone who was patient and kind who had a way with animals. She had a shed with cages where she cared for injured animals until they recovered enough to return to the wild.

Perhaps, Bree thought, Mrs. Stark was like that. Bree had seen her in town a time or two, dressed in long gauzy skirts and flowing blouses, her long black hair hanging down her back. And only once, when Bree rode past her house, had she glimpsed the woman watering the flower beds near her front porch. That time she'd been wearing a t-shirt and faded denim overalls.

Bree studied the raccoon. Flies flitted around the body. It looked dead. But what if it wasn't? What if it could be saved like that girl's cat in the movie? What if Mrs. Stark had magic healing powers, or at least the ability to be nurturing and patient like the witch?

A red pickup truck sped past, and Bree made a decision. She didn't want to touch the raccoon. She looked around and spied a plastic bag someone had tossed out a few feet away. It was weathered and dusty and torn, but it would do. She covered her hands with the plastic and picked up the raccoon, which was heavier than she'd anticipated. Carefully, she laid the raccoon in her bike's basket. That's when she realized that he was bloodied on his underside. Still, perhaps he could be saved. Or resurrected.

Bree pedaled back up the road and turned into the driveway. She remembered the children in the movie. They'd been afraid of the woman they thought was a witch. Bree felt a little afraid too. But there was the raccoon to consider.

She carefully lifted it from the basket and carried it with her to the porch. She decided to leave it at the foot of the steps, because she'd need at least one hand free to knock.

She was nervous, but she rapped on the door anyway and waited, rubbing the palms of her hands on her shorts. No one came. She knocked again. She couldn't see through the prismed glass of the front door, even though she cupped her hands around her eyes and tried to peer inside. Maybe Mrs. Stark wasn't home.

In the movie, visitors rang a bell outside the witch's house. Some boys rang the bell when they found a badger in a trap and left it for her to heal.

Bree retraced her steps and looked down at the raccoon. It hadn't moved. Most likely it was dead, but just in case it wasn't, just in case Mrs. Stark's magical powers could heal it, she decided to leave it where it was.

If she lingered any longer her grandmother would be in a tizzy because Bree was late for lunch.

That summer, Bree found two more injured animals near the crossroads and brought them to Mrs. Stark's place. The first was an opossum. Opossums were always getting hit by cars, it seemed. The second was a blackbird, its shiny feathers glinting purple in the sun.

Mrs. Stark wasn't home when Bree left the opossum where she'd left the raccoon. But when she'd come with the blackbird, although no one answered her knock, as she headed back to her bike, Mrs. Stark seemed to appear out of nowhere. She seized Bree by the shoulders, her face so close Bree could see into the depths of her eyes.

"You horrible little girl. Why are you leaving dead animals outside my door?"

"I—I thought—" Terror and panic shook Bree to her core. Mrs. Stark was not only angry, but her feelings were also hurt. Shame stole Bree's voice. She could imagine Mrs. Stark dragging her home and telling her grandmother what she'd done. They wouldn't understand. They'd think her ridiculous and stupid for believing real life could be like that movie. Or they might think she was just plain mean. What if everyone in town began to gossip about her the way they gossiped about Mrs. Stark? Bree already had enough trouble fitting in, having been abandoned by unfit parents to be raised by her slightly eccentric grandparents. She didn't need to give the local tongues any more ammunition.

Mrs. Stark let go of her and propelled her toward her bike. "Get off my property and stay away from my house. And if I ever see you around here again, I'll call the sheriff!"

Bree froze. She remembered vaguely, men in uniform putting her father into the back of a car with lights on the top. She'd been four at the time and hadn't understood why Daddy was leaving. But now she knew, if the police came to get you, it was a very bad thing.

"Go!" Mrs. Stark hissed. She pointed at Bree's bike.

Bree ran. She tore down the driveway, the sob begging to be released finally set free as she gained the road and pedaled toward home.

Chapter Twenty

Bree could not squelch the joyous anticipation shooting through her as she parked her car in the Sanctuary lot on a fine Saturday morning near the end of April. Griff and some of his men were preparing to clear the land for the community garden. Next week, the fence would go up and the week after that, they'd mark off the individual garden plots. A month from now, planting would begin.

Everything happened in a whirlwind of activity, and she found Griff to be relentless with the timeline once approval came through.

Bree had spent the three weeks since the board meeting hard at work getting the word out, notifying civic and high school groups and anyone else she could think of about the project. The local newspaper and television station ran preliminary stories and would be on hand opening day to do more.

A double buzz of excitement raced through her as she strode across the parking lot. Not only would she see Griff this morning, but the community garden would also turn from a rather vague idea into reality, thanks to him.

He was already there with his workers, supervising a bulldozer being off-loaded from a flatbed trailer. There were two smaller orange and black ground-clearing machines waiting nearby.

"Good morning," she called to him.

He turned and the breath caught in her throat. Could he be any more devastatingly attractive? He wore sunglasses against the brightness of the morning and was dressed in black as always. Instead of his usual thermal and flannel shirts, today he wore a long-sleeved tee. The breeze ruffled his hair, glossy as a raven's wing.

"Good morning," he said, rather curtly. "I didn't know you were going to be here."

His response almost sounded like another admonishment, but Bree ignored it. He was in work mode, and that's how he spoke to his crew. Still, his words tempered her excitement.

"Are you kidding? I want to be involved every step of the way. I want photos for the website." She held up her digital camera. "We need all the publicity we can get."

Griff eyed her from behind the dark lenses. "Fine," he said using the same brusque tone. "As long as you stay out of the way."

He turned back to see the bulldozer now on the ground. The trailer and truck were pulling away. He stalked off.

Bree wished she'd made some smart comment back to him, but his dismissive tone and his words temporarily robbed her of speech.

He swung up into the seat of the bulldozer and the engine soon rumbled to life. He hollered something to one of his crew and the land clearing began.

Bree stayed well back. The zoom lens of her camera was more than sufficient to take decent shots of the progress. All too often, she focused the camera on Griff, as he directed the dozer's scoop where he wanted it to go. Was it possible, Bree wondered, for him to be even sexier than she already thought he was? A hot guy on a big piece of machinery doing manly work proved to be a major turn-on.

Bree took shots of the other members of Griff's crew, all young and mostly men who followed the dozer's progress, waiting for their turn in prepping the ground. They, too, were staying well out of Griff's way, huddling together near a couple of pickup trucks and the tractor trailer.

"Hi there," Jenna said, joining her as she took another picture.

"Good morning."

Jenna carried a cardboard box containing trays of take-out coffee cups and a bag of donuts. "Need some help?" Bree asked.

"No, I'm fine." She looked over the scene and gestured with her chin toward the bulldozer. "Is that him?"

"That's Griff, yes."

Jenna mumbled something Bree didn't catch and didn't ask to have repeated. Jenna's attention turned back to Griff's crew. Several were eying the two of them like eagles spotting a squirrel.

"I think I'll go make some new friends," Jenna said. She marched off and Bree let her go. After a couple of days of silence following Bree's displeasure with Jenna calling the sheriff about the attack, they'd drifted back into their friendship pattern. Like an old married couple, they never stayed mad at each other for long. Such was the dynamic of their relationship.

Bree's gaze swung back to Griff. While the dozer idled, if she wasn't mistaken, he looked right at her.

One of the guys detached himself from the group and went to confer with Griff. Bree decided if Griff was going to be borderline rude, at least she could get a cup of coffee and a donut out of it.

She made her way toward Jenna and her new friends. Introductions had been made all around before Griff and the other guy joined them. "Jenna, this is Griffin Lancaster. He's the one making this all possible," Bree said.

Griff had the good manners to remove his sunglasses, Bree noted, as she made the introductions. "Griff, this is Jenna Scott, Sanctuary's head veterinarian."

"Nice to meet you," Jenna said dutifully, though her tone was unconvincing.

"Likewise," Griff all but growled.

The other man offered his hand to both Jenna and Bree in turn. "Um, I'm Tyler Dunn. Foreman."

"Charmed," Jenna said, turning up the wattage of her smile for Tyler. Her reaction was quite the opposite of how she'd greeted Griff, and Bree knew she couldn't be the only one who noticed.

Tyler was Griff's polar opposite. Blond haired and blue-eyed, he smiled easily, and friendliness radiated from him. He was just under six feet, lanky and loose-limbed. When Jenna had used the word 'charmed,' Bree knew she meant it.

While the rest of the crew took advantage of the coffee and donuts, Griff walked off toward his truck. He unfolded a set of site plans and studied them, his gaze going back and forth between the plot of land he'd cleared and the page in front of him. Then he put the blueprint away and lowered the gate on the truck bed. He withdrew a wheeled measuring device and walked it around the perimeter of the cleared area. Seeming satisfied with the results, he stowed the equipment back in the truck, retrieved the blueprint and came back to the group.

"Danny. Paul. You want to get those CATs fired up? Let's get the path cleared."

Two of the guys abandoned their half-finished coffees and jumped to attention. "On it." Griff walked them to the smaller orange and black CATs, reviewing what needed to be done to create the path to the garden.

Before Griff returned to the group, Tyler set his coffee aside. "Excuse me," he said to Jenna and Bree. He strode toward Griff. "I'll go ahead and get that earth churned up." He hopped on the bulldozer and brought its backhoe down and began digging through the cleared area in an orderly manner.

Bree's excitement reemerged and she was sure it had nothing to do with listening to Griff bark orders at the others. It was hard for her to envision a project like this on paper, but once it began to take shape, she could clearly see what the garden could be. There should be some statuary and maybe a fountain in the middle.

She wanted a curved wrought iron archway over the entrance with "Sanctuary Garden" in curly script at the top.

She pictured orderly plots, neatly labeled with flowers and vegetables. The people of the community working together, children of all ages learning about biology and horticulture.

She turned to where she'd last seen Griff. She wanted to share her excitement with him and thank him again for making this a reality, but he was already back at the open bed of his truck.

Jenna was busy picking up discarded cups and napkins before they could blow away. Bree knew she should help her, but instead she excused herself and hurried toward Griff. He was organizing wooden stakes and attaching short strips of neon tape to them.

"This is exciting, isn't it?" she said. She looked over the side of the truck bed.

"It was the first time I did it. Now, not so much."

"How many community gardens have you done?"

Griff gave her an odd look. "Oh. I thought you were talking about flagging stakes."

Bree laughed. "No. I meant I'm seeing your vision." She gestured toward where the garden and the path were taking shape.

When she turned back, she saw Griff still concentrating on the task at hand in what appeared to be an obvious attempt to tune her out.

Chapter Twenty-One

Bree bubbled with ideas, and he found her vision contagious even though he tried his best not to get caught up in it. He tried to ignore her, but she made it impossible.

Ever since he'd caught sight of her this morning in a pair of snug jeans and a sweater that complemented her curves, he'd had a few visions of his own. But they weren't about the community garden. His involved something more personal and in a much more private setting.

Not. Going. To. Happen.

No matter how many times he reminded himself of that, thoughts of her invaded his mind, stealing away his resolve to keep his distance from her, dangling the possibilities of a life after thirty-three out in front of him.

The possibility of a future. A normal life. A wife and a family.

He made himself slam on the brakes of his runaway dreams. This curse would end with him come hell or high water. He damn well intended to keep the promise he'd made to himself long ago. And no one, not Bree Mason or any other woman, was going to make him go back on it.

"You're not listening, are you?" she asked.

Griff drifted back into himself, realizing he'd managed to block the sound of her voice with his own internal angst. He rubbed his wrist against his pants leg.

"Griff?"

He glanced at her just as she took a picture of him. He frowned. He didn't like to be photographed and went out of his way to avoid it. He didn't like the way he looked in them, afraid a keen observer might see the animal inside him. "What'd you do that for?"

"I told you. I want pictures of the garden from start to finish."

"But you took a picture of me."

"You're part of the project."

"Delete it."

"Why? I'm going to take pictures of everyone here to-day. I want them all to have credit for the work they're doing. Especially you."

"I don't want credit."

"Too bad."

He fixed her with a look. "You're awfully stubborn."

She grinned. "What are you going to do about it?"

Several ideas came to mind. All of them appealing. None of them workable. Wiping that grin off her face with a kiss held a great deal of appeal. He'd like more than anything to see where such an overture might lead. Instead, Griff knew what he had to do.

"Nothing," he said, gathering up the stakes and hefting them over his shoulder. "Excuse me."

Bree watched him stride away to where Tyler was nearly done churning up the soil. It felt like Griff had punched her in the stomach. Her earlier excitement disappeared as if he'd stuck a pin in the balloon of her happiness and popped it.

She didn't know what gave him the power to take away her joy with his dismissal and rejection. Except she somehow allowed him to do it. She had to stop. Instead, she'd be as stubborn as he said she was. And she hoped, by the time she stopped being stubborn, he'd be eating his heart out over her.

She walked in the opposite direction, heading for the path. Danny and Paul had finished the clearing process, and now one of them was using the front loader of his CAT to pick up gravel from a mound and drop it in small piles along the path. The other used his front loader to spread and smooth it out. She took several shots of the activity from different angles.

Jenna came toward her with her box now filled with trash. "It's coming together, isn't it?" Bree said proudly as they surveyed the progress.

"It certainly is," Jenna agreed. Her eyes tracked Tyler's movements as he guided the bulldozer back onto the trailer. "What do you think?" Jenna said, inclining her head slightly in Tyler's direction.

"He's very friendly. He could be fun."

"You say that like it's a bad thing."

"Not at all. I just met him. What do you want me to say?"

"I just met Griff and I can tell you what I'd say. I'll take Mr. Fun and Friendly over the Grim Reaper any day of the week."

"The Grim Reaper? Don't you think you're exaggerating a bit?" Bree's gaze zeroed in on where Griff had started pounding his color-coded stakes into the ground.

"I mean, what's with all the black? It's depressing."

Griff's tee shirt molded itself to him, emphasizing his physique. He must work out, Bree decided. Or maybe all the landscaping work kept him in shape. She pictured him hefting fifty-pound bags of mulch, planting trees, building brick retaining walls. "It is a bit unrelenting, I guess."

"So is his personality. It's like he's got a dark cloud over his head or something."

Bree couldn't argue with that because she'd thought the same thing. Except she'd seen glimpses, rare and brief, that made her think there was more going on beneath Griff's surface.

"Where's Carter?" Jenna asked. "I thought he'd be here today."

"He wanted to be," Bree said. "But he had a conflicting family event. I'm sure he'll be here next Saturday."

"Well, unless you need me, I'm going to get rid of this." Jenna left with her box.

Bree decided to get a few more close-ups of the turned-up soil and the stakes. She ignored Griff and shifted her focus to Tyler as she came closer. She took a couple of close-ups of the stakes, their tiny neon flags flicking back and forth in the breeze.

"What are the different colors for?" she asked him.

"The green ones mark the perimeter for the fence," Tyler said, pointing to where Griff had nearly finished installing them. "The orange are for the irrigation lines and we'll use the yellow to mark off the individual plots."

"Isn't it a bit of early for that?" Bree let her camera dangle from the strap around her neck and pulled out a small pad and pen to take a few notes.

"That's why we use the flimsy wood stakes. They're easy to move," he said, and went back to laying out his orange tagged stakes.

Bree sensed Griff listening to their exchange.

"Thank you for helping out today," Bree said to Tyler.

"No problem. The boss makes it worth my while, don't you, boss?"

Griff grunted in reply.

"Oh. I thought all you guys were volunteering your time."

"We are," Tyler assured her. "But the boss trades us a paid day off in exchange for each day we volunteer."

"Oh. How generous," she said, more to herself than Tyler.

"Yep," Tyler agreed.

Griff stretched and surveyed the work. Bree grabbed her camera, knowing a money shot when she saw one. He stood with the trucks and bulldozer some distance behind him, the plot of churned soil with the brightly colored stakes in front of him. His sun-bronzed skin, dark glasses, and chiseled features set against the working-man backdrop. She was pretty sure what the community garden's web page would look like.

His gaze zeroed in on her when he heard the first click from the camera. She ignored his frown and took another shot.

"I thought I asked you to stop taking pictures of me."

She took another one as he advanced toward her. And one more before she lowered the camera and watched him. "You didn't. You just told me you didn't like it."

"I also told you to delete it."

"And I told you, you're a part of the project. What are you going to do about it?"

"I guess I can pull up my stakes and walk off and forget about doing any more work here."

"You wouldn't," Bree said.

"I might if you don't point your damn camera somewhere else."

"What is it you're afraid of?" Bree asked softly.

"Nothing."

She tilted her head. "No, it's not nothing. Something's bothering you, and I don't think it has to do with my camera."

"You don't know me well enough to psychoanalyze me," Griff informed her.

"Really?" She raised the camera and took another shot, even as he took another step toward her.

She whirled and started back toward the path where Danny and Paul were still smoothing the gravel with the CATs. She knew Griff followed her. Knew she'd pissed him off. *Fine. Let's have it out.* Maybe she'd find out what his deal was. Excitement mixed with anticipation surged through her once again, but it had nothing to do with the community garden and everything to do with the man behind her.

She heard the dull thud of metal connecting with wood and came to a stop, wondering what had happened and where.

"Bree!" Griff called from behind her. The panic in his voice caused her to turn around. His face was a mask of dread as he hurled himself at her, tackling her to one side. They stumbled on the tangle of vines and undergrowth and fell. An abandoned utility pole shook the ground where Bree had stood seconds before. The old, grey wood had cracked in half and toppled when the CAT backed into it.

Paul and Danny were next to them in seconds. "Sorry, boss. I didn't see that pole in the brush when I backed up," one of them said.

Griff ignored him, his focus on Bree. "Are you alright?"

"I'm fine," she said, although she wasn't. Her insides tremored in reaction to his arms around her, to the touch of his fingers against her hair.

"You guys okay?" Tyler called out as he and other workers approached.

Griff waved them off, his gaze still on Bree. "We're fine. Let's get finished up here."

Griff stood and extended a hand to help Bree up. When they were face to face, he brushed at the twigs and leaves and bits of dry grass in her hair and on the shoulder of her sweater. "You're an awful lot of trouble, you know that?"

She gave him a tremulous smile. "What are you going to do about it?"

His mouth set in a grim line and his hand dropped. "Nothing," he said, but she didn't think it was what he wanted to say.

Bree was nearly breathless. "Thanks for rescuing me. Again."

"It's what I do."

Chapter Twenty-Two

Things were moving too slowly. That's all Griff could think about as he drove to Madeline's home. Weeks had gone by since their first meeting. The day he'd seen her at Sanctuary she'd implored him to be patient. She'd begun working with a translator in Scotland on the old texts, but it was a laborious process. Both she and the translator had other obligations. She'd assured Griff she was putting as much effort into finding answers as she could.

When he finally heard from her, he'd tried to keep his impatience at bay. Maybe she didn't fully understand that this was *his life*. He needed answers *now*. Not weeks or months from now. His life was a countdown timer with not a hell of a lot left on the clock.

Still, she'd invited him to dinner, and he'd grudgingly agreed. Mostly, he told himself because he was sick of his own cooking and takeout meals.

He parked in her driveway and admonished himself for his frustration. He'd never had much hope that his life would go beyond this year. If Madeline didn't find an answer, nothing much would change.

She greeted him at the door and accepted the bottle of wine he'd had the forethought to bring. His mother would be appalled by his deteriorated social skills, and his abruptness which often bordered on downright rude. But how could he get close to anyone when he was what he was? He had to keep his secret. He'd never trusted anyone enough to share it.

Because that person might tell the wrong people? Because he might end up dead? No, it wasn't death he feared. It was changing to his animal state and being unable to transform back. Becoming a circus freak, part animal, part human. The pointing fingers, the disgust. Living out his life in a laboratory or worse, poked, and prodded and studied. Where he'd probably die anyway without leaving his mark on the world. Without leaving a legacy of any kind.

He followed Madeline to the kitchen. "Smells good."

Madeline retrieved two wineglasses and smiled. "It's my world-famous pot roast." She handed him a corkscrew.

He opened the wine and poured a glass for them both. A loaf of what looked like homemade bread sat on a wooden cutting board. She raised her glass and clinked it against his, noting his expression. "I assume 'cheers' isn't an appropriate toast this evening?"

"Not unless you have some very good news for me."

"Well, then, let's drink to acquiring knowledge, shall we?"

They each took a sip.

Griff reminded himself not to hope. Perhaps he could simply relax and enjoy the evening. The food. The wine. Madeline's company. Some stimulating conversation. Perhaps he could try, as they say, living in the moment.

The moment he had that thought, he rejected it. Not since childhood had he been able to live in the moment. Ever since he learned the truth, he'd been on a quest to find answers and a way to leave a legacy for his family before they were all wiped out by this wicked curse. Tonight would be no exception.

Madeline didn't keep him waiting. Once they sat down and began their meal, she said, "The translator has made some progress. Not as much as I would like, but he's shed some light on Emerald's intent."

Griff glanced up from the slice of bread he'd begun to butter. "Her intent?"

"Intent is a significant component of the curses of the ancients. At least as significant, if not more so, than the rituals themselves."

Griff said, "I never considered Emerald's *intent*." He'd always been too focused on how the curse affected him. "She wanted to make Colin's progeny suffer, I know. But you're saying she may have had intent beyond that?"

"I can't say with any degree of certainty. I can only tell you what my impressions are both from my own research and what the translator has sent me so far."

"I'm listening."

"It's hard to explain," Madeline said, as she loaded bits of meat, carrot, and potato onto her fork. She ate that bite and began to prepare another. She was methodical and precise, taking care to insure a pleasing combination of foods in each bite.

He ate without caring nearly as much, even though what she'd made tasted pretty good. He needed fuel. Taste was secondary. Plus, the sooner they finished eating, the more quickly Madeline could talk.

"I think what's happened is, our clever Emerald combined the ingredients from one or more concoctions to create a powerful brew. She poured into it her own feelings, and we can guess at what those were. Pain. Anger. Abandonment. Betrayal. Fear, even, though she might not admit it, for now she's pregnant. The father of her baby is gone, and her future is murky."

"Hatred..." Griff sat back. Hadn't he experienced those same emotions because of the curse? Emerald must have hated Colin as much as she'd loved him. As much as Griff and his predecessors had hated the curse they were forced to live under.

Madeline pointed her fork at him. "Most certainly. Now it's a matter of determining which spells, which ingredients, and which *emotions* were added to Emerald's concoction to create such a powerful curse. Untangling them may help us find an antidote."

Griff stared at his plate of half-eaten food. It sounded like an impossible task given the amount of time they had.

Madeline's hand covered his clenched fist. "Don't give up hope."

He gave a harsh laugh. "You're talking about trying to decipher some ancient code written in a dead language from a historical document. Untangling a mix of incantations, curses, spells, and ingredients, all with Emerald's *intent* added to the mix. What you're not saying is there's no easy way to determine exactly what she did, which parts of what spells she used, much less the recipe for breaking this curse. And even if you know all of that, her intent is always going to be a matter of guesswork. There's no point."

Madeline squeezed his hand harder. "Of course, there's a point. Your life."

He pushed her hand away. "I appreciate what you're trying to do, but there's no real hope. I may be closer to an answer than I've ever been, but it's still too far away."

Fire flashed in Madeline's eyes. She threw her hands into the air. "You don't know that. Where there's life, there's hope."

"Not for me."

"Don't do anything stupid, okay? I'm not going to give up. Even if you are. There's an answer here. I can feel it. You still have time."

"We're talking about months," Griff reminded her. "You can work your ass off to find answers, but if it comes too late, it won't matter."

"And if you give up, Emerald wins."

Griff looked away. "She's already won." He pushed his chair back. "Thank you for dinner."

He found his eyes watering blurring the road on the way home. He wiped them with his sleeve. *Don't give up hope.* Such an easy platitude to deliver when it wasn't your life on the line.

Chapter Twenty-Three

"What's with you these days?" Jenna asked irritably.

"Nothing!" Bree replied in mock outrage.

"Don't tell me you're still mooning over the Grim Reaper." Jenna reached for a tortilla chip, broke it in half, then in quarters and began nibbling the edge of one of the pieces, all while eying Bree knowingly.

"Don't call him that!" This time her outrage was real, although she had no idea why she should defend Griff, whose new nickname should be Mr. No Show. He'd handed supervision of the community garden over to Tyler. She'd learned this after dressing with care last Saturday morning and arriving at the site only to find Griff wasn't there. Much to Jenna's delight, however, Tyler was. And Tyler, unlike Griff, seemed equally delighted to run into Jenna.

Bree glowered at Jenna over the rim of her margarita glass. Some people had all the luck.

"My, my," Jenna said, unperturbed. "You have got a thing for him, haven't you?"

"I haven't got 'a thing' for him. I just thought he'd want to be more involved in the project. Especially after all the work he did designing and getting donations."

"Mmhmm. And after you featured him prominently on the garden's web page? But of course, that's only because of all his hard work, right?" Jenna took a sip of her drink. "Not because you have a *thing* for him. You do know he showed up shortly after you left last Saturday, right?"

"I'm aware." Bree had the sinking feeling that Griff had done so because he wanted to avoid her. "Can we please change the subject?"

Bree glanced around Dante's as if she'd grown bored. But the truth was, her feelings were as raw as they were confused. She couldn't justify the way she felt about Griff and didn't understand her obsession with him. She also didn't understand why there had been moments when she was sure he was interested in her, right before he shut down completely. Bree kept those thoughts and feelings to herself because she wasn't in the mood for a lecture or a warning from Jenna.

There was also the matter of the strange dreams she had every time she wore Griff's shirt to bed. It was always some version of the same dream. Running in the woods, coming up against a wall. An animal which turned out to be Griff coming after her.

"Fine. Let's talk about Tyler instead," Jenna said.

Bree raised an eyebrow. "He finally asked you out?"

"Not yet. But we did meet up for drinks last night."

"And?"

"I grilled him about his boss."

"Why?"

"For you, silly."

"Oh, for Pete's sake, Jenna. We're not in high school anymore." The last thing Bree wanted was for Tyler to tell Griff that her best friend was asking about him.

"Want to know what I found out?"

Yes! "I can see you're dying to tell me."

Jenna leaned forward. "Okay, here's the DL. Tyler's worked for him for two years and barely knows him."

Bree managed not to roll her eyes. "That's helpful."

"Isn't it?" Jenna ignored Bree's sarcasm. "He said they've gone out for a beer after work a couple of times, but even then, Griff didn't talk about himself. Strictly professional. Very serious. He never discusses his personal life, if he's been married, divorced, has children, nothing. Tyler doesn't even think he dates. He's got a Harley he rides on the weekends, but he never takes time off, never goes on vacation. All work and no play. Sounds like a fun guy, huh? Now I understand why you're so hung up on him."

Bree broke away from the brief fantasy she had of riding on the back of Griff's Harley, arms wrapped tightly around his waist, to say, "I'm not hung up on him."

"Please."

"Okay, I am," Bree admitted glumly. "But if it makes you feel any better, I don't know why I am. It's not like he encourages my interest."

"He's a fool."

"No, he's not."

"Is this Jeremy Syndrome rearing its ugly head again?"

"No."

"Are you sure?" Jenna asked. "Because it sure has all the earmarks."

"It does not."

"Oh, please. Griff is a loner, even if it sounds like he prefers it that way. You think he needs nurturing. You think you can save him just like all the other guys you—"

"Couldn't save?" Bree said bitterly.

"Baby," Jenna covered Bree's hand with hers. "You're my best friend. I don't want to see you get hurt, but you have a pattern..." Her voice trailed away as she withdrew her hand.

"I'm aware of my own history," Bree said. "I don't need you to remind me."

Jenna looked hurt. *Great.* Bree didn't want to fight with her best friend over a man who couldn't be bothered to give her the time of day. Damn him.

"Bree, I've never seen you like this. Ever since the attack, and *he* supposedly rescued you—"

"There is no supposedly, Jenna. I was there, remember?"

"Look, since you're already pissed at me, I'm just going to say this. I think he had something to do with the attack."

"Jenna!" Bree spluttered in outrage, hardly able to believe her own ears.

"I found black human hair on that flashlight. He has black hair. And he's human. Apparently."

"I explained all that. This isn't CSI, and I don't know how to treat a crime scene. He picked up the flashlight. It was in his house. It's entirely possible one of his hairs got on it there."

"There was more than one. And those hairs had been pulled out by the *roots*." Jenna leaned forward. "Consistent with being hit in the head. *By a flashlight*."

"You never told me that."

"What was I going to do? You were already mad at me for calling the deputy. You didn't want to file a report. You weren't hurt badly, and I figured it was a one-off. But now, this guy keeps showing up. I have a bad feeling. What do you think the chances are for a DNA match if I had the hairs from the flashlight tested against one of his?"

"Look, Jenna, I *saw* what attacked me. It wasn't human."

"And?" Jenna broke another chip and ate it.

"What are you saying, Jenna? That he's a *werewolf* or something? Don't they require a full moon before they transform? There wasn't one the night I was attacked."

Bree recalled the glimpse she'd had of black fur and amber eyes that night. She couldn't explain why a wolf, even a black wolf, didn't fit her impression. The animal had seemed more cat-like, if anything, though she couldn't explain exactly why she thought that either. Maybe because of the claw marks?

"I don't know what I'm saying, Bree. Maybe the trauma of the attack had you seeing things? Maybe someone was wearing a goofy Halloween mask. All I know is what was on that flashlight."

"I think you've read one too many books or seen one too many of those crazy horror movies," Bree said.

Except he lives underground, and he likes the dark.

Chapter Twenty-Four

When Bree got home, she changed into running clothes. She couldn't get away from Dante's fast enough. There was too much happening in her head, and she needed to counter the confusion of her thoughts with some intense physical activity.

She didn't even bother with her slow quarter-mile jog to warm up. She burst out of her neighborhood and onto her regular route past Griff's house at a full out sprint.

Jenna had stirred up her memory of the day Jeremy had died, and then she'd stirred up memories of Bree's less than stellar dating record. It was true. Bree often set herself up as a rescuer. Usually to guys who didn't want to be rescued. Always to guys who didn't believe they *needed* to be rescued.

But Griff wasn't like that, was he? What in the world did he need to be rescued from? By all accounts he was a successful businessman. If he had addictions, he kept them well-hidden. He was a loner who didn't like to socialize and didn't like to have his picture taken and apparently didn't date. So what? He wasn't hurting anyone. Being an introvert didn't mean you were unhappy. She couldn't fault him if all he wanted was to be left alone.

After the initial burst of speed, Bree dialed her pace back. There was nothing wrong with Griff. He didn't need or want her, so she didn't know why she had this desire to insert herself into his life, into his home. Into his heart.

She mentally shook herself as she passed by his driveway. Admit that's what you want, she scolded herself. You want him to fall head over heels. You want him to say he can't live without you.

This sick, unhealthy obsession messed with Bree's peace of mind, and there were moments she thought she *would* lose her mind.

Shake it off, she thought with a grim smile, as the Taylor Swift anthem blasted through her phone's speaker. Shake it off and get on with your life.

Griff stared at Sanctuary's community garden web page as he'd done every night for the past week. Contrary to his wishes, Bree had posted a picture of him right in the center of the page, giving him credit for instigating the project. Around that photo she'd arranged others with captions: "Clearing the Ground." "Creating the Path." "A Stake in the Future."

But Griff continued to fixate on the center picture, which stared back at him through dark lenses. His sense of unreality increased every time he studied the picture. *Is that me? Is that what everyone else sees? Or is it just what Bree sees?*

Maybe it was because of the shades, maybe it was because his eyes weren't visible, but Griff thought he almost looked normal. Like any other human being.

Tyler had given him a progress report last Saturday. The fence was up, and everything else had gone smoothly. The pipe for the irrigation system had been laid and it could all be connected to the water source whenever they were ready. Volunteers had shown up during the week, as Bree promised, and they'd cleared the plot of rocks and other churned up debris. Everything was going exactly as planned.

Griff rubbed his hands across his face and dug his knuckles into his eyelids. He knew everything Tyler had said already. He'd stopped by last Saturday once he was sure Bree had left. Griff checked the fence and the irrigation layout. He wanted to be there every step of the way. He liked overseeing his projects, liked to make sure the details were attended to, that the end result matched his original vision. Tyler was good, but he wasn't *him*.

After that first day on the site, Griff knew he'd have to back away. He couldn't risk seeing Bree again. He'd been doing okay until the utility pole got knocked down, when Griff ended up on the ground with his arms wrapped around her.

The memory of how warm and alive she felt in his arms plagued him, making him ache for something he'd never have. He thought he was strong enough to resist her, but he wasn't.

Kryptonite.

He couldn't get that song out of his head, any more than he could get *her* out of his head. But the more he was around her, the weaker his resolve got. He wouldn't be able to keep the promises he'd made to himself. He was only a few months away, and then it would all be over.

He closed the browser and shut down the computer, not sure why he tortured himself every night. Except it was no less than he deserved. And torturing himself was preferable to hurting Bree.

Chapter Twenty-Five

"What the hell is all this?" Griff stared at the mess in the middle of the garden. The carefully prepared ground had been torn up and paving stones were being installed. Four benches were stacked nearby while a fountain was being assembled. "Where the hell is Tyler?"

Bree separated herself from the group working on the fountain assembly and marched toward him. "Watch your language," she warned. "What is your problem?"

She was so close Griff took a step back to get her out of his personal space. He steeled himself to face her without flinching or showing how being this close to her affected him.

"My *problem*," he said, "is that someone apparently decided to completely change the layout here and add several features, including this." He gestured at the paving stones, which were set in a circle smack in the middle of the garden. "And that." He pointed at the fountain. "And those." He indicated the benches. He glared at her. "I'd like to know who's responsible."

She grinned at him. "I am."

"You didn't discuss it with me."

"Because you're never here when I am. In fact, I think you go out of your way to avoid me. But why would you?"

She peered at him as if she expected an answer. Griff crossed his arms and frowned. "You don't go changing things in the middle of development. This changes the entire layout. It throws off the symmetry of the plots and changes the requirements for the irrigation system."

"All of the plots don't have to be the same size, do they?"

"What difference does it make? They're not going to be now thanks to you. If you'd mentioned this at the beginning, I could have worked it into the plan."

"I *did* mention it," Bree said. "The day you were clearing the land. But you weren't listening."

Griff recalled tuning her out, not wanting to get caught up in her enthusiasm. He'd been more concerned about controlling his emotions when he was around her.

"I discussed it with Carter and we both talked to Tyler about it, since he seemed to be taking over for you."

"He never mentioned it," Griff said.

"Maybe he did, and you weren't listening."

"If it's about one of my projects, I listen."

"To *him*, you mean."

"Where is he, anyway?"

"He's right there."

Tyler came through the front gate with Jenna Scott grinning from ear to ear, and she was laughing. Griff hated them both at that moment. For being happy. For finding joy in each other's company. For laughing and being carefree.

"Oh, hey, boss." Tyler said.

Griff nodded to Jenna and said to Tyler, "Looks like I'm behind on your updates."

Tyler squinted. "How so?"

"He's upset he didn't know about the fountain and the benches," Bree said. She smiled sweetly at Griff.

"Oh, yeah. I didn't think it would be a problem. Is it?" Tyler asked Griff.

"You had to change the irrigation layout, didn't you?"

"Well, yeah, but since we hadn't connected all of it, it wasn't that big a deal."

"And we lost some of the plots."

"Yes, but Bree said—"

"Let me guess," Griff put in. He swung his gaze back to Bree. "Bree said she's in charge, so what she says goes."

"I managed to get the benches, the fountain *and* the pavers donated, and I *asked* if it wasn't too much trouble before the project was too far along, would it be possible to create a courtyard in the middle. Tyler thought it was a great idea."

"Did he? Well, maybe next time you let Tyler in on one of your great ideas he'll see fit to inform me."

"Sorry boss. I didn't think it was that big a deal." Tyler looked from Bree to Griff and back.

"It's not," Jenna said, joining the group. "Somebody's just got a bug up their butt, and it has nothing to do with a fountain or a courtyard."

"Are we cool?" Tyler asked Griff. "Because the fountain looks like it's ready to be installed."

"Yeah. Go on. We can talk about this on Monday."

"Are you *trying* to take all the fun out of this project?" Bree asked after Tyler stepped out of earshot.

Is that what she thought? "No, I—"

"Because that's what you're doing," she said in a low tone. "You seem determined to burst my bubble and everyone else's even though the garden was *your* project. Tyler's been here every Saturday overseeing *your* plans and doing a great job, by the way. And then you waltz in and bust his chops—"

"Don't tell me how to manage my employees," Griff growled.

But Bree was on a roll. "I'm *excited* about this. Do you know we got such a huge response to the garden we had to do a drawing to see who would get a plot? The board is already planning to expand it for next year because there's so much interest. I thought we'd be working on it together. But we're not and that was your choice and now you're pissed about it—"

"I am not—"

"Do you know how much work I put into this? How many calls I made to get the fountain and the pavers, and the benches donated? How many volunteers have shown up to put this all together? But it seems like you can't be bothered to be part of it. You show up when you please and you criticize everyone who's been working on it, and I *do not* appreciate your attitude."

Griff bit the inside of his lip to keep from smiling. Bree was magnificent in her outrage, which she had every right to. He'd been behaving like an ass, and she'd called him on it, and he loved her for it.

No, he warned himself. Don't go there. Don't even think about loving her for any reason. Or being attracted to her. Or wanting to stay right here next to her for the rest of the day. Working with her. Being a part of something. Thinking about the future. Because chances were by the time everything in this garden was harvested, he'd be dead.

"Don't you have anything to say?" Bree asked him. All the ire had gone out of her.

Griff looked over the garden and the workers. They'd moved the fountain into place. Tyler was on his knees, hooking it up to the waterline. A couple of volunteers were attaching advertising plaques to the benches. He could see Bree's vision. He could picture her there in the courtyard, relaxing on a bench, gazing at the fountain. Maybe there was a man with her. Only it wouldn't be him.

"I'll see you next Saturday."

Chapter Twenty-Six

Bree watched Griff stalk away. Again. He did that a lot. Even though she was sure that wasn't what he wanted to do. Why was he so contradictory? And why was did she think she could read him? He seemed to do the exact opposite of every signal he gave off. She didn't understand his behavior because it made no sense.

Even when she'd been practically yelling at him, it hadn't seemed to bother him. If anything, it seemed like he enjoyed watching her speak her mind. But whether her words had any effect on him, she couldn't say.

Still, she looked forward to next Saturday. It was the garden's grand opening and everyone who'd been awarded a plot would be there, ready to plant. And she'd be more than ready to see Griff again.

Absently, she scratched her wrist. She looked at the remaining scar which had finally faded to a pale pink outline to see that reddish welts had risen to outline its design more clearly. Rubbing the prickliness for relief only made it worse. Maybe Jenna had a tube of anti-itch cream in the vet clinic.

Once Jenna and Bree were in her office and Jenna had washed her hands, she waved her friend over and donned a pair of latex gloves. "Okay, let me take a look."

Bree showed her the mark on her wrist, which no longer itched as maddeningly as it had before. The redness had dissipated, although it was still an angry shade of pink.

"I don't think it's contagious," Bree said, mildly amused at Jenna's overabundance of caution.

Her friend glanced up. "Best to be on the safe side until we know what we're dealing with. It works both ways, you know. I don't want to cause any infection by touching it. It'll be easier if you're seated."

Bree took the chair next to the desk and pulled her sleeve up. Jenna bent over the wound, gently probing it with her fingers, stretching the skin this way and that. "This almost looks like a brand, doesn't it?" She glanced up at Bree. "Like there's a design or something."

"That's what I thought, too. It's weird because all the other scratches healed just fine."

"I don't think this is a scar. Not in the way you'd normally think of one, anyway." She slid her chair over to a set of drawers near the exam table and pulled out a magnifying glass, then wheeled back. She performed a closer and more thorough examination under the magnification.

"There's definitely a design here. I'm seeing clear edges. But it's fading, even as I'm looking at it." She sat up straighter and moved the magnifier away, gently rubbing her gloved thumb across Bree's skin. "Look."

Sure enough, the symbol had faded into barely visible pink lines, the design a blur between them. "It's weird, isn't it?" She pulled her sleeve down. "It doesn't itch like it did before, either."

Jenna pulled off the gloves and dropped them in the waste bin. "Bree, this is beyond weird. You noticed this after that animal or whatever it was attacked you, right?"

"I don't know what you mean by 'whatever it was,' but yes. I thought it was a scrape or something at first."

"It hasn't healed, and it doesn't behave like a normal scar. It's usually barely noticeable, right?"

"Right."

"But at certain times, it reddens and itches."

"Yes."

Jenna looked at Bree's wrist again, even though she couldn't see the skin. "It's behaving more like an allergic reaction."

"But to what?"

"This began the night of the attack, which means it was either caused by whatever attacked you—"

"Whatever *animal* attacked me," Bree corrected.

"Or it was caused by him."

"Griff?"

"When he found you after the attack... did he touch you?"

"Um." Bree's brows knit in concentration as she tried to recall every detail of their first encounter. "Yes. I was a bit wobbly, and he steadied me. He held my hand on the way to his house."

"He could have done this."

"Done what?"

"Caused this reaction."

"I said he took my hand, Jenna. He didn't maul me."

"Maybe he did it while you were asleep at his place."

"Now you're being ridiculous." Bree stood.

"Am I? When did you first notice it?"

"After the attack, when I went inside with him."

"After you had contact with both him and the animal."

"Yes."

"Well, something fishy's going on. You've got this scar that doesn't act like a normal scar, and a guy you're obsessed with who doesn't act like a normal guy."

"I get it, Jenna. You don't like him."

"I don't like the way he looks at you."

Jenna's deadly serious tone threw her. "What?"

"Like he's hungry for you."

A chill went through Bree. "He does not."

"He does," Jenna insisted. "I've noticed it every time I've seen him. He'd like to devour you."

"Then why does he do everything he can to avoid me?"

Chapter Twenty-Seven

Every time, Griff thought, every damn time I'm near her, this happens. The inflammation and prickling sensation on the inside of his wrist faded the further he drove away from Sanctuary. He knew what it meant, and it terrified him. He had to fight the overwhelming urge he felt to possess her, this instinct to mate with her. He used to be certain he was strong enough to withstand his animal-like impulses. But his certainty was beginning to waver.

The mark on his wrist first appeared sometime after his thirteenth birthday. His brother had one as well. When his mother saw them, a sadness came into her eyes unlike anything Griff had ever seen before. Sadder even than the day his father died. She'd put her arms around their shoulders and steered them into what had once been their father's study. There, she explained in no-nonsense detail what would eventually happen to them and what they had to do. What precautions they'd have to take.

She handed them each a letter left for them by their father with more information about the curse they were under, and what he had gone through, and his father before him.

They'd discussed it in their bedroom later, hardly able to believe what they'd been told. "What if it's true?" Greg whispered in the dark. When their father had first tried to tell them about the curse, they'd been too young to understand. Greg had boldly stated he didn't any of it, but that had been more out of denial than anything. Now the facts were too hard to ignore.

"We'll get through it," Griff assured him with a confidence he didn't feel. "Dad did."

"Until he died."

Griff could hear the despair in his brother's voice. He loved his twin, even though Greg's quiet, sensitive nature often got on his nerves. Greg preferred board games or jigsaw puzzles to football or riding bikes with the other kids in the neighborhood. He liked to draw and was quite a good artist. Books were some of his best friends.

The day of the new moon, their mother drove them to another city two hours from their home. Before dusk, she dropped them off in a wooded area close to a shopping mall. She'd prepared them as best she could, along with their father's instructions.

Griff thought they knew what to expect. In a way, he was curious and excited with a sick kind of anticipation. Transforming into an animal? It was like being in some fantasy movie. Things like this didn't happen in real life, only in myths and legends.

Greg reluctantly left the van, and they watched their mother drive away. She would wait for them at a pre-arranged location nearby when it was all over.

They were taken by surprise when the transformation began. They'd stepped deeper into the woods as darkness fell. Ambient light from the mall parking lot barely penetrated the gloom. In their animal states, they could make out little detail of each other. All Griff could see of Greg was the gleam from his eyes and the shadow of dark fur. He could safely assume that's what Greg saw when he looked at him.

They loped off in different directions. Instinct leading them to hunt for suitable prey. Griff wanted to get this over as soon as possible, return to human form, and be normal again. He waited patiently, roaming between parked cars, keeping his eyes on the mall exits until he saw a lone woman heading for her car, keys in hand. She walked with confidence, head swiveling, on the lookout for any threat.

But she didn't have eyes in the back of her head, and Griff's paws made hardly any sound on the pavement. He attacked from behind, knocking her down, sinking his claws into her, drawing blood, snapping and snarling, terrorizing her while she struggled to get free, to turn, to fight back.

Almost as soon as it began, it was over. The moment he knew he'd done what needed to be done, he leapt away and raced for the safety of the woods. He didn't stop running until he was deeply hidden in the brush. He lay there panting, adrenaline pumping through his veins.

When the painful transformation began, he moaned, trying to stifle his natural reaction, so great was his fear of discovery. When it was over, he lay on the ground for long minutes, stunned by what had happened. He knew what to expect, but nothing could have prepared him for the actual event. He patted himself, hardly able to believe he was whole and human again, wearing the same jeans, tee shirt, and jacket as before.

He sat up and got his bearings, then crept back to the edge of the woods where he could see the parking lot.

He sighed in relief when he saw the woman he'd attacked wasn't there. She hadn't been injured badly then. She'd gotten up, brushed herself off, hopped in her car, and gone home. A bit bruised, a bit bloody, but no injuries from which she wouldn't recover.

Griff found his mother waiting in the minivan exactly where she said she'd be. She offered him a sympathetic smile when he got in, but they didn't speak. What could either of them say?

They waited for Greg for another hour, until he finally joined them.

The three of them rode home in silence.

Chapter Twenty-Eight

On Monday, without explaining himself, Griff apologized to Tyler. But very little got to Tyler, and Griff sometimes envied the man's easygoing nature.

Griff spent the rest of the week mentally preparing himself for Saturday. Of course, Bree would be there. She'd probably be taking more pictures. He promised himself he'd try to be pleasant. If she took his picture, he'd make himself smile. Or at least not frown.

He'd help the gardeners. He'd maintain a comfortable distance between himself and Bree.

He was lying to himself, and he knew it.

Bree told herself she didn't care whether Griff showed up for the garden's opening day or not. But he was there with his crew when she pulled up to park. They were helping the guys from the local nurseries unload more donated plants.

Long tables manned by volunteers were set up for registration. There was coffee and donuts and balloons. The local news reporters were on site, milling about with cameras and microphones. And, not wanting to waste such a great opportunity, pets were offered for adoption in a separate area.

Bree refused to seek out Griff. The crowed of people here today meant their paths might not even cross. Worshipping him at a distance would have to be enough. It didn't matter if she felt more alive than she ever had when she was close to him or that a kind of excitement she'd never felt before bubbled under her skin whenever he looked at her.

It was a dumb crush on an apparently unobtainable guy. Nothing more.

Bree spent the first part of the morning dealing with the press. The reporters wanted to interview everyone involved. Candy Simmons, Sanctuary's public relations coordinator, was on hand to squeeze out every bit of positive publicity from the event.

Candy insisted on numerous photos with key parties, which included some of Griff and his crew. Bree noticed Griff seemed calmer than usual. He didn't object to the cameras this time. He might, she thought, even be smiling.

Bree managed to keep her distance from Madeline Stark as well, only nodding to her politely when she joined Carter and Charlotte Young from the extension service for photos before they began assisting the gardeners.

Jenna was helping at the refreshment stand. Bree stood next to her as the event wound down. "What a success," Jenna said as they watched the gardeners milling about. "You should be proud."

"I didn't do that much," Bree said. "But I am pleased with the result."

"Oh please. You got the Grim Reaper in on it. Without him—"

"None of this would have happened. And stop calling him that," Bree said for what seemed like the tenth time.

Griff wore a black polo shirt today with his black jeans and boots. A wristwatch with a wide black leather strap covered one tanned wrist. Jenna elbowed Bree. "I bet he wears black underwear, too."

"Would you stop it?" Bree said in mock irritation. Though she wouldn't admit it to Jenna or to anyone else, she spent a considerable amount of time wondering what lay beneath all those black clothes. Lots of solid muscle, she already knew. But did he have a hairy chest? Was he partial to boxers or briefs? Were there any tattoos?

"Careful. You're drooling," Jenna teased.

"I am not," Bree said irritably. She couldn't help but stare while Griff helped a small boy pat down the soil around a plant. Bree was too far away to hear what the two were saying, but there was something about Griff's relaxed posture, his genuine enjoyment of the interaction, his huge frame next to the boy's small one that tugged at Bree's heartstrings.

Griff stood and brushed the dirt off his hands. He looked right at her, and Bree didn't care if he'd caught her watching him. She didn't look away. He needs a family, she decided. She knew exactly what was missing from his life. People who loved him.

That's what she wanted to do. Love him. Yet he kept pushing her away.

Chapter Twenty-Nine

He'd survived the grand opening of the community garden, but Griff had another problem. He'd transplanted Bree's Christmas cactus into a bright red ceramic pot that made him think of Bree every time he saw it in the greenhouse. The pot was *enthusiastic*, or something. Upbeat. Optimistic? All those things certainly described Bree. She'd had his attention from the first moment he'd seen her, and she'd held him in her grip ever since. She just didn't know it. At least he hoped she didn't.

He'd been a monumental ass the last couple of weeks, and he was surprised she hadn't tracked him down and asked him point-blank what was going on. Thank God she hadn't. He hated behaving this way, but he didn't have a choice. He kept reminding himself of that.

He'd been staring at her cactus nightly, ever since he'd transplanted it. He'd fussed over it more than he did most of the plants he experimented with in his greenhouse, making sure it was adequately watered and the all-natural fertilizer he'd added was doing its job.

As a result, the cactus was healthy again, probably healthier than when Bree first got it. But what was he going to do with it?

He knew what he *should* do. Return it to her. She'd never mentioned the plate he'd returned, but he assumed she found it. Had she also assumed he'd taken her sickly plant?

He knew one thing. He was sick of wondering what he should do, tired of asking himself these questions night after night for which there didn't seem to be any good answers. Sick of torturing himself.

He missed her. For the past three Saturday mornings, he'd woken up feeling sad. He wanted to be part of building the community garden. It was a fun project, and God knew he could use some fun in his life. But every misstep he made with Bree made his life more difficult. He wished he'd never suggested he could help with the garden. He hadn't realized at the time how hard it would be not to give into his yearning for her.

Enough!

He picked up the red pot and marched out to his truck. If he returned it to her, he'd at least regain his peace of mind while he worked in the greenhouse.

He turned into her neighborhood before he remembered that Bree didn't live alone. How had he forgotten? She'd mentioned some guy named Pete the first night. Was he the guy in that picture on her desk? Had they been high school sweethearts?

No. Bree wasn't married. At least he didn't think she was. She didn't wear a ring. She didn't *act* married. And she'd never referred to Pete, a husband, or a boyfriend since. At least not to him. Plus, she always acted interested in him. Maybe she'd been living with the guy and the relationship had deteriorated into nothing more than roommates sharing expenses.

How was that possible, Griff wondered. He'd never take a woman like Bree for granted. She'd be the center of his universe. He parked and grudgingly admitted she kind of already was.

He listened to the *tick-tick-tick* of the truck's engine cooling. The outside light above her front door was on, but it was hard to tell if anyone was home. Only one way to find out. If she wasn't, he would leave the plant on the doorstep. He didn't have to knock or ring her doorbell. He could do a plant-by the same way he'd done the plate-by.

Coward.

Damn right.

He wasn't sure what he was more afraid of: Bree or his own feelings.

It could be a brief exchange. He didn't have to go inside if invited. He could simply explain about the cactus, hand it back to her, tell her it was nice seeing her, and leave. What could be simpler than that?

He knocked, which to him seemed more informal than ringing the doorbell. He waited. A minute ticked by. Nothing happened. He rang the bell, hearing it chime inside.

He glanced around at Bree's relatively quiet neighborhood. The developer had left a lot of the old trees intact. Streetlight glowed against the gathering darkness. The air had that soft quality to it as the cooler air breezed down from the mountains, replacing the earlier heat.

The townhouses, though relatively new construction, must be high quality. Griff couldn't hear anything going on inside Bree's unit. But maybe that was because there was nothing going on. Maybe she wasn't home.

Then the door popped open, and his head whipped around at the sound. Bree stood there, wrapped in a terrycloth bathrobe, squeezing her wet hair with a towel.

"Griff!"

Her appearance temporarily robbed him of speech. He imagined himself dropping the cactus, not caring when the pot broke, and the dirt exploded across the steps. Of backing her into her house, taking her in his arms, and somehow finding his way to her bedroom. Finding his way to her.

"Uh…"

She looked at him expectantly, her gaze briefly taking in the potted cactus.

She stepped back. "Would you like to come in?"

Chapter Thirty

Griff didn't consciously think about what he was doing until after he crossed the threshold, and she closed the door behind him. Then he knew a moment of panic. He was in her house now. Her personal space. What if the mysterious Pete was there? Griff knew one thing. If a guy showed up at the door unexpectedly to see his woman with some lame excuse like, "I repotted your plant," Griff wouldn't be happy. *Repotted her plant, huh? I'll just bet you did.*

"Come on back," she said. He followed her to the kitchen, which opened onto a cozy TV room and eating area. "I just made tea. Would you like some?"

"Uh…" Griff tried to take in the space. He couldn't help it. She'd seen his house. He wanted to see hers. Maybe that had been his subconscious ulterior motive all along. If he knew her better, he'd know exactly what he'd never have, exactly what and who he was pushing away. Or maybe he could convince himself that she wasn't the one after all, based simply on her taste in home furnishings.

Wrong. Her living area was clean and comfortable. Her sofa made him think of oatmeal and featured soft, over-stuffed pillows. There were four cushioned chairs around the round polished oak dining table. An armoire housed a television and entertainment equipment. Books, DVDs, and CDs lined the shelves. The mantel above the small fireplace held framed photos and knick-knacks. Griff saw no indication of a man living here.

Windows were everywhere, and French doors led to a small deck at the back. He noticed a skylight above the kitchen island.

"Where's Pete?" he said almost absently, staring up at the light.

Bree turned with mugs she'd retrieved from a cupboard and looked at him. "Pete?"

"Your... boyfriend?"

Her brow furrowed. "Sorry? I don't have a boyfriend."

Griff looked at her and frowned. "The night we... met, I asked if there was anyone you could call, and you said Pete was at home, but he'd be sound asleep by then."

She grinned. "Oh, *Pete*!"

"I didn't think much of a guy who'd let his girlfriend or wife go running at night without knowing when to expect her back. A guy who wouldn't be going out of his head when you didn't show up."

"Yeah, I wouldn't think much of a guy like that, either." Bree poured the tea into mugs from a whimsical teapot covered with purple pansies.

"So? Who's Pete if he's not your boyfriend?"

Bree giggled when she looked up again. "Pete's a dog."

"A dog?" Griff hadn't seen evidence of a pet, either. Why hadn't it barked when he'd knocked and rang the bell?

"A beagle/terrier mix, if I'm not mistaken."

"Where is he?"

"He was adopted. Instead of having one of my own I foster dogs from Sanctuary. Usually if we're overcrowded or there's one who needs to be socialized or who needs special attention for one reason or another. It's always a temporary situation."

"Oh. When you said 'Pete' I figured he was human."

Bree pushed one of the mugs toward him. "Sugar? Milk?"

"No. I—this is yours." He thrust the pot toward her across the island's counter.

"Oh. Thank you." She took it from him and set it on the granite countertop. "It's beautiful, but you didn't have to bring me anything."

"I didn't. It's yours."

"I have to be honest with you. I'm not good with plants."

He had to smile. "I know. This is *your* Christmas cactus."

"Mine?" Her brow knit. "You mean... the one by the front door?" She looked from him to the cactus and back.

"Yes."

"But—but I thought it was dying. Or already dead. Then it disappeared. You're saying you...?" She stared at him, mystified.

"It's what I do." He picked up his mug and sipped the tea. It was fragrant with notes of orange and cinnamon.

"Well, thank you. It's beautiful," Bree said, staring at the healthy plant in the bright red pot. Gently, she fingered the fronds. "You should keep it," she said. "I'll probably kill it."

"I can't keep it."

"Why not?"

"It makes me think about you too much." He shouldn't have said that. He'd let his guard down. He wanted to get comfortable with her in her house. He wanted to stay forever.

"What's wrong with that?"

"It's better if I don't."

"Better for who? Or is it whom?" She smiled, and Griff knew he was teetering on the edge of a cliff. If she kept smiling at him, if he kept seeing that delighted glint in her eyes, he wouldn't be able to walk away. A panicked voice inside his head screamed, *Get out now while you still can!*

"Better for both of us," he said with finality. He set his mug on the counter and turned toward the door. "Good night."

He got back in his truck and drove off. Cold sweat broke out all over his body. He wasn't strong enough to resist Bree and if he kept circling her, he knew there'd come a time when he'd fall into the very situation he wanted to avoid at all costs.

Bree stared after Griff, mystified. Everything in her wanted to run after him and tell him not to leave, insist he explain himself. He owed her that much.

It makes me think about you too much.

He thought about her and was attracted to her. But those were bad things, apparently. Maybe Griff was more messed up than she realized. Maybe he had a psychological condition which kept him from behaving normally around women, especially one he was interested in. She wondered what it was called. Hot-and-cold syndrome? Come-close-then-skedaddle disorder? Encourage/push-away-Bree-until-she's-completely-insane pattern?

Maybe there was another reason. Something embarrassing like erectile dysfunction. Or maybe his equipment was... small. Or maybe he simply had intimacy issues.

Whatever his problem, she was not going to chase after Griffin Lancaster. She refused to make a fool of herself over him. She hadn't figured out if his messing with her was intentional or not. She didn't want to believe that because it went against every instinct she had about him. She was sure he was at heart a decent, if somewhat screwed up individual, who wouldn't intentionally hurt another human being.

As she poured Griff's tea down the drain she noticed the place on her wrist had become more pronounced. She stared at the pattern of the markings, stymied once again by the imprint's strange behavior. After locking up she took her tea with her into the bedroom. Where she'd probably spend another sleepless night trying to ignore her longing for Griff.

Chapter Thirty-One

A couple of weeks later Griff sighed as he turned away from the kitchen sink and reluctantly made his way to the front door. He knew it was her. She was the only person who came to his house. The only person who knocked on his door in such a determined, insistent manner. Even though he couldn't see her, he knew it was her.

He debated about not answering. It seemed small and childish of him, but it was tempting, nonetheless. He'd been in her company too often these past couple of months. It was a struggle not to give in to what he felt every time he was with her. Not to reach out and touch her hair. Not to ask her out for coffee or a drink.

So far, he'd succeeded. He cringed inside every time she gave him one of those interested looks tinged with confusion. She didn't understand why he hadn't asked her out. And he couldn't explain it to her. And if she kept pushing, if she kept giving him those looks, if she kept showing up uninvited and knocking on his damned door, he was afraid he might lose control. And then all hell would break loose.

He yanked the door open. He tried to look like he wasn't happy to see her even while everything inside him came alive just because she was right in front of him, breathing the same air as him.

"Hi," she said a bit breathlessly while she took in his expression and his stance, surely noting that he hadn't greeted her.

"Hello." He tamped down the urge to invite her in.

"Are you busy? Am I interrupting?"

"Yes."

"Oh, well, this will only take a minute. I brought you something." She held a gift bag out toward him. Red tissue paper obscured the contents.

He glanced at it, then back at her. "What is it?"

"It's a tie. For the donor recognition dinner."

He made no move to take it. He didn't need any more reminders of her. "I have a tie."

"Of course, you do." She continued to hold the bag out toward him. "This is a red tie. That's our theme. 'Give Red a Bed like Fred.' Candy Simmons does all our PR. Gratis, of course. She came up with that after this guy named Fred adopted a stray Irish Setter. I don't know if you saw it on the invitation or not, but it's red tie only."

"I might not even be there," Griff said.

"But I have your name on the RSVP list. You sent a check."

"Check, sure. Happy to help. Attendance isn't mandatory, is it?"

Her face fell. "Of course not." She rallied in the next instant. "You don't need a date, do you?"

"I don't date."

"Oh?"

"Women."

"Oh. *Oh!*"

Griff bit the inside of his lip to keep from laughing as she drew the obvious conclusion. Even for him, this was taking it a bit too far. "Or men, if that's what you're thinking. I'm not interested in dating. Period."

She lifted her chin and stared him down. "Got it." She shoved the bag at his chest and let go forcing him to take it or let it fall. "Okay. Maybe I'll see you at the dinner. Maybe I won't. The tie's a gift, so you might as well keep it. No strings attached."

She turned and stalked back to her car without looking his way again. She started the engine and Griff watched until her taillights disappeared. He closed the door and stared at the gift bag while his earlier sense of elation dwindled to disappointment.

The following Saturday evening Griff knotted a tie, a *black* tie at his throat and stepped back to look at the results in the full-length mirror. Black was his thing. Him and Keanu Reeves. It's all he wore down to his underwear. It suited him, reminded him he wasn't allowed to have color or joy in his life. It blended right in with the black cloud that followed him everywhere. *Red tie only* indeed. He sincerely doubted he'd be denied access to the event because he didn't comply with that ridiculous sartorial requirement.

The gift bag with the red tie sat on his dresser, mocking him. He'd seriously considered not attending the Sanctuary dinner at all. But he wasn't a coward. He knew he could control himself around Bree. There'd been a couple of close calls, but he'd proven it more than once. Whether he liked it or not, he was a part of the community. Without his efforts, the community garden wouldn't exist. Every time he and Bree crossed paths, he made sure the contact between them was as brief as possible. Even if he had made contributions to Sanctuary for his own selfish reasons, he deserved a place at the dinner.

He'd go. Alone. In his black suit. Besides, his business thrived on the kind of people who would be there. Wealthy retirees with lavish homes who belonged to elite country clubs. The kind of homes and clubs his company excelled at servicing.

These were also the kind of people who would be enamored with a cause like the Lancaster Memorial Botanical Garden. The kind of people who also believed in leaving a legacy. The more support he had for the project, the better. Even if it meant suffering through an appearance at a social event such as this dinner.

He'd eat the rubber chicken, be pleasant for a couple of hours, and rub the right elbows. As soon as he could he'd escape and, if he was very lucky, since his contribution to Sanctuary was at an end, he'd never see it or Bree Mason again.

Three hours and many rubbed elbows later, Griff was more than ready to make his escape. He'd given an extra ticket to Tyler, and Jenna Scott had made sure he was at her table. Griff couldn't help but notice how often they leaned close to each other as if sharing a secret, smiling into each other's eyes.

Griff was at a table with people he didn't know and didn't particularly want to. But he'd forced gregariousness, making conversation, mentioning the botanical garden at every opportunity.

At one point, he'd had to stand and be recognized by Bree as the driving force behind the community garden. If he'd known he'd have to navigate through the tables to accept an engraved plaque from her, he would have made good on his threat not to attend. During his remarks on stage, Carter made mention of the expansion plans already underway for next year's planting season, as well as the work to revitalize the orchard, which only reminded Griff he wouldn't have any part in it.

The evening had been torture, and he'd sought solace at the bar as soon as dinner and the speeches ended. He sipped at a Jack on the rocks, a rare indulgence. He tried to tell himself lingering at the bar wasn't just so he could catch another glimpse of Bree tonight. When he finished his drink, he would head home. Alone.

Bree had looked stunning in a silky red wrap dress that clung in all the right places. A red ribbon was tied in a pretty bow around her neck. The makeup she wore made her eyes look huge and smoky and sexy. Her lips were tinted with a subtle red, and her hair was fuller and wavier than he'd ever seen it.

She'd given him the same polite greeting she'd given all the guests as they'd passed through the receiving line at the entrance. A brief handshake. "So glad you could make it." And other than the presentation of the plaque, she'd pretty much ignored him. Just the way he wanted it, he reminded himself.

Except it was killing him.

The event room was dotted with red. Every man but him had donned a red tie, while the women either wore red or accessorized with it. The PR campaign had been effective. When the woman sitting next to Griff asked about his lack of a red tie, he told her he forgot.

All evening he'd watched Bree. Even though he was seated two tables away from her, his seat faced hers.

He'd logged every smile, every time she laughed or became animated when she spoke. Since she never even looked at him, she couldn't have noticed him watching her. Thank God.

"Pinot grigio, please."

Lost in his own glum thoughts about Bree, Griff didn't realize she now stood right next to him.

The bartender stepped away to pour her a glass of wine. Griff slid a glance in her direction. "Hello."

She allowed her gaze to flicker toward him, but only for a moment. "Hello." She smiled at the bartender when he set the glass in front of her.

"Nice party."

She took a sip of her wine. "Glad you enjoyed it."

"I didn't say I enjoyed it."

"Didn't you?" She refused to look at him. She drank some more wine.

Griff drained his glass, although there was hardly anything left except ice cubes. He set the glass on the bar and told himself to walk away. A minute ticked by. Then another. It was like they were the only two people on the planet.

The bartender approached, but Griff waved him away.

When he didn't leave or speak, Bree turned to him. "You know what I don't get?"

"What's that?"

"You're interested."

Griff stared at her. He hoped she couldn't see the panic in his eyes.

"But it's like you don't want to admit it. Like you're fighting it."

"I don't—"

"Oh, spare me. You've been watching me all night. You do it all the time. I don't know what your game is, even though I've spent an awful lot of time trying to figure it out. Why don't you just tell me the truth? Or get over yourself and tell me why you haven't asked me out."

Her eyes blazed at him. Now was his chance. He'd have to be cruel. If he wasn't, what would follow would be even more cruel. He fixed her with a dismissive look and said what he had to say. "The reason I haven't asked you out is because I'm not interested in you. I don't want you. I'm not attracted to you. Simple as that."

He saw the light die in her eyes, replaced by pain. He'd hated a lot about himself for a long time, but in that moment, he truly despised who and what he was. He pushed his glass to the back of the bar, ready to walk out.

But Bree seized his wrist and shoved the cuff of his shirt higher. He hadn't worn his watch to cover it because the shirt cuff wouldn't button over it. She stared at the puckered skin there. He knew she recognized what she saw. She ran her thumb over the design. At her touch, it became inflamed, causing him to gasp in reaction.

He yanked his arm back and turned away, drawing on every bit of inner strength he possessed to do so.

He didn't make it more than a step before he heard her hurl the word, "Coward," to his back. She couldn't have chosen a more hurtful insult.

Chapter Thirty-Two

Griff kept walking, but it wasn't easy when everything in him wanted to go back to her, to explain, to take away the hurt he'd seen in her eyes.

Be cruel to be kind, he reminded himself. Except everything she felt, he felt, an excruciating addition to his agony.

He got into his truck and took several deep, shaky breaths before he started the engine. Sadness weighed him down as he drove home. Her parting shot still rang in his head, bringing back everything and everyone he'd lost.

He'd accused his brother of cowardice after his death. Greg had become increasingly withdrawn with every episode of transformation, and while neither of the brothers had liked this new development in their lives, Griff had grudgingly accepted it.

The wounds he inflicted were more psychological than physical, and he only had to draw blood using those razor-sharp claws before the animal inside him calmed. Of course, by then, he'd traumatized his victim.

The morning after the first attack, both he and Greg sported claw marks to match those they'd inflicted. Though they healed quickly, they served as reminders of the pain they'd caused.

Griff began to look through the research his father had left and became certain there had to be a way to break the spell they were under. He'd begged Greg to help him find it, but his twin accepted what was as his fate. Transformations every third new moon until death at age thirty-three. Rather than face such a future, he'd hung himself from the rafters of the garage when they were nineteen.

"*Coward*." Griff hadn't held back his bitterness and sense of abandonment as he and his mother stood at the gravesite. The other funeral goers had withdrawn, leaving the two of them alone.

"Not everyone's as strong as you are," she said. "Nor as brave or determined."

"I'm sorry, Mom. I just—he could have helped find a way out of this. We could have done it together."

"He didn't believe there was any other way."

"He gave up." Griff didn't want to hate his brother for abandoning him, but he couldn't help it. He'd lost the other half of himself, the only person who shared his experience. Griff resented such weakness. He vowed never to give up. There had to be a way to end the curse.

And now, after all these years, Madeline Stark was his last hope. If she and her translator didn't come through with *something*, his quest and his life would be at an end.

He parked in his driveway but stayed in the truck. The irritation in his wrist had dwindled to an annoying tingle. His limbs were heavy, his mind dull, and his spirit broken.

Getting yet another glimpse of what he could have, what he might have had in a different life, made it easier to understand why Greg chose suicide. While Griff never seriously considered it, over the years he'd come to understand the appeal of letting go.

The curse would end with his death, but somewhere inside him, he had a need to break Emerald's spell. She'd been an evil, vindictive woman whose vengeance had harmed countless innocents. Any justification she'd had was long since paid with his ancestor's death. He simply couldn't let her win. There had to be another way. Had. To. Be.

He dragged himself out of the truck and inside his cold, dark house where he'd been fooling himself living in the shadows was all he deserved, convinced he'd never be free to enjoy living in the light of day.

He yanked off his tie and hung up his clothes, exchanging them for comfortable pajama bottoms and a tee shirt.

In his office, he pored over the schematics for the botanical garden once more. He'd accomplished that, at least. Assuming Bree didn't throw a wrench into the plans because of his rejection.

Somehow, he didn't think she'd renege, even if she could. Bree Mason was a woman of her word. His impression of her was she saw things through to the end.

He stared at the pages, but Bree's face super-imposed itself over them. He'd hurt her, but maybe, in some small way, he could still make it up to her. He could show her how he felt after he was gone, even if it would be little comfort to her.

He began revising his plans, sketching out the idea he had to create a section in her family's name. He envisioned it surrounded by wrought iron fencing. The entrance would be a pergola covered with wisteria. He could picture an apple tree and a profusion of perennials, like the ones he'd seen poking through the weeds, planted long ago by Bree's grandmother. Wildflowers and native shrubs to attract bees and butterflies. He added benches near the fences. A fountain wasn't an option, but perhaps a sculpture of some kind. He made a note to find or commission the right one.

He'd fund this section personally and create a plaque to be posted near the entrance. "For Maybree Anna Mason, who gives Sanctuary to all." Something like that. "Contributed by Griffin Henry Lancaster." Then she'd know, if she ever visited the garden once it was complete, which would be well after his demise. Would she visit? Or would it be too painful? She might only want to banish the memory of him, of ever having met him.

He closed his eyes against the sudden rush of pain. Squeezed them tight, holding in the emotion that threatened to bubble to the surface.

After his mother's funeral a few short years after his brother's, he'd vowed never to give in to useless, foolish tears.

Tears never did anything except to make him feel more helpless, and he refused to wallow even further in his misery.

"There has to be a way out," he said as he clipped his notes and drawings to the existing plans and rolled them up. "Has to be."

Early the next morning, Griff stared into the inky blackness of his bedroom. He wished he could close his eyes and shut off his thoughts once and for all. If he didn't see Bree's face or hear the echo of his own hurtful words, he could finally stop hating himself.

It was no use. He got up and went to the kitchen. He'd hardly slept at all. His body bore the weight of the world. He sipped coffee while he stared at the dim outlines of his furniture and fixtures without really seeing them. All he could see was Bree before he'd walked away from her.

He had to get out of here before he drove himself nuts. Before he did something stupid and tried to see her. Tried to explain something she'd never understand. No. The only way to keep from hurting her further was to stay away from her. Far, far away.

Griff set his mug on the counter. A half hour later, he was on a narrow two-lane that curved back into the mountains. The powerful engine of his Harley roared in his ears, its noise drowning out his painful thoughts.

He never wore a helmet, hoping, he supposed, he'd be more likely to die and be put out of his misery in the event of an accident. He'd had the bike for five years and never had an accident. Figures, he thought grimly.

Then again, what if he *was* involved in a bad accident that required months in the hospital or a rehab facility? What happened during the next change? He'd have to perform an attack somehow. A nurse. A respiratory therapist. An aide.

And then everyone would know. They'd ship him off to a lab or something for further study. Or stick him in jail for assault. As far as he knew, none of his ancestors' transformations had been detected by outsiders. He prayed he'd be as fortunate.

Normally, a long ride soothed him. But his thirty-third birthday loomed before him like never before, and the ride did nothing to calm his agitation.

Chapter Thirty-Three

Bree awoke late the next morning, wishing she'd never wake up again. She stared at the familiar, comfortable bedroom she'd always loved. She might as well be in a prison somewhere surrounded by blank walls and iron gates with only a crust of bread and a few stale drops of water to sustain her.

The weight of Griff's words lay heavily on her mind and created an ache in her heart. She'd never get over what he'd said. Her thoughts went round and round, looking for an explanation for his behavior and came up empty. Nothing he did or said made sense to her.

I don't want you, I'm not interested in you, and *I'm not attracted to you,* did not jibe with *it makes me think about you too much.*

If he wasn't attracted to her, if he wasn't interested in her, then why think about her at all? And if he *was* attracted and interested, why did he go out of his way to not only avoid her, but to hurt her? No, this was beyond hurt. He'd stabbed her in the heart, and she'd been bleeding all night. It was a miracle she hadn't bled to death by now.

She felt as if all the life had drained out of her. Her lifeblood was seeping away, and she couldn't stop it. There were no words to describe this kind of misery.

She had been weirdly connected to Griff from the first time they met, and seeing the mark on his wrist only confirmed it. And it seemed he not only knew of their connection, but he also chose to fight it with everything he had. While she became more and more attracted to him, obsessed even, he didn't even have the decency or the courage to explain it to her.

She closed her eyes, begging sleep to come back. But all she saw was Griff's face. All she heard were his words.

Not attracted to you, not interested in you, not attracted to you.

The sound reverberated through her brain like an echo, and she couldn't make it stop.

She had to get out of here before she lost her mind. She threw back the covers and dressed. She needed to be out in the open, physically exert herself. It was the only thing that might stop last night's highlights reel from playing over and over in her head.

She hadn't hiked in months, but there was a trail she used to love about an hour's drive north. Steep and challenging with incredible views. It was exactly what she needed. She concentrated on packing a knapsack with water and energy bars and a few emergency supplies. In her car, she plugged in her road trip playlist and let it blast through the speakers, hoping it would drown out everything else. Hoping the music could fill up the emptiness inside her heart.

She parked and stared at the marked trailhead assailed by doubt. She wasn't sure she could do this. No, that wasn't quite right. She wasn't sure she *wanted* to do this. Hike alone. Be alone.

She caught a glimpse of herself in the rearview mirror, and she didn't like what she saw. She looked haunted. Hunted. Fearful. Weak. Things she despised. She was not weak, and she was not afraid. Griff did not have any power over her. This *fantasy* she'd been feeding on about him was her own doing. It was all in her own mind, right? And she needed to get it out of her head.

She got out of the car, adjusted her backpack, and headed for the trail. No one passed her on the way up and only a couple of hikers passed her on their way back down. She made it to the top in two hours. She was hot, sweaty, and anger had begun to crowd out the pain. Blindly she stared out at the mountains and trees and valleys, rivers, and streams, ate an energy bar without tasting it, and washed it down with water.

She started back down the trail and with every step her anger grew. How dare he? Who did Griffin Henry Lancaster think he was? He had no right to treat her the way he had. He was the kind of person who dangled a treat in front of a dog, made him jump for it, then held it higher and higher so the dog could never reach it, while he stood there and laughed.

And she was the dog. No wonder she felt like such a fool. If she'd been smart, she'd have refused to play his game. As it was, she'd set herself up for humiliation, kept coming back for more and in the end, she'd allowed him to kick her where it hurt before he walked away.

She was moving too fast down the steep trail, slipping and sliding on fallen leaves. She forced herself to slow down while icy rage filled her. She made her steps more deliberate. Never again, she promised herself, would she let Griffin Lancaster get close enough to hurt her. Hopefully their paths would never cross again. Which would be for the best.

She was going to change her pattern. Stop looking for guys to rescue, stop looking for guys who wanted to play games and never wanted to be caught.

By the time she reached the parking lot, she was a mess and breathing hard. She was also delightfully, physically exhausted. She'd drive home, take a shower, and go to bed early to catch up on the sleep she'd missed last night. All because of him.

After her shower Bree walked into the kitchen and froze. The first thing she saw was the bright red pot holding the Christmas cactus. She'd been touched that he'd nursed her cactus back to health and brought it to her.

It makes me think about you too much.

Liar! What it did was make *her* think about *him* too much. And it would. Every damn time she walked into her kitchen. She'd see it and she'd remember. *I don't want you. I'm not interested in you. I'm not attracted to you.* The memory of his words would never go away.

Even though she was ready for bed, she threw a sweat-shirt on and picked up the pot. She killed the car's lights and parked at the end of his driveway. It was growing dark, but there was still enough light for her to see where she was going. She hefted the pot and got out, glad she'd worn her running shoes.

His house was dark. Wasn't it always? Even if he was still up, he couldn't see her approach and certainly wouldn't hear her footsteps crunching in the gravel. She passed his hulk of a truck and paused about six feet from his front door. The thick oval-topped portal made her think of the door to a hobbit's house. An asshole hobbit.

She hefted the pot close to her right shoulder and hurled it at the door. It hit with a dull thud, then dropped to the stone walkway and shattered. The cactus spilled out along with the dirt, a sick, broken mess. Good. Because that's exactly how she felt.

She ran back to her car, hit the gas, and drove a quarter mile before she bothered turning on the headlights.

Chapter Thirty-Four

"You look like shit."

"Well hello to you too." Bree had allowed Jenna to corral her into a drink at Dante's and now Bree eyed her friend over the rim of her wineglass.

Jenna frowned. "What's with all the black?" she asked, indicating the severe cut of the blouse Bree wore, along with a charcoal pencil skirt.

"It's what I felt like wearing today."

"You wore black yesterday. And Monday. It's him, isn't it? The Grim Reaper? Is he choosing your wardrobe now?"

"He's not doing anything. Black is a slimming color. You can't go wrong with black."

Jenna gave her a knowing look. "You two sure looked cozy at the bar after the dinner."

"Trust me, we weren't."

"Tyler and I saw you as we were leaving. You had a hold on his wrist, and you were looking into each other's eyes."

Bree could only imagine how their interaction might have looked to an outsider. "It wasn't what it looked like."

Both she and Jenna ignored their usual chips and salsa. Bree wished she'd asked for a bottle of sangria instead of a glass. She'd like to chug the entire thing and sink into oblivion, where thoughts of Griff and questions from Jenna couldn't follow her.

"What was it then?"

Bree tilted her head back to stare at the rustic ceiling rafters, willing herself to hold her tears at bay. Jenna reached across the table and squeezed her arm. "Bree, what? What did he do?"

Bree shook her hair back and faced Jenna. "He didn't do anything. In fact, he doesn't want anything to do with me."

"What?"

"I believe his exact words were 'I don't want you. I'm not interested in you. I'm not attracted to you.'"

"He said those things? To your face?"

Under other circumstances, Bree would have found Jenna's incredulity hilarious. Instead, she took another fortifying drink of sangria. "He did."

"He's a damn liar," Jenna said as they each reached for a chip. "What the hell, Bree?" Jenna shoved an entire chip into her mouth instead of breaking it up, a sure sign of agitation. "I don't get it," she said with her mouth full.

"Me neither."

"I could have sworn he was into you. The way he looked at you."

"I thought so, too." Bree didn't even try to hide her disappointment.

"Oh, sweetie. And here I am dying to tell you about me and Tyler."

Bree couldn't help but be happy for Jenna, even if her friend's joy was like a dagger through the heart. "So, tell me."

"No, let's finish our conversation about *him* first. He says these things to you and then what? Turns around and walks out?"

"After I called him a coward, pretty much, yeah."

Jenna sat back and crossed her arms. "No. I refuse to believe my judgment where men are concerned is that impaired. Everything he said to you is a lie. The question is why would he lie?"

"Does it matter? If he's not going to follow through, then I've lost him anyway."

"You can't lose what you never had, Bree."

"Fine. Then I've lost any chance I had with him. It's all the same. I'm still a mess."

"Sorry. I know. I hate this for you."

"I hate this for me, too. Now tell me about you and Tyler. God knows I need something to take my mind off my dismal love life."

"Sure?"

"Positive." Bree signaled the server for another round. Two was her limit, even though they would do nothing to take the edge off her misery.

"Well, after the dinner we spent the rest of the weekend together."

"Already? Sounds serious. And you look happy." Bree tried to smile. "In fact, you're glowing."

"Yeah, but now I feel like a shit. If it wasn't for you, I'd never have met Tyler. Now I'm happy and you're sad. Not exactly fair, is it?"

"Jenna, come on. It's not your fault. Be happy. Please. I need to believe it happens. I need to know *someone* gets to live the fairy tale."

Relieved, Jenna let the joy she felt spill out of her. "I think I'm in love with him, Bree. Honest to God. He's so sweet and he's—"

"Good in bed?" Bree said with a genuine smile.

"God, yes. And the stamina. I mean, I know he's only a couple of years younger than we are, but Oh. My. God." Jenna pretended to fan herself with her hand.

Their drinks arrived, and they hit the chips and salsa more heavily.

"Maybe you are in a fairy tale," Jenna said, having apparently given it some thought. "Beauty and the Beast."

"If I recall, after Belle falls for the beast, he turns back into a handsome prince, and they live happily ever after."

"Yeah, well, yours is more like a Grimm fairy tale. He starts out as a beast and he's still a beast at the end. Love does nothing to change him."

"Maybe he can't change," Bree said.

Jenna remained adamant in her view of Griff. "Or maybe he doesn't want to."

Chapter Thirty-Five

Everyone had left the office for the day, and all was quiet in Sanctuary when Bree walked out to the garden. Fulfilling her vision, a wrought-iron sign curved over the gated entrance proclaiming, "Sanctuary Community Garden." Blossoming flowers scrolled around a horn of plenty spilling its bounty.

She thought the garden would be peaceful. That was the other thing she'd wanted. The fountain in the middle of the courtyard spilled trickles of water into a pool where they were recycled. The four benches surrounding it were at right angles to each other.

She sat on the bench facing the far corner of the garden where she'd foolishly started her own tiny plot. She didn't know why she'd bothered. Probably because the day planting began, Griff had shown up, like he'd said he would. She got caught up in the excitement of seeing him again, even though he barely acknowledged her presence other than the basic civilities when Candy needed them for photographs.

God, would this feeling of complete humiliation ever leave her? She felt small and worthless and no matter how many times she tried to talk herself out of it, to tell herself that Griff was only one person and his opinion of her meant less than nothing, she couldn't convince herself.

For some reason, his opinion of her meant everything. And to hear him say he wasn't interested, wasn't attracted, didn't care... It made her heart feel like a squashed tomato, whose thin skin allowed its fruit and seeds to leak everywhere.

Even if he was lying about how he felt, nothing changed. Even if he had good reasons for lying, she'd never know what they were, and the result was the same.

She wished she could cry. Maybe it would make her feel better. But her eyes were dry and gritty from lack of sleep. She felt hollowed out. Her ache went beyond tears. She was just... lost.

She'd never felt like this before. She didn't understand it because it made no sense. It was like Griff had infected her somehow, or put a spell on her, and there was no cure or antidote. He'd gotten under her skin and into her blood. "Like a vampire," she muttered. He was draining the lifeblood from her.

She decided to inspect her plot. Her plants were already struggling. *Great.* She had never been any good at gardening. Her grandmother shooed her away from her flowerbeds because she always pulled up the wrong plants when she tried to weed, or she stepped on the baby buds. Her ineptitude got her sent to the barn where her grandfather and the animals seemed to appreciate her. She'd felt more at home there anyway.

But every bit of greenery she encountered gave up if she so much as breathed on it. She compared hers to the healthy plots on either side. Their plants looked happy and were thriving. Some were already blooming.

Still in her work attire, Bree squatted and began pulling up the sickly stalks one by one. She yanked them out by their roots and tossed them aside. Exactly what Griff had done to her heart. When she got done pulling them out of the ground, she planned to trample on them. Put them out of their misery.

"Are you okay?"

Bree thought Jenna had left with everyone else and hadn't heard her approach from behind, but she didn't stop what she was doing.

"I'm fine."

Jenna came closer. "Why are you pulling everything up?"

"They're dying." *I'm dying.*

Jenna stared at what Bree had done. "They aren't dead yet. They're still green. Mostly."

"It's only a matter of time. You know I've never been good with plants." *Or men. Or relationships.*

"Want to go get some dinner? Or better yet, come over to my place. I'll cook."

"I'm not hungry."

"You need to eat."

Bree stood and brushed her hands together. "I don't *have* to do anything." She checked her black slacks for dirt but saw none. The beauty of wearing the color of death. "But thanks, anyway."

Jenna went to her office to pick up the supplies she'd forgotten to take when she left earlier. She'd need them first thing in the morning because once a month Sanctuary offered a free clinic for those who couldn't afford veterinary fees. The county had offered space in a maintenance facility several miles away. It wasn't ideal, but it was close to the communities where her services were needed the most.

Jenna hated to see Bree moping around the way she had ever since the donor recognition dinner but didn't know how to help. Bree didn't want help, anyway, always insisting she was "fine."

She wasn't fine. She'd lost weight and she'd lost interest in almost everything. Bree did what she had to do every day, like a robot. Maybe the change wasn't noticeable to everyone, but it was glaringly obvious to Jenna.

After she placed the last of the supplies in the trunk of her car, a black truck cruised past and parked near the path to the garden. She recognized the truck, and her blood began to boil. Bree was long gone, but Jenna decided it was way past time she confronted Griffin Lancaster.

She stalked around the office building. He had already reached the garden entrance and opened the gate. She watched him stroll along the paths, fingering a staked tomato plant, hunkering to examine something in the soil nearby.

"*Excuse me.*"

Griff straightened as Jenna approached.

"What do you think you're doing?" she asked.

"Checking for vermin."

"That should be easy for you."

"It is kind of what I do."

Jenna stopped a few feet away from him. "I meant you'd recognize one of your own species."

He stared at her. "Is there a problem?"

"I don't like you and I don't trust you."

"That's fair, considering you don't even know me."

"I know enough."

"Do you?"

"I know you hurt Bree."

"I didn't want to."

"Of course, you didn't. Men never *intentionally* hurt women, do they? Just stay away from her."

"Believe me, I'm trying."

"Good."

Griff watched Jenna spin around and retrace her steps. The gate clanged shut behind her.

He shouldn't be here, but he couldn't stay away. He always made sure Bree's car wasn't in the lot. By the time he arrived, everyone had usually left for the day.

He loved how the garden had taken shape. Each plot was tagged with the gardener's name. Some were groups, some were individuals. He walked up and down each row as darkness fell until he reached the far corner and saw plants uprooted and tossed aside in the middle of the path.

He approached carefully, not wanting to crush the half-dead plants under his boots. He stared at the mess and had a feeling he knew who it belonged to, but he bent to peer at the sign, anyway. *Bree Mason.*

He'd noticed the plants in her plot were struggling the last time he'd stopped by. They were furthest from the irrigation system and weren't getting their fair share of water. He'd filled a can from the spigot and watered them himself, but it hadn't been enough.

Bree had given up on them. She must have ripped them from the ground and tossed them aside. *Exactly what she thinks you did to her.*

Griff stared sadly at the bent and broken plants before he gathered them up as gently as he could and carried them back to his truck.

Chapter Thirty-Six

Griff adjusted the throttle and the bike thrust itself into the wind. Tomorrow it would be two weeks since the Sanctuary awards dinner. Two weeks since he'd seen Bree. Almost two weeks since he'd paused in the act of pulling a clean tee shirt over his head and heard something hit his front door with force.

When it happened, he'd padded down the hallway and across the living room, turned on the outside lights, and peered through the peephole but could see nothing.

After he slid the deadbolt back and eased the door open, he saw the broken pot, a pile of dirt, and a Christmas cactus. His heart broke all over again.

Griff had knocked off work early today because he couldn't stand being around Tyler one more second. He was happy and upbeat all the time, but he was especially annoying ever since he'd started seeing Jenna Scott.

Their relationship had only intensified. Although he and Tyler didn't discuss their personal lives, Griff noticed

Tyler checking his phone much more regularly and doing a lot of texting on his lunch break. Plus, he had the satisfied look of a man getting laid on a regular basis. Griff wished he could remember when he'd had that look, but he knew the answer. Never. Which only added to his irritation.

Tyler could afford to have a normal relationship with a woman. He didn't have to hide who he was from the world. Tyler could fall in love, get married, have a family, and a nice long life. Griff wanted to punch Tyler just to wipe the smug grin off his face. Before Griff took out his frustrations on his foreman, he'd walked off the job site, got in his truck and left.

He drove home, changed clothes, got on the bike, and took off. He didn't care where he was going. Somewhere he didn't have to think about that shattered pot all over his front steps. Where he didn't have to acknowledge what drove Bree to take such action.

I understand, he wanted to tell her. *I know I hurt you. I know I was cruel. But I didn't have a choice.*

He took the mountain curves too fast. Traffic was light but still he passed with impunity, cutting it close on the narrow two-lane, with the cars coming in the opposite direction. In fact, he made every maneuver that made sensible drivers hate motorcyclists.

If the last two weeks were any indication of the future, Griff didn't know how he was going to get through the next few months. Bree was all he thought about. It was like she had taken over his mind, from the moment he'd first seen her to the shattered pot at his front door.

He couldn't stand what he'd done to her, and he couldn't stand knowing he'd never see her again. The knowledge ate him up inside, making it nearly impossible to concentrate on anything. These rides were the only thing that gave him any respite, where it was just him and his machine and all he had to think about was the ribbon of pavement in front of him.

That wasn't quite accurate. In between thoughts of Bree had been thoughts of Madeline, and her last phone call. The translator had made more progress, but it was still slow-going, so Madeline had asked him to cut to the chase and start from the last page of text and work his way back in the hopes he would find what they needed faster.

"How's that going to help?" Griff had asked irritably. He'd been close to telling her to call the whole thing off. This expensive, ridiculous quest. He should simply accept his fate. Should have accepted it long ago.

"I'm not certain it will," Madeline said. "But I'm assuming if the incantations and the recipes used to create the curse are at the front of the book, the methods for lifting them and all the antidotes will be at the back."

Griff thought for a moment. "But don't you have to know what spell or curse you're under before you can figure out which method will end it?"

"Honestly? I'm not sure. All I could think of was the time factor. Maybe, if we uncover antidotes, the translator can try to cross reference it in the body of the text and find the exact curse each one applies to."

"Sounds like a long shot."

Madeline agreed. "It's not an exact science."

Griff reminded himself to be gracious. "I appreciate everything you're doing. The translator too. If the effort fails—"

"You'll die."

For some reason hearing someone else admit it made Griff smile. "I was going to say, there's still a huge tip in it for both of you."

He could hear Madeline bristle. "I'm not in this for the money."

"I know you're not. Bad joke."

It was dusk now, and the light had taken on the grayish quality it sometimes did when the temperature dropped in the lower elevations, where areas of almost-fog set in. Griff was close to turning around and heading home. The empty weekend stretched in front of him, and Griff knew what he'd be doing both days. Exactly what he was doing now.

He pushed the bike around another curve, leaning in low over the handlebars as the bike tilted beneath him. As he straightened for the next curve, he saw something coming toward him. A minivan trying to overtake a heavy, slow-moving utility truck. For a moment they'd be blocking the road.

Here was his chance. A head-on collision. End it all now. Escape from the agony the days ahead would bring. Nothing but time spent without Bree while contemplating the end of his existence.

But the van was a family vehicle. Even in the split second of time he had to observe and process what was about to happen, he could see a man and a woman in front. The woman had turned toward the backseat. Griff glimpsed at least one car seat back there. Maybe two.

Even if they didn't die, they'd probably be scarred for life knowing they'd been in an accident that had caused the death of the guy on the motorcycle. And what if they were injured? Disabled for life? Because of him.

He couldn't do it. The van was beyond the point where it could have tucked back in behind the truck. Griff didn't pause to wonder what the driver had been thinking. If he had a death wish like Griff's, it was too damn bad. Griff wasn't going to be his instrument of destruction.

He throttled back, and swerved to the shoulder, of which there was very little. Just six or eight inches of thin gravel bordered by brush covering the incline.

The bike skidded across the gravel, and since Griff had already prepared to take the right-hand curve, he headed even more right than he'd planned, straight down the ravine.

He did his best to slow the bike's momentum as branches slapped at his face and overgrown weeds and brush dragged at the wheels and against his boots. He thought he'd be okay. He got the bike under control. He could hear the rush of water from a creek somewhere below him. The ground grew rockier but also slick with fallen leaves. The bike skidded and he almost laid it out on its side.

He didn't want to let go of it. He loved that damn bike. But just as he righted it, the front tire hit a log buried under leaves and vines. The bike flew out from under him, cartwheeled forward and crashed on the rocks lining the creek bank.

Chapter Thirty-Seven

When Griff came to, he was staring up into an almost dark sky. The stars winked at him through the branches overhead. He assessed himself for a moment before he sat up with a groan. He was sore as hell and there was a lump on the back of his head, but otherwise he was uninjured. He'd had the wind knocked out of him, he decided, and maybe the knot on his head caused a moment of concussion. It hurt like hell.

"Crap," he muttered. He wasn't sure if it was because of the predicament he found himself in, or that the crash hadn't finished him off. Maybe it was both. No one from the minivan or the truck had come to check on him. He didn't know how they could since there was nowhere for vehicles to safely pull over. Maybe neither driver even realized what had happened to the guy on the bike.

Using his cell phone's flashlight, he picked his way to the bank of the creek. He could barely make out his bike where it had landed on the big wet stones. The water wasn't deep, but the rocks hadn't been kind.

From the gearbox he took the utility flashlight he kept there and checked the bike over. The damage was far more than cosmetic.

He maneuvered down the bank. With a grunt, he stood the bike up and pushed it through the brush back to the road.

He should have had his headlight on. He probably could have avoided the accident.

Luckily, his cell phone had a signal, so he put in a call to Bear. Griff didn't know Bear's given name, but he assumed it was something other than Bear. And he was pretty sure a guy who customized motorcycles for a living wasn't going to be too happy to get a call on a Friday night, but he was Griff's first choice. The guy lived and breathed Harleys. If Bear couldn't help him out, he'd call a towing company and see if they could send a flatbed.

Bear answered. "It'll be a while," he grunted. "And it'll cost ya."

Griff wasn't surprised, but he agreed to Bear's terms because there was no one he trusted more with his bike.

Besides, money held little meaning for him. It couldn't save him. His will bequeathed percentages of his estate to worthy causes, with the bulk of it going to completing the botanical garden and to other conservation organizations. Hell, he might leave the bike to Bear. No one else he knew would appreciate it more.

He leaned the bike against a tree, made himself as comfortable as possible, and waited.

The thoughts he'd been trying to escape returned, but they were like a leopard changing its spots. He stopped shying away from thoughts of Bree and started asking himself *what if?* What if he'd been killed earlier? He'd be dead in a few months anyway, but this near miss had changed his perspective. He'd thought about going to his grave never having a chance to see Bree again, never apologizing, never trying to explain why he did what he did to push her away.

She deserved better. She deserved an apology, or at least an attempt at honesty. Maybe she'd understand. Maybe she wouldn't. He didn't have to tell her everything. He could tell her he was dying. That he only had a short time left, and he didn't want to get involved with her because it would be too painful. It was all true, after all.

He mentally patted himself on the back. Why hadn't he thought of this weeks ago? It was such a simple solution.

He checked the moon calendar on his phone and came to a decision. A day or two after the next transformation, he'd contact Bree. Unburden himself and help her understand why it was for the best.

He continued to go over all the possible scenarios, what he would say, her likely response, until he heard the rumbling diesel of Bear's truck. He straightened and flashed his light as the truck came around the curve.

Chapter Thirty-Eight

What Griff thought of as "the weirdness" began. As always, he'd scouted his hunting ground early. He parked the truck a good distance away and hiked back to the area he'd chosen before darkness fell. He needed the privacy of the woods for the transformation, somewhere he wouldn't be discovered while it took place.

He lay face down on the ground because he'd learned long ago it was the best position to be in. Even after all this time, he still couldn't understand how it happened. The change defied all known science—chemistry, biochemistry, physics—as well as any other science one could name.

His father had tried to explain before he died. "That's because it's not science. It's a curse. A powerful, powerful curse that can't be broken."

"Like magic?" Greg piped up.

"Yes. Like magic. But not the fun kind you're thinking of. This is evil magic. *Black* magic. A horrific, sinister curse dreamed up by a vicious, sadistic woman."

Greg shrank back, sorry he'd asked. But eventually both boys came to understand that what they would experience was deadly serious.

First came the disoriented feelings. Everything in his line of vision became wavy, as if he were on a ship in troubled waters being tossed from side to side. He had to close his eyes against the undulating landscape.

He began to shiver as though a layer of ice had formed under his skin. Next came the burning fever that melted the ice. Each stage only lasted minutes, possibly seconds. He'd never timed it, focused as he was on enduring what was happening to his body, but each phase caused excruciating pain.

Next, he felt the prickling of his skin that meant soon every inch of him would be covered in fur. The coarse black fur of a bear or perhaps a panther, although he was neither of those. His limbs and hips would pop and shift in a way that made it natural for him to travel on four feet instead of two.

He braced himself for the longer period of torment as his muscles and ligaments protested their realignment.

He panted his way through it, not uttering a sound, holding his breath when he wanted to howl in agony.

Over the years, he'd become creative and efficient in locating prey. He researched trash pick-up days and college class schedules. He knew when shifts ended at hospitals and clinics. When restaurants and nightclubs and gyms closed for the night. He'd pace the shadows, watch, and wait for his opportunity.

Sometimes he got lucky and sometimes it was exhausting when the circumstances weren't optimum. He needed a woman alone in a fairly isolated area. Parking lots were often too well-lit or had too much traffic. Public parks were usually a good bet. Sometimes women, *like Bree*, jogged alone at night in dimly lit surroundings. Bars and convenience stores often provided fertile hunting ground. He'd been surprised how many women were not at all careful about or aware of their surroundings.

The trick was not to repeat the pattern or the location. Sometimes that meant a long drive earlier in the evening. But the very last thing he wanted was to get caught. Or shot.

Once he'd gone after a woman holding a heavy bag of groceries, juggling her keys to unlock her front door. He'd knocked her down and attacked as milk spread across the porch from the busted container and oranges rolled down the steps.

He hadn't realized a German Shepard had been cooped up in the house all day and was desperate to get out. The dog went wild, pushing on the door she'd unlocked, tearing at the wood. The shepherd snarled and snapped and barked in an effort to get to the woman.

Griff did what he had to do quickly, but not quick enough because the dog must have hit the door latch just right, allowing him to break out and give chase back toward the woods. Fortunately, the dog never caught him. It stopped abruptly at the edge of the lawn, barking hysterically.

An invisible fence, Griff realized later, and effective dog training had saved his ass. That time he'd come to as always, fully dressed, exhausted and drained, in the same place where he'd transformed. After he dragged himself up, he made it back to the truck, but barely had enough energy to drive home.

He always knew when the transformation was complete. The moment when he became more animal than man. He was unrecognizable as his human self. He had no idea what his animal state looked like, only that his fur was black upon black. His eyesight sharpened in the darkness; his hearing became hyper-sensitive. His animal instincts took over, focused on his only purpose. He rose on all fours and sniffed the air before he took off through the middle of the forest.

From his earlier research, he knew that this wilderness area backed onto the town of Collinsville. The city had created a trail at the outer edge of the woods for the use of its citizens. Just beyond the trail, the residential areas began.

He was panting by the time the woods began to grow thin. He paused and swept his gaze from side to side. Once he crossed the trail, he'd be in a populated area with homes and streets and sidewalks. He prowled behind the houses closest to him and moved west toward the main section of the town.

His ears twitched, and he raised his nose to catch any scent that might lead him to his prey. Collinsville hadn't found money in the budget to add lighting to the trail yet. The backyards were dark, but light from windows helped guide him.

He circled around swing sets and picnic tables and barbeque grills. After he jumped a fence, he paused to listen to a stereo blasting "Mustang Sally" from one of the homes and the volume turned all the way up on an episode of *Law & Order* from another.

He padded along until he saw a flash of something on the sidewalk as he passed from one backyard to the next. He picked up his pace and whipped around the corner of the house, and saw someone on the sidewalk, alone.

He gave chase to the woman, who was running full-out toward the town center. Her arms were pumping, her shoes making a hollow clackety-clack against the concrete, dark hair flying out behind her.

She looked back over her shoulder once and he saw the whites of her eyes. He sensed the raw fear in her. Had she seen him? He didn't think so. He'd stayed in the grass while he gave chase, waiting for a better moment to pounce, but the look back slowed her down, which was to his advantage.

He poised and sprang, knocking her to the ground. She fell awkwardly, her shoulder scraping along the uneven concrete. She might have tried to cry out, but the fall knocked the wind out of her.

He jumped on top of her, claws out, raking them down her body, hearing the rip of material as her top snagged on his nails. He dug deeper until he drew blood, until the damned curse was satisfied. She tried to struggle, to scream, but his weight on top of her made that nearly impossible.

"Come back here, bitch!"

Griff stilled. He stared down at his victim. Someone else was after her. She was panicked with fear, her eyes huge, her mouth open as she gasped for air. He leapt away and raced between two houses to the safety of the backyards.

He kept himself hidden but peeked around the corner of the house to see his victim struggle to her feet. She looked in the direction from which she'd been running and took a few staggering steps away. One of the sleeves of her shredded blouse hung down, exposing most of her arm.

She wasn't wearing running clothes. She looked like she'd dressed for an office job, in a silky white blouse, a slim skirt in a dark color, and low-heeled shoes.

Heavy footsteps pounded the sidewalk behind her. "You better stop right there, Caitlyn," a man's voice warned.

Griff crept forward staying in the shadows below the front porch so he could see.

The woman, Caitlyn, was now jogging in a slow uneven gait away from her pursuer. He could hear her labored breaths. One thing Griff always did was make sure his victims were able to recover from his attack. He made sure they were ambulatory, that even though they were in shock, they could get back to their homes or cars or find help.

The hair on his back stood at attention, warning him of a dangerous situation. He lowered himself to the ground and crept closer.

"Goddammit, Caitlyn, you better stop or else." The man, clearly built for stopping a tank, but not running, was nonetheless gaining on the woman.

He was so muscle-bound his arms stuck out from his sides, and he ran awkwardly. But that didn't keep him from catching up to the woman called Caitlyn, who did her best to put distance between them.

Caitlyn stumbled on, her breathing labored by fear and tears, but he caught her, grabbing her viciously by the arm. She cried out as he spun her around and shoved her causing her to lose her balance. Her head hit the concrete with a sickening thud.

"Now you listen, bitch," the man yelled as he kicked her prone form in the stomach. "You don't go *anywhere* unless I say you can. Now get up."

Before the man could kick her again, the animal sprang forward, claws out. He landed on the man's chest, which should have knocked the man to the ground. But the guy was built like an oak, solid muscle, with a neck the same width as his head.

"Goddammit!" The man swore as sharp claws raked their way across his upper torso. He reared back with a fist and the animal ducked, but not fast enough. He dropped to the ground and snarled, circling around behind the woman who still lay prone on the sidewalk. Behind him, a door opened, and a porch light came on. "What the hell's going on out there?"

The animal caught the strong scent of blood. He stared down at the small slick puddle dribbling from beneath the woman's head. Another scent came to him, the scent of death.

Too late, he perceived the change in the air around him. He didn't prepare for the kick that sent him sprawling.

He recovered quickly, ignoring the pain. He heard a pop of metal on leather as the two circled each other. The man had pulled out a deadly looking knife with a thin blade.

"I don't know what's going on out there, but I'm calling the police!" shouted the voice from the porch. The door slammed shut.

The animal and the man squared off. The animal growled low in his throat. This man had killed Caitlyn. Griff wanted to make it right, but he knew his time was limited. He couldn't risk capture. Already, sirens sounded in the distance.

The dim light from the porch did little to dispel the darkness. The man squinted. The animal knew it had the advantage. The man stopped moving, as if sensing more than seeing that there was something out there, just beyond his reach.

The animal leapt, operating on pure instinct, and sunk his teeth into the man's thigh. He drew blood, knowing somehow, in some small way, he had to avenge Caitlyn's death. A death for which he was partially responsible.

The man howled in pain, sliced down with the knife, and staggered back until he fell. The enraged animal pounced, claws out, knocking the knife away, snapping at the guy's head, tearing through his skin, ripping his ear.

The animal wanted to kill the man. It's what he deserved. But the animal pulled back, regaining control, just as swirling red and blue lights appeared on the road, approaching fast.

Griff leapt away, took one last glance at Caitlyn's lifeless body, and limped back to the woods before the reverse transformation began. Before he was discovered.

Chapter Thirty-Nine

Griff grunted in pain and his skin prickled all over, as if being singed by fire where each tuft of fur withdrew. He heard the crack of his joints and ligaments as they twisted and popped back into place and became arms and legs once again.

He panted his way through it, always wondering if this was what women in labor went through, their bodies changing and expanding to accommodate the expulsion of another being that lived inside of them. God, he hoped not. He wouldn't wish this pain on anyone. Except for the man who had thrown Caitlyn to the ground, cracking her head open. He had killed her. But Griff had helped by hurting her first, slowing her escape. He'd only added to the fear she'd felt in her final moments alive, and that was something he could never take back.

He hadn't killed the man, but he'd desperately wanted to. If he hadn't already felt so surrounded by death and destruction and hopelessness, maybe he would have. Still, Griff hoped he'd scarred Caitlyn's killer enough that he would wake up every morning wishing he was dead.

Once the agony of the transformation ended, he lay upon the damp ground, fighting nausea and feeling especially disoriented. Being injured and heartsick tonight further slowed his recovery.

He'd never killed anyone. They were always traumatized and bloody after his attack, but alive and usually not that badly injured.

He knew from the welts he felt rising on his own skin that he hadn't hurt Caitlyn badly. Nothing beyond the usual marks deep enough to draw blood, nothing more. Even now, he could feel them coagulating and sticking to his shirt and jeans.

He had to get back to his truck and get out of here. He didn't know what kind of police force Collinsville had, but whatever cops were available would begin prowling the neighborhood if Caitlyn's killer told his version of what happened, including the attack by some kind of animal. Unfortunately, Griff had left a bit too much evidence behind. The police would believe the man's story.

They might even believe he'd had nothing to do with Caitlyn's death and blame that on the same mysterious animal.

Griff pushed himself to stand and groaned at the throbbing pain shooting down from his right hip to his thigh. What was almost worse was the pain from the knife cut across his shoulder and down his upper arm. Most awful was the sour metallic tang of another man's blood on his tongue.

Carefully, Griff slipped off his shirt and probed the gash with his fingers. He hissed in pain, but determined the cut was long, but not deep. It would be more of an inconvenience than anything else. His tee shirt had absorbed most of the blood and was stuck to the wound. Griff couldn't change shirts anyway until he got home. He eased his shirt back on. Even if the blood soaked through the black cotton, it wouldn't be glaringly obvious.

The kick the man gave him with a couple of hundred pounds of solid muscle behind it had walloped him good. He'd be limping for a day or two. He could only imagine the size of the shoe-shaped bruise he probably had on his hip.

He fought his way back through the forest, his sense of direction never failing him. He knew he should hurry, but he couldn't. The disoriented feeling dogged him, as did the sadness over a senseless death, and the guilt he felt for his part in it.

He reached the parking lot and headed toward his truck when a pair of headlights flashed. Griff warned himself not to slow down or appear surprised or concerned when the police car stopped behind his truck.

The car's headlights were the only source of light. The driver's side door opened, and a sheriff's deputy stepped out. He adjusted a spotlight so it shone on the truck, just as Griff approached from the shadows.

He'd taken the cop by surprise without meaning to and the guy fumbled for his sidearm, aiming it over the roof of his cruiser at Griff. "Halt! Police! Hands in the air!"

Ignoring the objection from his left shoulder, Griff raised his hands. He hoped he didn't open the wound and make it start bleeding again. "What seems to be the problem, officer?"

"Is this your vehicle, sir?"

"Yeah."

The cop pressed a mike attached to his collar and spoke into it, giving his location and requesting backup. He kept his weapon trained on Griff. "Mind telling me what you're doing out here?"

"Hiking."

"At night?"

"Is there a law against that?"

"In the dark? Without a flashlight?"

"I've got a light on my keyring," Griff said, which was true although he hadn't used it. "But I'm not going to reach for it."

"Good idea."

Griff couldn't recall ever feeling this weary. But more than weariness, he felt despondent. And sick. His arm muscles began to protest.

"How long is this going to take?"

"Backup's on the way."

"Look, would you mind if I leaned on the hood of your car? I'm not armed."

The cop motioned him forward. "Do it slowly," he said. "One hand at a time."

Griff did. His biceps and injured shoulder thanked him as he leaned heavily on the hood of the patrol car, arms braced, hands flat. "This is the last time I go hiking out here," he muttered.

A few minutes later, another deputy arrived. He parked his car in the opposite direction from the first one so his headlights lit up Griff and the driver's side of the truck. The two deputies engaged in a brief conference. "Driver's license and registration," barked the first one. "Where are they?"

"In the truck."

The second deputy came around behind Griff. "Keys?"

"Right front pocket."

"Take them out. Slowly."

He removed the keys and held them up.

"Unlock the truck."

Griff used the key fob. The deputy opened the driver's door. "Where?"

"License is in my wallet under the front seat. Registration is in the center console."

"Step back here," he told Griff. "Keep your hands where I can see them."

The first deputy circled around toward them, weapon still raised. Griff couldn't blame them for being cautious. Paranoid, even. God knew they had reason given all the attacks on cops in the past couple of years.

"Any weapons in the vehicle?"

"No."

The deputy shone a flashlight under the seat and found Griff's wallet. "Take your wallet out. Remove your license, please."

Griff did as instructed so he could get this over. He swayed slightly, fighting exhaustion.

"Get your registration." The deputy positioned himself closer to the bed of the truck. Just in case, Griff supposed, he came out with a weapon and started firing.

Griff stepped onto the running board, leaned over the seat, and came back with the piece of paper.

The deputy took it. "Wait here." He nodded at the other deputy, who lowered his weapon but didn't holster it.

With Deputy Number One still covering him, Griff closed the door and leaned against it, arms at his sides. He averted his head from the headlights and the spotlight. All he wanted to do was go home to mourn.

"You been in a fight or something tonight?" the deputy asked.

Griff straightened. "Why do you ask?"

"Looks like you got a split lip or something."

Griff wiped the back of his hand across his mouth. It wasn't his dried blood that came away. "Took a tumble while I was out there," he said. He didn't embellish the story.

"Hiking after dark. Not the smartest idea."

"It wasn't dark when I set out," he said. "I lost track of time." He glanced toward Deputy Number Two, still seated in his patrol car.

Griff never understood why it seemed to take cops so long to check on a driver's license and registration. The patrol cars were all equipped with computers that should respond to a request for information instantly.

But Griff knew they'd find nothing. No outstanding warrants. No unpaid tickets. No violations of any kind.

Eventually, the second deputy exited his vehicle and returned Griff's ID to him. "You were out hiking in the wilderness area this evening, sir?"

"Yes."

"Anywhere near the Collinsville city limits?"

Lying did not come easily or naturally to Griff. "No."

"Kind of dangerous to be out in the woods like that after dark, isn't it?"

Griff figured that to be either a rhetorical question or the guy was fishing, so he didn't answer. "Can I go now?" he asked.

"You come across any wild animals out there?"

"Heard some rustling, but I couldn't say from what," he said. "Might have been opossums or raccoons."

"Nothing bigger?" the deputy asked. "Like a panther or a bear?"

"No. Nothing like that. What's this all about, anyway?"

"Thanks for your cooperation, sir. You're free to go."

The deputies climbed back into their vehicles and lined them up so their driver's sides were next to each other, and they could rehash what he'd told them. Griff didn't wait around. He got in the truck and headed for home.

Sorrow and self-loathing had seeped into every part of him by the time he parked the truck outside his house. He got inside and locked the door behind him. The gloom of his home welcomed him, although he didn't find it as comforting as he usually did.

He stripped and stepped into a hot shower, bracing his hands on the wall while the water poured over him, rivulets running down his face, mixing with tears. He howled and beat on the stone walls as if inflicting pain would somehow relieve his own.

It didn't.

Chapter Forty

Griff knew once he fell asleep, he'd be tormented by nightmares. They'd become part of his existence; a part of the exquisitely designed torture Emerald had thrown into her noxious brew.

The dreams had escalated the older he got, but they were always worst right after an attack. He'd relive everything he'd experienced, but there were parts of the dream where he was also in his victim's body, in her thoughts and her mind. He got to experience more than just the physical suffering he inflicted. He felt her fear, her shock, her trauma.

Emerald wanted every one of Colin's descendants to know exactly how she felt after what Colin had done to her.

Entwined in every dream, looking on from a distance, was a woman he now knew was Emerald. She always looked smug and satisfied, an evil leer infusing her features as if she found satisfaction in what she'd created.

Which, of course, she did. What could make her spirit happier than knowing the revenge she'd sought had been so effective? To know that generations of Lancaster men had suffered at her hands, after the one she'd wanted had slipped through her fingers.

He woke aching and exhausted, not sure if he had it in him to face the day. In the mirror, he could see how haunted he looked.

"Get it together, Lancaster," he growled.

He showered and dressed and made coffee, but his limbs were heavy, his spirit in the trenches. The only thing that soothed or motivated him on days like this was work.

The initial preparation to create the botanical garden started today, and he needed to be on site with the university people and the state reps. Someone from the National Arboretum Society was to be on hand as well. Griff struggled to generate some enthusiasm for the day.

The botanical garden commemorating his family was important. It was going to be his legacy... his family's legacy. Except now it didn't seem like enough. Perhaps, having finally achieved his goal, he couldn't see the point of it anymore. Not when it also seemed to magnify so many other things he wanted but would never have.

He stopped in the greenhouse to check on Bree's recovering plants. He'd transplanted each of them into their own pots, added some nourishment, and monitored the watering. He felt confident they would recover. The *Aster linariifolius* even showed buds. He made a mental note to include those in Bree's corner of the botanical garden. They grew easily and were native to the area. If Bree hadn't yanked hers out of the ground, it might have survived.

He didn't know how to make thoughts of her stop. He might have been the one who'd sunk his claws into her, but she'd definitely wormed her way under his skin.

More than anything, he wanted to see her. Talk to her. Explain himself to her.

But not today. Not when he was feeling this low and vulnerable.

Two days later, he had a message from Madeline. She wanted to update him on her progress. They agreed to meet the following evening at her place.

He followed her into the kitchen and once they were seated at the table with mugs of ginger tea, she said, "It's news. But it isn't good news."

"There's a way to end the curse that doesn't involve me dying?"

"Yes."

"What is it?"

When Madeline finished explaining, Griff slammed his fist down on the table, making the tea mugs jump. He shoved his chair back and paced to the wall of windows at the end of the kitchen, hands on hips. "That isn't a solution. It's bullshit. It's still a death sentence."

Madeline remained silent in the face of his frustration and disappointment.

"I wish I'd never come to you," he said. "I wish I didn't know." He slumped back in his chair. "I should have done what my brother did. Given up."

"Surely you don't mean that."

"Why not?" Griff snarled. "The end result is the same. What difference would there be if I died then or die now? It's still the end of a miserable, useless existence."

"I disagree."

"That's your prerogative."

"I know this isn't what you wanted to hear," Madeline began.

He flung himself back into his seat. "You think?"

She refused to back down. "But I have an idea I think you should consider. One that will contribute to the legacy you want to leave. Beyond the botanical garden, I mean. A way your family will always be remembered."

Griff eyed her with suspicion. "The garden's enough."

"I think you should leave the research, the documentation, the translations, everything. Make it public."

"No. Absolutely not. I can't believe you'd even suggest it."

"Listen to me. This is of historical significance. We have evidence of the true power of the granny women who populated Appalachia. We have proof of where that power came from and in this case, exactly how it was used."

"It's an embarrassment. It's shameful. Not exactly the legacy I want to leave. It's *not* how I want my family to be remembered."

"But don't you see? This is a way to make sure they'll never be forgotten. Yes, they were victims of a curse. But that's the value of what was done to them. We have Holocaust museums, for God's sake. We built an entire memorial for the 9/11 tragedy. Civil war monuments, The Tomb of the Unknown Soldier. All those things are there to document history, Griff. The people they memorialize, many of them were victims of something evil and cruel and unspeakable, just as your family was."

"What if someone figured out how it worked? Used it the way Emerald did? That's some kind of legacy to leave. Here's a curse you can cast on your worst enemy. Great idea."

"Oh, for heaven's sake." She threw up her hands in annoyance. "Do you really think that's going to happen? Besides, you can't stop everything being made public. It would be better if you were on board with it, but frankly, you'll be dead. Not only won't it matter to you at that point, but I'll be free to do what I want with the documentation you gave me."

"I want it back."

"You can have it."

"You made copies."

"Of course, I did," Madeline nearly shouted. "I had to. I couldn't risk anything happening to your originals."

When Griff still didn't speak, Madeline modulated her tone. "You may not understand, but I have a stake in this too. Emerald was my great-grandmother, the curse on your family, inadvertently or not, also cursed my family. It's part of our legacy as well."

"The deaths," Griff murmured.

"Yes. The stupid, pointless deaths brought about by one woman's vindictiveness."

"And with my death, it all ends."

"Yes," Madeline said. "The same way it ended with my daughter's death."

"You're right. I can't stop you."

"I'd rather do it with your blessing, though. It would mean a lot."

"Let me think about it."

"There's something else. Just a minute."

Griff lifted his gaze to the ceiling as Madeline rose and left the room. "Please, God. No more."

When she returned, Madeline had something in her hand, which she placed on the table. Griff looked at it curiously.

"What is it?" he asked, scooting closer. It looked like a string of corroded and blackened metal beads, five or six inches long, with a medallion of some type in the middle.

"Whatever concoction Emerald cooked up to create the curse would have to include something given to her by whoever she directed the curse at."

"My great-great-grandfather." Griff found himself afraid to even touch the strand, though the medallion intrigued him.

"My mother not only saved those old texts, but there were also other items she kept as well. I took another look through my grandmother's things and found this. I remembered Colin brought Emerald trinkets whenever he visited. I believe that's what this is. It might be the last thing he gave her."

Griff looked up from the dull patina of the metal spheres. "Was it expensive?"

Madeline shook her head. "These cheap bracelets were made by the thousands and sold everywhere around that time. They were of a nickel alloy, which created a shiny silver-like surface, but the metal corroded quickly and left a green circle around the wrist."

Griff almost laughed, though there was little humor in what he was seeing. "God, Colin was a piece of work, wasn't he?"

"Imagine how Emerald would have felt. She'd given him everything. Her youth. Her innocence. Her love. She was even carrying his child. And this cheap piece of garbage was his parting gift to her. I can imagine her rage."

"So can I," Griff said, recalling his most recent night-mare.

"I think the mark on your wrist—the same one all the men before you had? It's from the stamp on the medallion. The shape is the same, but you see why the design is so ill defined."

"Because the imprint is from a cheap piece of crap." Griff found himself morbidly amused.

"Apparently, this kind of mark was common with the type of curse Emerald cast."

"It transfers," Griff said. "During the attacks."

"It can," Madeline agreed, "based on what I read. But in most cases, it heals like the other wounds."

Their eyes locked on each other. "Except when it doesn't."

"There are certain... incidents, apparently when the victim retains the imprint."

"Like a bond," Griff said.

"Exactly. It creates a lasting connection between—"

"The animal and his ideal prey."

Madeline swallowed visibly her eyes huge. "Yes."

"It's another form of torture."

"Yes."

"Because Emerald wanted her victims to know what it felt like to go crazy with unfulfilled desire."

"Yes."

"Because if they gave into it, destruction would follow."

Madeline looked away. "I hate that I have part of her in me. That someone in my family could be that cruel or hateful. Those moments when I have given into my darker side, I look at them now and I think, what if I'd kept going? If I'd fed those feelings, encouraged them?"

"You'd be like her."

"It's terrifying to think that I have such capability."

Griff gave her a ghost of a smile. "No. Not you. You use your abilities for good."

"I'm sorry nothing good came out of my efforts."

"Nothing I can use, anyway," said Griff. "I tried not to get my hopes up, but it's been hard not to. The bottom line is I'm no worse off than I was before. It's my fate. I accept it."

He stood. "Thanks for everything, Madeline. And if you want to make everything public after I'm gone, well, as you said. I'll be dead. It won't matter to me."

She followed him to the door, and he allowed her a brief embrace before he left.

Chapter Forty-One

The following evening, Griff turned into his driveway and frowned at the patrol car parked in the turnaround.

What now?

His brain had been buzzing all day, zipping from thoughts of his conversation with Madeline to the development of the garden and supervision of the jobs his crews were working on.

He'd also decided to meet with Tyler and see if he had any interest in running the company once Griff couldn't. Of course, he'd couch the question as "if" he couldn't.

In truth, Griff wasn't certain Tyler was up to the task, but there was no reason the company couldn't go on with someone else at the helm. But if Madeline went public with the Lancaster family history, he'd want to change the name. Griff felt like he owed it to his employees, some of whom had been with him for years, to at least put a plan in place.

As if that weren't enough, thoughts of Bree hovered around the edges of everything else on his mind. He wanted to offer her both an apology and an explanation for his behavior. Admit what an ass he'd been and hope the fact that he was dying would allow her to forgive his cruelty. Then, maybe, he could at least die in peace. If that didn't work, there was also the corner of the garden created just for her in memory of *her* family's legacy. He hoped it would count for something.

But when he saw the same female deputy who'd visited him before emerging from the patrol car, he experienced a moment of panic. It passed quickly, though. He assured himself her snooping around would reveal nothing of value to any investigation. There was no real proof that he'd done anything illegal, at least, not in his human state.

"Deputy," he said.

"Mr. Lancaster. I'd like to ask you a few more questions."

Griff halted a few feet away and forced himself to stay at ease. "About what?"

"Could we step inside?"

"We can talk out here. I don't expect this will take long."

Gardner frowned. Griff wondered why she wanted to enter his home. To snoop around, maybe? Before she could speak again, Griff said, "What's this about? I know for a fact that Bree Mason is completely recovered." *Except for the mark on her wrist.*

"There was another attack. On a woman over in Madison County a few nights ago."

Griff waited, reminding himself that she hadn't asked him a question, and he wasn't about to volunteer anything.

Her frown deepened. "She died."

"I'm sorry to hear that." Griff wondered what the official ruling would be on the cause of death. He knew he wasn't directly responsible.

"Cause of death has yet to be determined," she admitted.

"Look, Deputy, it's been a long day, so if that's all you wanted to tell me..."

"You were there."

Griff stared at her, but before he could speak, she said, "Your name came up from the investigative reports. Deputies questioned you about the incident."

"And I told them I was hiking."

"They also said you were limping. And bleeding."

Griff waited her out. He was speaking with her voluntarily and she wasn't asking him questions. She was feeling her way along, hoping he'd say something incriminating. He warned himself not to. "I waited too long to head back and it got dark. I tripped and fell."

"Thing is, there was another witness to the woman's death. Claims there was an animal there, but he never got a good look at it. Coroner says the deceased had injuries that appeared to be caused by an animal. Just like Ms. Mason's injuries back in early March."

Gardner lifted a brow, encouraging Griff to respond. He crossed his arms and rocked back on his heels, which sent her frown into scowl territory. "The witness says he kicked the animal. Also claims he defended himself with a knife which we found on the scene."

"Look, Deputy, this is all very interesting, but I don't own any kind of animal, so—"

"They tested the blood found on the knife." The deputy gave him a knowing look. "Funny thing, though. The blood on the knife? It's human."

In the face of Griff's silence, she went on. "Doesn't match the victim's blood, or the witness. What blood type are you, Mr. Lancaster?"

Griff debated about answering. But why should he? Anything he gave her would only fuel her suspicions, not allay them. Truth was, like millions of other people, he had the most common blood type of all. But if she wanted that information, she could damn well get a court order to obtain it.

"Deputy, I admire your tenacity, but it seems like you want to accuse me of something although I'm not sure what. However, as I said, it's been a long day."

He turned away from her and strode to the door. "I know it's you," she said to his back. "I may not have all the answers, but I know you have something to do with all these attacks." Griff got inside and leaned against the door, telling his heart to slow the hell down. "I'm going to prove it!" The thick oak muffled her parting shot, but Griff still heard it.

No. You're. Not.

Deputy Gardner would never be able to prove anything. Of course, she wouldn't have to once everything was made public after his death.

He couldn't help but think about how many cold cases going back decades would be solved once the truth was out. In some way, he'd have the last laugh. Or maybe

Deputy Gardner would, since she'd be proved correct in her suspicion of him.

It doesn't matter.

He kept telling himself that. None of it would matter once he was gone. The world would keep spinning. Maybe it would cause a furor at first, but eventually it would become the kind of ancient history no one would remember or care about.

And that, for some reason, was the most depressing thought of all.

Chapter Forty-Two

Bree slogged through her nightly run. She didn't know why she continued to make the effort because she didn't care anymore. She went through the motions of her life, but all the flavor had gone out of her existence. She faked her way through each day. Only Jenna could tell something was wrong, but Bree couldn't bring herself to admit how Griff's rejection and the separation from him had affected her. She didn't understand it herself.

It wasn't like her to build a romance novel fantasy when a guy gave off signs that he wasn't interested. Evidently, she didn't want to see those signs or acknowledge they were even there. Instead, for some reason she didn't understand, she chased after a guy who'd been running away.

And yet, she knew she hadn't imagined those moments when Griff looked at her a certain way. But he hadn't done anything to make her think he wanted her, had he?

He'd been polite at times, kind, and even helpful. Then abrupt and dismissive. Rude, in fact, if she was being honest.

But aside from that confusing encounter when he returned her Christmas cactus, not once had he shown anything more than professional interest. She'd foolishly been pursuing him the whole time, and he'd what? *Tolerated* her behavior?

Perhaps she'd been mistaken during the recognition dinner. She'd been so sure she'd *felt* him watching her, even though she'd avoided direct eye contact with him. Maybe she read so much into his actions that she'd set herself up for crushing disappointment. It all felt wrong to her, like a woman with no self-esteem going after the wrong man because she wanted to be treated like dirt.

And how did he have the same mark on his wrist as her? Had he also been attacked? If so, why wouldn't he tell her? Her thoughts had gone round and round on those questions for weeks. If she couldn't snap out of this funk, whatever was causing it, her only solution would be to seek professional help.

She hated herself for jogging the same route past his house every night. It was a kind of punishment, a comeuppance she obviously deserved. Putting herself in the vicinity of his home was her version of a hair shirt.

Even if something was *drawing* her there, she refused to give it power over her. Why should she change her routine because of him?

She made it to the turnaround and started back. It was easy to go through the physical effort of running right now. She had plenty of self-loathing thoughts to keep her mind occupied. Often they were so loud they crowded out the music from her phone's speaker. Music she used to enjoy.

She jogged on, trying to ignore the headlights she. Her heart started to pound, and not from exercise. It could only be him. Why did she continue to run past his house, knowing the possibility existed that they might cross paths?

She drew nearer to the black mailbox hidden in the foliage. Instead of turning on her flashlight in the gathering dusk, she fantasized for a second about being hit, her body tossed into the air and dropped onto the pavement. Put her into a nice, long coma and when she woke up, she wouldn't remember Griffin Henry Lancaster.

No, with her luck she'd end up maimed and paralyzed for life and still remember everything. If she ever got so low she couldn't go on, she could always throw herself off a cliff or something. That made her picture Jeremy, dropping out of sight, his voice swallowed by the sound of rushing water.

"Don't be an idiot," she muttered. People who fantasized about suicide thought about death in the abstract. Remembering Jeremy's last look of terror before he lost his grip shook her out of that notion.

She used to despise women who believed they couldn't live without a man. Now she sympathized with them. Because now she understood loss. But why did she feel it so sharply for something she'd never even had?

The vehicle slowed and pulled into *his* driveway. Griff got out and closed the door. Getting his mail, she figured. She was far enough away it was possible he hadn't seen her. She slowed to a walk, hoping he'd get his mail, return to his truck, and disappear. But also hoping he wouldn't disappear. Hoping he'd notice her.

Dammit.

She kept walking even though he didn't approach his mailbox. She'd walk on by like the Dionne Warwick song. *Walk on by.* Pretend he wasn't there. Then she'd go home and wish she could cry.

"Bree," he said when she got close.

She stopped. Looked at the shadowy outline of him. The truck's headlights were pointed away, but she could still see him, and he could see her. She couldn't imagine what he could possibly have to say to her. Nothing she'd want to hear.

I don't want you. I'm not interested in you. I'm not attracted to you.

She didn't need to hear those lines from him again. Not when she had the recorded loop constantly playing through her head.

She started to walk again, giving him a wide berth. "Bree," he said again. "I want to talk to you."

Too bad for you. You had your chance. I think you've said enough. And yet it still took all her willpower not to turn back around.

"Bree, I'm sorry."

She stopped. Turned. How was she supposed to respond? Was she supposed to tell him it was okay? Because it wasn't. It would never be. He'd *killed* her. She'd been slowly dying ever since he'd said those words. Every day she'd gone without seeing him, every day she'd gone without hope of being with him. It would never be okay. An apology changed nothing.

She turned away and picked up her pace.

"Bree."

She refused to turn around, even though something inside of her tried to make her.

"Bree. Please."

She heard his footsteps behind her. "Bree, wait." He caught her. His fingers closed around her arm.

She whirled around. "Get your hands *off* me. What is wrong with you? *Why* can't you leave me alone?"

"I want to apologize."

"No, you don't. You're like that animal. All you want to do is hurt me."

He stepped back as if she'd kicked him in the stomach. Even in the dim light, she could see the pain in his eyes. Like that of a wounded beast.

Her wrist itched like mad. She panted in outrage, very much aware of her inner voice telling her to get the hell out of there *now*. While another more stubborn part of her waited for something more from him. An explanation. A declaration of some sort. *Something.*

"You're right. I'm an animal and I can't..." He looked away.

"Can't what?"

"I can't... give you what you want. Be what you want. Isn't your instinct telling you to go? You should listen to it." He made to move back to the truck.

She scratched at her wrist. All her conflicted feelings coalesced into a kind of understanding. A feeling she understood but had done her best to deny, because it made no sense to her. And yet...

"You know I'm in love with you."

He froze. "Don't," he said without turning around.

"Don't what?"

"Just...don't."

"Why do you keep pushing me away?"

He flexed his fists and turned to face her. "Because of who I am. What I am."

Bree took a step closer. "That doesn't make any sense."

"I know."

"Hey! You stopped *me*. Stop with the fucking riddles. You got something you want to say to me then fucking *say it*!"

Bree took another step. Her wrist was on fire. Griff looked desperate. "Bree, don't come any closer."

"Are you afraid of me?"

"I don't want to hurt you." The words sounded strangled.

"Then don't."

"It's—I can't... it's not that simple."

"And we're back to riddles." She pounded the heel of her hand against her forehead. "Why do I keep doing this to myself?" She turned.

"Bree, wait. Please. Let me explain."

She whirled to stare at him. "I've *tried* to let you explain. Repeatedly."

"I know. You have to understand, this is probably the hardest thing I've ever had to do in my life."

He stepped closer and trailed his fingers through the ends of her hair. He almost smiled as he looked into her eyes. "I'm sorry," he said. "I'm so sorry. I shouldn't have said those things. I know they hurt you. I shouldn't have said any of them."

"Because they're not true?"

She wanted him to kiss her. Not gently. Like he'd been starving for her. He'd crush her to him, the way she'd wanted him to, the way she'd dreamt he would. His mouth sealed against hers. His tongue exploring and caressing and demanding. She wished, oh how she wished, he'd never let go of her. Her skin heated. She couldn't breathe.

As if he knew she needed some space, he stepped back. Questions swirled through the haze in her brain. He peered at her intently, brushed his forefinger along the back of her hand.

"Come in and let me explain. You deserve that much."

She drew a shaky breath and created more space between them. "If I come with you now, even if I don't like the explanation, I might never leave."

"Trust me. After you hear what I have to say, you won't want to stay."

A chill ran through her, and yet she felt more alive in the last five minutes than she had in the weeks since she'd seen him last.

She took his hand, noticing again how her wrist burned and throbbed. "Let's go."

Chapter Forty-Three

The moment the door closed behind them she kissed him. Everything she'd saved up since that first night, every thought, every fantasy poured itself into her kiss and transferred to him. And he responded to her.

Not attracted, my ass.

Just as she'd fantasized minutes ago, the kiss went on forever. Bree was caught up in the wonder of it. She was right where she wanted to be. Right where she was *supposed* to be. In his house. In his arms. He picked her up off her feet. Her arms twined around his neck. He held her easily and carried her through the dark living room.

Their presence tripped the motion detectors in the hall and Bree could tell even though her eyes were closed that the lights came on. But the lights went out as soon as they stepped into his bedroom, where it was beyond dark.

She opened her eyes to the weird sensation of not being able to see anything at all. But she didn't need to. She let her other senses take over, feeling everything. The soft bedspread against the backs of her legs. The rough denim of Griff's jeans against her. The solid form of him under his tee shirt and the arousal beneath the denim.

She heard every breath they took, felt their heartbeats, her pulse rushing in her ears. Griff's work-rough hand went beneath her tank top, and his calloused fingers caressed her, his thumbs brushing against her nipples through her sports bra. She moaned with pleasure at his touch.

He pulled at the top, and she briefly broke the kiss, lifting her arms so he could take it off. She slid her hands underneath his shirt, and he sucked in a breath. His skin was hot, and the hair on his chest silky soft.

"Take this off," she whispered, tugging at the hem of his shirt until he complied.

She buried her face against him, drinking in the scent and feel of his skin. She traced a path of kisses along his throat, his jaw, his ear, before finding his mouth once again.

He cupped her bottom as his fingers inched inside the leg of her shorts. Inside her panties. Her breath caught at his touch on her bare skin.

It wasn't enough for him either. He tugged at her shorts, pulling the elastic band down until they dropped to her ankles. Then his hands went back to what they'd been doing before.

She found his belt buckle. Nothing tricky there. She undid it and the snap of his jeans. Lowered the zipper. Panting in excitement, she pushed the jeans down. Boxers or briefs? She explored his backside first. Soft. Cotton. Snug and tight, extending down his thigh a little. Boxer briefs.

His erection pressed against her, hot and hard. His fingers slid against the crotch of her damp panties, and she forgot to breathe. She gasped. Again. And again. She could feel herself melt against his touch. Hotter and wetter than she'd ever been. He knew how to touch her, and where. The right pace. The perfect amount of pressure. Again. Once more. She went up and over the edge. Lost. Mindless.

He stilled, letting her have the moment while she clung to him. A sheen of perspiration covered them both. She caught his scent, the one that made her think of freshly mowed grass. She tasted the saltiness of his skin and sensed the desire burning beneath.

She worked his briefs down until his erection sprang free. She held it tight, letting her palm glide against him while she caressed the tip of his shaft with her thumb. He bent her back, his mouth at her throat before he pushed her onto the bed and eased away from her.

He untied her shoes and took them off. Then her socks. The other movements she heard were him removing his boots, socks, and finally his jeans and briefs. While he tugged her panties off, she pulled her bra over her head, snagging the phone with its wristband along with it. She wasn't sure what had happened to her flashlight.

He settled himself against her, that huge, hot part of him pressing between her thighs. He played with the ends of her hair. She could feel his breath above her.

"Are you sure you want to do this?"

"Don't you?" If he said no, she'd have no choice. She'd have to kill him.

"You know the answer." He kissed her again, his lips trailing along her throat to her shoulder. His hands covered her breasts. Caressing. Kneading.

"Then why are you asking?" She was nearly breathless. Coherent thought became a challenge.

"Because you didn't let me explain. And if we do this, there's no going back."

"I don't want to go back. I *can't* go back. I was dying without you. I don't know why, but I was."

"You'll die being with me, too."

"Please don't send me away." Bree didn't care how pathetic she sounded. How needy. She had to make him understand even if *she* didn't understand.

She must have succeeded because he came alive and consumed her. Touched her everywhere with his lips and his hands. Oh, those clever, clever hands. That devious tongue. Brought her to that peak again and filled her as tumbled over it.

She cried out into the darkness, and he swallowed her scream, took it inside himself, just as he came inside her. She was falling, tumbling, head over heels, into the darkness. And only he could save her.

Chapter Forty-Four

Bree's mind floated somewhere in the dark. Griff lay where he'd collapsed, partly on top of her, his face in the crook of her neck. She loved his breath against her skin, his bigger body covering bits of hers. She had no idea how they'd got beneath the covers, but it was like being in a cocoon together. Her last thought before she fell asleep was that she never wanted to be anywhere else.

When she woke the all-encompassing darkness surrounded her. She had no sense of time. Had she slept for minutes or hours? She shifted experimentally. Griff occupied his own space next to her. Still, his body radiated heat in her direction. She wondered if she could find her way out of this room without disturbing him.

She made it to the edge of the bed before he spoke. "Where are you going?"

"Bathroom. If I can find my way there."

He shifted and seconds later soft recessed lighting chased many of the shadows from the room. She looked over her shoulder. "Thanks."

The otherwise tidy space was now littered with their discarded clothes and shoes. She picked her way carefully to the door.

In the bathroom, her reflection looked much different than the first time she'd visited. She looked thinner, for one thing. She hadn't been eating much these last few weeks. Food had lost its taste. Jenna noticed her weight loss, but Bree had brushed her concern aside. She thought she hadn't lost *that* much weight, but apparently, she had lost more than she'd realized. Was there something about this mirror, she wondered? Some magical power that forced her to confront the reality of what was right in front of her?

She stared at herself. What else might the mirror reveal? Things she already knew. Griff also had some sort of dark magical power that drew her to him. From the first time they met she hadn't wanted to leave. She'd never stopped thinking about him, never stopped hoping for the possibility of them together, even when he'd crushed every bit of that hope and she thought she'd die still wanting something she'd never have.

But they were together now. She'd already told him she wouldn't leave. She could only hope he didn't want her to.

When she got back in bed, he was on his side, facing her. He'd tracked her from the door. She adjusted her pillow so she could be close to him and look into his eyes. Gently, she rubbed the slight furrow between his brows. "What's this frown for?"

He captured her hand and pressed his lips to her palm. "I hurt you. I'm sorry. But I'm only going to hurt you more."

"Please don't make me leave. I'll die without you."

"Don't say that."

"I know it must sound crazy, but it's true."

"It's not crazy. That's the whole problem." He searched her face, and she didn't flinch. She'd never been more certain of anything. He must have understood her conviction. But she could see it made him sad. He rolled away from her to the edge of the bed and sat up, dropping his head into his hands. "Oh, God. What have I done?"

His anguish was so real, it pierced Bree's heart as if she could feel everything he felt. She pressed up behind him and slid her arms around his waist. "You haven't done anything. Except love me."

"I shouldn't have. I tried not to."

"Why?"

He turned so he could see her. "Because I'm dying."

She heard him, but she didn't want to believe it. A chill ran through her while her mind refused to accept the possibility.

Yet, in a way, it explained everything that hadn't made sense about his behavior. Why he constantly pushed her away, even when he didn't want to. But Griff didn't look sick. He didn't act sick. "Is it a brain tumor?" she whispered. That might explain his contradictory behavior. Why he didn't appear to be ill yet.

Something about her question amused him, but he didn't smile. "No."

"What then?"

He searched her face while something warred inside him until he came to a decision. "I'm...cursed."

Now it was her turn to frown. "What do you mean?"

"It means I've only got a couple of months left."

"You're truly dying? Why aren't you sick?" When he didn't answer, she squeezed his shoulder. "Griff, tell me."

He stood. "We should get dressed."

Bree's mouth went dry, and her mind went blank. She hadn't seen him naked. She'd touched and sensed and imagined, but it hadn't prepared her for the impact of seeing his sculpted body. Again, came the image of a romance cover novel. The shoulders, the chest, the abs. Bree thought he was just about perfect. Except for trying to push her away.

"You're staring." A corner of his mouth quirked up.

She brought her gaze to his face in time to see it. "I can't help it. I keep thinking we're in a romance novel."

"More like a tragic love story. If you're looking for a happy ending, you've got the wrong guy."

"Come back to bed."

"Bree, we need to talk."

"We can talk in bed." On her knees, she walked to the edge of the bed in order to reach him. She put her hand flat on his chest, enjoying the tickle of hair against her palm, noting the solid wall of muscle beneath his skin.

He grew aroused, with just that touch. Or maybe seeing her naked begging him to return to the bed did it.

She trailed her hand down to his cock and circled her palm around its swollen length. "Please?" she said, looking up at him from beneath her lashes.

He gave what sounded like a growl before he surrendered. This time around things were wild and crazy between them. Bree couldn't process everything at once.

The physical, emotional, and psychological impacts occurred simultaneously. She needed lots of time to savor
every second of being with Griff. Every touch, every kiss,
every nuance of their lovemaking. But so anxious were
they to be joined again, minutes later they were both
panting from satisfaction.

Chapter Forty-Five

After lying together a while longer, Griff said, "Do I get to talk now?"

"If you must." She pressed her lips to his throat.

"Stop doing that. It's distracting. I mean it." He held her close, her head below his jaw. His lips grazed her hair.

"All right. I'll behave. Talk."

"I'm cursed," he began.

"I wish you'd stop saying that."

"Please let me explain. This is hard enough as it is. There will be a Q & A afterward."

"Okay." she said, knowing she'd do just about anything he asked of her.

"Five generations ago, my great-great-grandfather became involved with a woman. I wouldn't be surprised if there was more than one.

"Colin Lancaster was a charmer, but he was despicable when it came to women. He used them and literally abused them.

"But there was one woman he maintained a liaison with for years. Emerald MacCallam. She spent those years learning witchcraft trying to come up with a potion or cast a spell to make him hers alone. But none of the potions or spells worked. She wasted her life pining after him. No other man would have her because their ongoing relationship was well known.

"When his wife died, she thought he'd finally come to her, make an honorable woman of her. But he didn't. Instead, he found some rich young thing and married her. When Emerald found out what he'd done, she cursed him. She'd lost her chance at a life with a husband and children because of him. She poured all her sadness and hate into the curse, and she had plenty of it after twenty years of his treatment.

"It took me a long time to put all the pieces together and there are things I only learned recently. But I know for a fact my great-grandfather was the first to be affected. And every male in the line since. It's going to stop with me."

Bree had been lulled by the sound of Griff's voice as he stroked her hair, his heart beating beneath her ear.

"But what's the curse?" she asked.

Griff sighed. "Every third new moon, the curse turns Lancaster men into animals."

Bree propped herself on an elbow so she could see Griff's face. "Animals?"

"The closest thing I can compare it to is a werewolf, but it's not that."

Bree sucked in a breath, her gaze locked with his. She remembered the attack. The night they met. The strange behavior of the animal she couldn't quite see or describe. "That—that was you."

He nodded. "We're compelled to hunt for a female. To attack. Inflict pain. We must draw blood before we can change back."

"But—but you brought me back here. You *rescued* me." She sat up, pulling the sheet over her chest.

"I normally don't attack near my own home. I usually plan things out better."

"You *plan*? Who to attack?"

"Not necessarily who. More where and when. To reduce the risk of getting caught."

"But you don't—you don't..."

Griff lifted an eyebrow. "Mate with them?"

"Yes."

"I'm an animal, not a rapist." He kept a straight face, but there was an underlying tone of humor in his voice.

"Are you trying to be funny? Because this isn't funny."

He reached out and stroked her hair again. "I know it's not. But I swear it's the truth."

"So, you don't... sleep with the women you attack."

"Except for you."

"Why me?"

"Do you remember the song that was playing when I knocked you down?"

Bree's brow furrowed. She shook her head.

"There was a line in it about walking on the dark side of the moon."

"*Kryptonite*, by 3DoorsDown."

"I was unnaturally drawn to you when I first saw you at Sanctuary, but I froze when I heard those lines."

"You were unnaturally drawn to me while I was trying to figure out why I was so obsessed with you."

"What are the chances, do you think, that you were listening to that song while I was walking on the dark side of the moon."

"I don't know. How often do you...?" She paused and, unable to say the words, made her hands look like claws.

"Depends. Three or four times a year. How often do you run by my house?"

"Almost every night for two years. It's my favorite route because it's almost exactly four miles round trip. The road dead-ends and there's hardly any traffic."

"Funny thing is, I'd never seen you running before. We've lived two miles apart for all this time."

"Do you think there's a connection? That this was meant to be?"

"What do you think?"

"I think from the moment I ended up in your house I didn't want to be anywhere else. I still don't."

"And I don't want you to be."

"You left your mark on me," Bree said in wonder. She pressed her wrist to his but felt nothing but the warmth of his skin. No inflammation or burning or itch. She examined both wrists, running her thumb across the pink outlines of the razed patches.

"Why did you say those terrible things to me?" Bree couldn't keep the anguish out of her tone. Even knowing it wasn't true, it still hurt.

"Because you're my Kryptonite," Griff said.

"I make you weak?"

"Where my resolve is concerned, yeah. I had to be cruel, so you'd stay away from me. But every day since I wanted to die. The look on your face that night haunted me."

"I wanted to die too."

Griff ran his fingers across her ribs. "By starving your-self?"

"Subconsciously, maybe. You sent me away because of this stupid curse. Because you didn't think you could tell me. But now I know. I'm not crazy about it, but I can live with it."

"That's just it, Bree. You won't have to."

"Why? There's a way to break the curse?"

He hesitated. "No. There isn't. I'll die on my thir-ty-third birthday. It's part of the curse."

Bree's eyes widened. "When's that?"

"The end of November."

"No." Bree barely breathed the word. She stared into his eyes, willing him to take it back. Under any oth-er circumstances, she'd have doubted his story. Who wouldn't? Part of her wanted to hit rewind, go back and make it so none of it was true. How clever would he have to be to make it all up and how gullible would she have to be to believe every word?

But she did believe. She could see the truth and the sadness in his eyes.

"There must be a way out of this. We could research it. There must be experts—"

"Don't you think I've tried?" Griff shouted. His outburst startled her, and she drew back. He threw the covers off and got out of bed. He yanked open drawers and rifled through his closet. She didn't know how he could find what he was looking for. Everything in it was black.

He donned underwear, a shirt, pants. His voice settled to a calmer, matter-of-fact tone. "My father left me every bit of research he had and let me tell you, it was exhaustive. I was ten when he died. He'd been consumed by the need to find a way to break the curse. Since then, I've consulted genealogists. Anthropologists. Historians. Witches. Warlocks. Mystics. You name it. I've looked for a way out."

"I'm sorry about your father."

"His death certificate lists cause of death as cardiac arrest. He was thirty-three when he died. So was his father. And his father before him. My brother knew what was coming and didn't wait for the end. He killed himself when he was nineteen. Don't think I haven't considered it."

Bree stared at him. She hadn't imagined the dark cloud above his head. Shadows enveloped him, and they had nothing to do with the room's lighting.

He locked eyes with hers. "Dead man walking. That's me."

He stormed out of the room. Bree sat frozen in the middle of the bed. She finally had everything she wanted. And it was running through her fingers like grains of sand.

Chapter Forty-Six

After Bree gathered her scattered clothes and put them on, she found Griff in the kitchen. He was using a spatula to prod at some kind of egg concoction cooking in a skillet. A mug of coffee sat on the counter next to the stove.

"You need to eat," he informed her.

"I'm not hungry."

He squinted at her. "Don't kill yourself over me. I'm not worth it."

She slid her arms around him and pressed her cheek against his arm. "Why are you being like this?"

He dropped the spatula and held her. "I *want* to spend a lifetime with you and it's killing me, knowing I won't get that chance." He looked into her eyes. "Plus, I was incredibly stupid last night. And this morning. Not using protection. You need to take the morning-after pill.

"It's okay. I'm on birth control."

"I can't take a chance. I know it's my fault and I hate like hell that I'm asking, but please do this. Trust me, you do not want a child of yours to go through what I've been through. This curse ends with me. It has to."

More sadness washed over Bree. That romance novel future she'd envisioned for them had crashed and burned with this morning's revelations. She didn't have it in her to tell him no. "All right," she said.

They held each other for a long time. Bree sniffed. "I think breakfast is burning."

"Dammit!" Griff yanked the skillet away from the flame. He lifted the edge of the contents with the spatula. "It's extra brown, but I think it's still edible."

Bree grinned at him. "Great. Because I'm starving."

"That wasn't funny." He smiled.

"Yes, it was." She poured herself coffee.

He smacked her bottom. "Behave or I'll send you home."

She leaned against the counter and sipped. "You can try."

Griff dropped bread into the toaster and picked up his mug. "What do you have planned for the day?"

"After a trip to the drugstore, you mean?" With her mug she gestured at their surroundings. "This."

"And by 'this' you mean?"

"I told you if you let me in, I wouldn't leave."

"I did let you in, didn't I? I shouldn't have, but..."

"You couldn't resist me any longer." She grinned.

"True." He wanted to smile back at her, but how could he explain his own selfishness? Could she understand that he wanted to be happy, even for a little while, before something he had no say in destroyed him? He wasn't even sure she would see how unfair it was to her. All he knew was how horribly guilty he felt.

Over breakfast Bree said, "This whole curse thing..." She pointed her fork in his direction. "It's for real right? It isn't just some twisted plot to get me into bed, is it?"

She wanted to lighten the mood, but she knew what he'd told her was no joke even if it all sounded too far-fetched to be believed. Somehow, she knew, deep in her bones, it was all true. It explained her obsession with him, the matching marks on their wrists, the sense that she'd die without him.

Griff scraped his hands over his face and then back through his hair. "I wish I was that clever and inventive."

"You didn't need to be." She fixed him with a look. "After I landed on your couch that first night? I didn't want to leave."

He looked grim. "I told myself I was strong enough to keep you out of this. You're part of it now because I couldn't walk away last night."

"I wouldn't let you." She pushed back her chair and went to him. "Look, I won't claim to completely understand but I *want* to be part of it. I don't want to be anywhere else but here."

"I wasn't going to tell you about the curse." He wrapped a strand of her hair around his finger. "After I apologized, I was going to tell you I was dying and wanted to spend my last few months in peace and leave it at that." He let the strand of hair slide away.

"But I didn't give you a chance."

"Once you kissed me, I couldn't think about anything except how much I wanted you."

"You still could have lied to me. You didn't have to tell me about the curse."

"You deserved the truth. To deceive you..." His gaze shifted to the strand of her hair he had wrapped in his finger before coming back to her. "Would be to dishonor what we have."

Bree took his hand in hers. "More than anything, I want you to be happy. What do you want?"

"I want you."

After their trip to the pharmacy, they enjoyed a long, slow lazy day of talking, sharing, and lovemaking. An interesting joint shower. Scrounging in Griff's kitchen for food. The two of them savoring every minute they had together.

"I want to see your research," Bree said after they'd scraped the last remnants of chocolate chip ice cream from the bottom of the carton.

"It won't change anything."

"I know, but I want to understand all this. Besides, I'll be seeing it with a fresh set of eyes. Maybe there's something you missed—"

"There isn't."

He dropped the ice cream carton in the trash and tossed the spoons in the sink.

Bree watched him warily. "I'd still like to see it."

"Fine." He stalked away down the hall. She thought better of following him. A little while later, he returned and sat a fat binder and an accordion file folder next to her. A big rubber band was wrapped around their combined three-inch girth. "Read it and weep," he said.

"Not the best choice of words."

She saw the corner of his mouth quirk up. "Pun intended. Sorry."

"Is this what the rest of my life will be like? You and your bad jokes?"

"I don't know. But it's what the rest of mine will be like."

"Griff, dammit!" She slammed her hand down on top of the file. "This is your life we're talking about. There has to be a way out of this."

"There isn't. Even if there was, I can guarantee you it wouldn't be something either of us wants."

Bree felt a prickle. He knew something. But he wasn't going to tell her. And she wasn't going to push him. He'd been through enough today. He'd opened up more than he probably ever had with anyone. He should be allowed to be happy and not constantly worry about something he saw as inevitable.

She went to him and slid her arms around his waist. "I can think of something pleasant for right now, though. Something we *both* want." She smiled up at him.

Chapter Forty-Seven

"You're *moving in* with him?" Jenna exploded. "As of Friday, you weren't even speaking to him."

"Things changed," Bree said.

There was no way to explain her relationship with Griff. She couldn't tell Jenna about the curse. Jenna couldn't understand how she'd fallen for him so hard and so fast to begin with. She'd been suspicious of Griff all along, and this sudden change in their relationship would only add to her distrust of him.

"You told me what an ass he was. There must have been more to it that you didn't tell me."

"And I'm not going to tell you now," Bree said sweetly.

"You were moping around here for weeks. You weren't eating, you were barely sleeping. I was seriously worried about you."

"I know. I appreciate your concern."

"Maybree Anna Mason. Have you forgotten that I'm your best friend?"

"Of course not."

"We have an agreement. We listen to each other. We don't judge. We don't give unasked for advice."

"We also don't lecture," Bree inserted.

"I don't trust this guy."

"So you've said."

"He hurt you," Jenna reminded her.

"Yes. He did."

"Badly."

Bree was losing patience. "Is there a point to this?"

"I don't want to see you get hurt again. Frankly, based on the past couple of weeks, I'm not sure you'd survive."

"It's going to be fine," Bree said. "Stop worrying about me."

"I can't. With you, it comes with the territory."

After work, Bree went home and packed a suitcase. When she arrived at Griff's he was already there. He opened the door and she fell into his arms. They kissed hungrily and stripped their way to the bedroom.

Once there, Bree gasped. Griff had lit candles and placed them all around the room. "I want to see you," he said.

"You have lights, you know."

"Not as romantic," said Griff, giving her a rare smile. "I'm tired of holding back. I want to make every moment with you special."

"Me too. I want every bit of you I can get so I can remember."

The candlelight burnished his skin to gold. She used all her senses to absorb the taste and feel and sight and sound of him making love to her.

She lay in his arms afterward, stroking the hair of his chest. "Tell me the rest of it."

"The rest of what?"

"The curse. There's more, isn't there?"

He was quiet for such a long time she thought he wasn't going to answer. His fingertips brushed lightly up and down her arm. "I don't think it's an intended part of the curse, not exactly. It's more of a side effect."

She propped her chin on his chest and he reached out and wound a strand of her hair around his finger. "We cursed Lancaster men, once we find the woman of our dreams—"

"The dream doesn't last."

"It'd be better if we didn't find them. If we didn't get involved—"

"You wouldn't be here."

Griff smiled sadly. "That's kind of the point. It's like the curse's way of keeping itself going. I thought I'd make it all the way to thirty-three without ever finding someone, and then..." He didn't finish.

"I'll take whatever time I can get with you. I won't regret a second of it. I promise."

He brought her in for another kiss. "Me neither."

Later, after a meal they'd prepared together, they lay on the sofa while the fire burned down to embers.

"I know guys hate it when women ask them this, but what are you thinking?"

Griff was playing with her hair again. "About what you said earlier."

"Which part?"

"About being with each other as much as we can and not regretting it."

"I meant it."

"I know." After a minute, he said, "We should write a bucket list."

"No. I don't want to think about you dying."

Griff adjusted his position so he could look into her eyes. " But it wouldn't be about dying. It would be about living. We can list all the things we'd like to do and do as many as we can together."

"Squeeze a whole lifetime into a couple of months?" She feathered her fingers through his hair and smiled. "Sex. That's number one on my list."

He chuckled. "What else?"

Bree thought for a moment. "Maybe we could go somewhere nice for dinner one night."

"Sure. How about hiking? You like that, right?"

"Yes. I want a ride on your Harley, too."

"You got it. Bear's almost done with the repairs. We'll take the bike, pack a picnic, and go for a hike."

She traced her index finger across his bottom lip. "Let's find a remote trail where no one else goes. After lunch, we can make love."

Griff made a sound of agreement and kissed the tip of her finger. "I like the way you think."

She grinned. "We could also see a movie."

"No chick flicks or rom-coms."

"Fine, then no sci-fi or shoot em ups or gritty war dramas."

"Straight up comedy, okay?"

"I wouldn't mind a few laughs. And some popcorn. A big bag with lots of fake butter. And soda with lots of ice. And gummy worms."

"At theater prices? Sounds like you're an expensive date."

"I'm worth it."

They laughed. After a few minutes, he sat up. "Stay here."

"Where are you going?"

"Just. Stay. Here. I'll be right back."

Bree was about to get up by the time he returned. He knelt in front of her and took her hands in his.

"What are you doing?" she asked.

"I didn't plan this, so don't laugh, okay?"

"Okay."

He cleared his throat, his heart in his eyes. "I always wanted to say this to the woman of my dreams, but I didn't think I'd ever have the chance. Bree, I want to spend the rest of my life with you. Even though it's going to be a short one." He held up a ring. "Will you marry me?"

Her breath caught in her throat. "Seriously?"

"As a heart attack."

"Don't make jokes."

"Sorry."

"You're not that funny."

"I know."

"And your timing's horrible."

"Got it. Now about that 'marry me' question?"

"Of course. Yes."

"Your hand, please?"

He slid the ring onto her finger. It almost fit. White gold twined in a circle to create the band and a ruby set in the middle of flower petals.

"It's so pretty. So delicate. Where did you get it? And when?"

"It was my mother's."

"Oh, Griff."

"She was crazy about my dad. He had the ring made special for her because she loved growing things, especially roses. It just about killed her when he died, and later when we lost my brother. She held out until I finished college. I think she wanted to make sure I could fend for myself so she could be at peace."

"Oh, Griff." She hugged him.

"We don't have to get married," Bree told him later when they were in bed. "It's enough for me that you asked."

"I want to, though." He turned on his side so he could look at her. He sifted her hair through his fingers. "But there might be a reason why you wouldn't want to marry me."

"Trying to back out already?"

"You started it."

"Point taken."

"I thought the only legacy I could leave would be the botanical garden. I'm not going to be here when it's finished, but all the pieces are in place for its completion. There won't be any children to carry on the Lancaster name."

"We could have a girl."

He ran his hands through her hair. "I'd love a daughter. But it's too risky." He thought for a moment before he said, "There's no record of any daughters born into Colin's line in all these years. For all I know, that might be part of the curse as well. Females might be affected too, just not in the same way." His gaze faltered. "But here's the thing. Once I'm gone, the legacy of the curse might become public knowledge. I won't be here to prevent it. And you might not want your last name to be tied to mine."

"I can always keep my name," Bree pointed out. "I'm not saying I would, but if that's what's bothering you..."

"I just thought if I was married." He lifted a hand and let it drop as if he wanted to drop the subject altogether.

"If you're married...?" Bree prompted.

He looked into her eyes. "I've thought a lot about my legacy. About leaving something behind so my family won't be forgotten. That's why the botanical garden is so important to me. But marrying you? It's proof that I meant something. That somebody loved me."

"Somebody does."

His eyes softened. "Plus, as my wife, you would automatically inherit my estate."

"You have an estate?"

"It's not huge, but I haven't been unsuccessful. I have some cash in reserve, some investments. This place. I like the idea of you being here if you want it."

"Alone."

"You wouldn't have to be."

For some reason, Madeline Stark flitted across Bree's mind. Her family had died. She'd never remarried. Never had more children. Was that because her heart was completely, irrevocably broken?

For Griff's sake, though, she summoned a smile. "You're right. I wouldn't have to be."

Chapter Forty-Eight

When Jenna heard the news, she exploded. "I can't believe you're marrying him!"

Bree calmly continued to pack for her honeymoon. "I know you can't."

"You only just moved in with him!"

"I know."

"Does *none* of this raise any red flags with you?"

Jenna had been beside herself ever since she'd barged into the townhouse five minutes ago. She'd ignored every rule that had kept them best friends since their teens. Normally, Bree would have resented Jenna voicing her disapproval. But this time, she understood it. In her place, Bree would have behaved the same way.

"Jen, please calm down. Do you want a glass of wine?"

"No, I damn well do not want a glass of wine. What I *want* is a believable explanation as to why my best friend, my normally level-headed best friend, I might add, is taking off and marrying a man she hardly knows on a—a whim!"

Bree turned to look at Jenna. "It's not a whim."

"Then what is it?"

"Would you believe me if I said fate?"

"No."

"It's what I want."

"But it's so sudden!"

"That doesn't make it wrong."

"Is he in a cult? Is this a cult thing? Blink twice if it's not safe to talk here."

"Jenna..."

Jenna chewed her lip arms akimbo as she watched Bree fold clothes and set them in her suitcase. "Oh my God, *fine.* I'm sure in a few months we'll be talking about what a mistake this all was."

Bree flinched. That stung harder than she'd thought. How was she going to explain this... after? She shook herself and continued to pack.

"So, where are you going?" Jenna pestered.

"I'm not sure. An island in the Caribbean. St. Bart's? St. John? Griff made the arrangements."

"I'll bet he did," Jenna said darkly. "A compound with lots of his friends and a creepy ass reverend. Whatever you do, don't drink the Kool-Aid, Bree."

Bree stopped packing and stepped in front of Jenna. She hugged her. "Please stop worrying. Trust me. You have nothing to worry about."

"This isn't like you," Jenna mumbled against her shoulder. Bree let her go. "You haven't been yourself since you were attacked. Ever since you met this guy."

Bree stepped into the bathroom. Jenna was right, but Bree didn't want to give her any more ammunition. As it was, Bree was finding it difficult not to explain everything to her best friend. But she knew Jenna. Jenna wouldn't believe it. She'd want proof. She'd want to do her own research. She'd never stop warning Bree away from Griff and Bree simply didn't have the time to waste trying to make Jenna understand. Instinctively she knew no one would understand. What was between her and Griff was theirs alone.

"I wish you'd bring me one of Griff's hairs so I can compare it to the ones from your flashlight."

Bree paused in the act of gathering a few toiletries. "I'm not going to do that," she said.

"Because you think he's the one who attacked you and then rescued you?" Jenna put air quotes around 'rescued.'"

"Because I was in his house. Because he picked up the flashlight and *it* was in his house. We've been over this. One of his hairs could have easily transferred to it."

"Uh huh."

Bree knew she hadn't convinced Jenna, but she didn't care. "Are you done yet? Are you going to stand up for me, or not?"

"If I have a DNA sample, he'll be easier to track down when you disappear," Jenna mused. "Like that girl who went to Aruba and—"

"God, Jenna! I'm not going to disappear! Nothing bad is going to happen to me!" Bree cried in exasperation.

Except very soon I'll be a widow. And when that happens, I'll want to die.

Jenna froze at Bree's outburst, her eyes wide. Jenna's questions had rubbed Bree's emotions raw. She thought she had them under control. She was going to marry Griff with her eyes wide open now. He'd told her everything, and it hadn't changed how she felt. She wanted, as he said, to live life to the fullest in the days they had left together. But knowing she was going to soon lose him haunted her.

She stared at Jenna, knowing her best friend deserved some kind of explanation. "He's dying, Jen." The moment the words left her tongue, her eyes filled with tears.

"Dying?"

"That's why." She gestured to the open suitcase on the bed. "All of this. Why he pushed me away for so long. Why I'm marrying him now. Why it's all so sudden."

"Maybe I will have a glass of wine after all."

Bree nodded numbly. Jenna handed her tissues from the box on the nightstand and led her to the kitchen. Once they were seated with glasses of pinot grigio, Bree said, "He doesn't want anyone to know, Jenna. You have to swear you won't say anything. Not even to Tyler."

"But why?"

Bree stared at the ceiling, willing back her tears. "Because there's nothing to be done. He doesn't want pity. He doesn't want to explain or talk about it." She brought her gaze back to Jenna's. "I'm telling you, and only you, because—because I had to."

"So that explains the dark cloud over his head 24/7. He's always looked pretty healthy to me. What's he dying of?"

"The details aren't important. What's important is that we spend whatever time we have left together."

"Still, maybe something can be done. Maybe there's new research out there for whatever he has—"

"There isn't. Trust me. I've seen the reports. I've seen the expert opinions. This is real, Jenna."

"That's why he pushed you away! That's why he acted like he wasn't interested! Ding! Ding! Ding!" Jenna swirled her finger in the air above her head and Bree smiled.

"Yes. But he was as miserable as I was and when he apologized and explained, none of what happened before mattered. I want to be with him for as long as I can no matter what. He knows how hard it's going to be, how hard it already is. But we're going to cram as much living as we can into the time we have left."

"A wedding. A honeymoon. A lifetime in... How long does he have?"

"Not long. A matter of months."

Jenna leaned forward. "Oh, Bree, I'm so sorry. I've been such an ass to him this whole time."

"You didn't know."

"I should have trusted your judgment."

"You had your reasons not to."

"Still want me to stand up for you?"

"More than anything."

"I'll be there," Jenna said. "But I swear to God, if he does *anything*, if he hurts you again—"

"He won't, Jenna."

"He better not."

Three days later in the hotel room bed in St. Bart's Griff nuzzled against Bree's ear. His breath tickled her, and she wiggled back against him.

"What do you want to do today?"

"This," she said. "Just this."

Six hours after the wedding at the courthouse under Jenna's overprotective gaze, Bree and Griff had arrived at the island resort. The first two days were filled with sun, surf, and sex. Griff had been determined to pack as many experiences into their short honeymoon as possible. They'd taken a charter fishing boat out. The restaurant chef cooked the fish they'd caught and served it to them for dinner. They'd snorkeled. Walked hand in hand along the beach. Taken a historic tour of the island.

Poked through the merchandise in the exclusive boutiques. And made love. Bree was exhausted.

Griff chuckled and buried his face in her hair. "You want to stay in bed all day?"

"Why not?"

"We could order room service," he said. "Champagne. Chocolate-covered strawberries. Belgian waffles. Whipped cream."

"Eggs Benedict. We need protein."

He kissed her neck. "My practical girl." He picked up the phone.

Bree set her plate on the room service cart and snuggled back under the covers. "I'm stuffed."

"You're not going back to sleep, are you?" Griff pushed the cart outside and hung the Do Not Disturb sign on the door. "You can sleep when I'm dead."

Bree groaned. This seemed to be the only way Griff could face the inevitable. "More gallows humor. What am I going to do with you?"

"That depends. Are you going back to bed?"

"I don't know. I might not sleep. But I'm not going to get up, either."

Griff paced toward the bed like a big cat and leaned over, a glint in his eyes. "I have an idea."

"Uh oh."

"I think you'll like it."

"Probably."

"Get naked, lay on your stomach, and close your eyes."

"Um." Was this a test of how much she trusted him? She complied with his request.

"Stay there."

Chapter Forty-Nine

She heard him pad away into the bathroom. When he returned, he tugged the sheet to her waist and straddled her, the hair on his legs prickling against her hips. Bree's mind began to conjure up all sorts of possibilities. He moved her hair to one side. Nothing happened for a moment except she could sense movement above her.

His hands landed on her back. He slid them up to her shoulders and down to her waist. She picked up notes of sandalwood and jasmine. Scented oil. His fingers dug into her shoulders, and she groaned as her muscles loosened under his touch.

He kneaded her neck, her delts, her arms. All along her spine and down her back. Heat built wherever he touched until Bree felt like she was melting. He reached her tailbone and tugged the sheet lower and paused as he added more oil.

He caressed her waist and slid his hands down over her buttocks, his thumbs gliding along the crevice between.

She turned to liquid inside as everything tensed and loosened at the same time. His knuckles dug into her glutes before he slid his palms flat along the backs of her thighs.

A sound between a sigh and moan escaped her as he massaged his way along, taking his time, his thumbs gliding between her thighs without any apparent sexual intent, which only turned her on more. She wanted him to touch her *there.* But he didn't.

He kept going, down to the backs of her knees, along her calves to her heels. He added more oil as he massaged her feet in turn, without tickling her, until even her little toes had been administered to.

"Want me to do the front?"

Bree wanted to shout *Yes!* but wouldn't it be more fun to drag this out? Didn't Griff deserve the same treatment he'd just given her?

"Bree?"

"I'm thinking."

He trailed a finger up between her legs, all the way to her neck, where he kissed her.

"How about if I give you a massage?" she asked.

"I can't lie on my stomach."

"Why not?"

"You get one guess."

She felt the press of him against her backside. "We can work around that." She sat up and crawled over him. "Lay on your side then. I'll do the best I can."

"You could work on my front."

"We'll get to that."

She dribbled oil into her hands and rubbed them together and started with his shoulders. God, she loved touching him. Loved looking at him. Loved his body and his mind and his heart and his soul. Loved knowing he was hers.

She loved all the rock-hard muscle beneath his skin. Her massage was more sensual than therapeutic.

She kneaded his shoulders and arm and back until she reached his waist before she drove her knuckles into his buttocks. She let her thumbs glide along the crevice. Then back up, her nails scraping his skin ever so slightly. He twitched and groaned. "Naughty girl."

She laughed in delight. "You started this."

"I know," he said.

She ran her hands along the backs of his thighs, pressing her thumbs against his hamstrings. "What's the matter? Am I driving you crazy?"

"Yes."

"Are you turned on?" She peeked over him to get a glimpse of his massive hard-on. She progressed to the backs of his knees. She'd read somewhere they were an erogenous zone.

"I was turned on before we ordered breakfast."

Bree giggled as she caressed his calves. She took her time with his ankles before pouring a couple more drops of oil and beginning on his feet. She explored his calluses before moving on to his toes, sliding her fingers in between each one.

He turned onto his back and looked down at her. "Are you done yet?"

Her gaze shifted from his eyes back to his swollen cock. She licked her lips. "I might be."

"Bree... whatcha doin'?"

She crawled toward him, then stopped halfway and took him in her mouth. He gasped and his fingers tangled in her hair. She wanted to please him, but after a minute, as if he sensed what she was thinking, he said, "Come here."

She moved up to straddle him and lowered herself onto his cock. She was slick and wet against him. How could she not be? He half sat up, holding her close, deeply inside her. They were locked together with their eyes wide open. Bree could see everything in his eyes. Their past, their future, and this present moment. He buried his hands in her hair and kissed her.

Their tongues and lips clashed and sought and satisfied while they rocked together. Bree twined her fingers through the silk of his hair. Griff slid a finger between them, adding just enough pressure where she needed it so that she came, clenching hard around him before he spilled himself inside her.

They collapsed, Bree half on top of Griff, their limbs tangled. Sandalwood, jasmine, sex, and sweat hung in the air. The bed was a mess.

If only every day could be like this.

They must have dozed. Bree wasn't sure because lately reality merged with her dreams anyway. But even dreams came to an end and tomorrow they'd fly home. Back to reality and an insistently ticking clock.

But they had the rest of today to enjoy each other. They didn't have to talk about how they felt here. They were attuned to each other and could almost always follow each other's thoughts. Except sometimes, she'd rather he didn't know what she was thinking, because she didn't want to add to his sadness.

"Hey," she said softly. "You want to take a shower?"

Griff opened one eye, then closed it. "That depends. Will there be a repeat performance?"

Bree chuckled. "That's kind of up to you."

He looked down at himself. "Doesn't seem likely. But you never know."

While in the shower, they decided to call housekeeping to put the room back to rights while they poked through the boutiques in town one last time. The bed would still be there when they got back.

Holding hands, they wandered through the bustling retail district. When they passed a shop window displaying brightly patterned island clothing, Bree tugged Griff inside. She said, "Tell me again why you only wear black?"

"It goes with everything."

"That's not a good enough reason."

"I'm... color blind?"

She looked at him. "Are you?"

He smirked. "No." Then he became serious. "It reflected my mood when I was adjusting to what happened to me. I got used to it, I guess, and started wearing it all the time."

"You wore the red tie I got you at our wedding," she pointed out.

"That was for you." He squeezed her hand.

She squeezed back. "I know. Now I want you to do something else for me. Let's find a shirt for you. One that isn't black."

"Bree?"

"What?"

"Are you trying to change me?"

"Of course not! I'm trying to change your depressing wardrobe to something less funereal."

Their gazes crossed as a silent communication passed between them. "All right. One shirt," said Griff "But I get to pick out something for you, too. And you have to wear it. Agreed?"

"As long as it's not black."

"Oh, it won't be."

"Damn I've got good taste," Griff proclaimed as Bree twirled in front of him in her new outfit. He'd chosen a figure-hugging mini dress featuring bright red hibiscus on a turquoise background.

Bree teetered on the sparkly high-heeled sandals he'd chosen. "It's not too short?"

He gave her a comical leer combined with an eyebrow wiggle. "There's no such thing as too short. It shows off your legs."

She adjusted the baby hibiscus hair ornament she'd tucked into her updo. "You look divine," she informed him as he stepped forward and took her in his arms.

She'd wanted to ease him into color, so she'd selected a navy blue shirt highlighted with pale yellow hibiscus. He'd paired it with new khaki slacks.

"I feel ridiculous," he informed her, his eyes merry. "But I guess it looks okay. Thank you."

"We're going to dance, right?" Bree queried.

"Definitely." He started to move as if music was already playing for them. "Then eat and drink and enjoy every last second of our honeymoon."

Bree followed his lead as he held her close. "Then we can cross dancing off our list," Bree said.

"Uh huh. And me wearing something besides black. I bet that was on your list, wasn't it?"

"Maybe."

He swung her into a dip, and she squealed. "Wasn't it? Tell the truth."

"Yes, okay." He let her up. "But I'd live with you wearing only black forever if I had the chance."

He cupped her head in his hands and looked deep into her eyes. "I know you would." He kissed her. "And if I had a chance at forever with you, I'd never wear it again."

Chapter Fifty

"Tell me everything," Jenna said at six-thirty in the morning. On her first day back, Bree had suggested a coffee-and-donut get-together in her office before things got busy. She didn't want to waste one moment of her after-work time in Dante's.

Jenna seemed to understand and agreed to meet before Sanctuary's normal business hours.

Bree blushed. "I'm not going to tell you *everything*."

Jenna giggled. "Not about that. Although you are glowing, if you don't mind me saying so." She eyed Bree over the rim of her mug. "Was the honeymoon wonderful?"

"Wonderful doesn't even begin to describe it. We had such a great time. Jenna, we did everything. Fished and snorkeled and walked along the beach. Shopped, dined, danced."

"You got the grim reaper to dance? Nice tan, by the way. Are there any tan lines?"

"Jenna!" Bree laughed. "I thought you agreed to stop calling him that."

"I know. I know. I'm just having a hard time picturing him dancing. But I'm happy for you," Jenna said. "And how is Griff?"

"He's wonderful. Jenna, I love him so much. We have such a good time. And I know he loves me. I mean I really *know* it."

"That's great."

Bree ignored Jenna's less than enthusiastic tone. "So, what did I miss here?" Bree said. "How are things with you and Tyler?"

"Also, wonderful. He hasn't said anything about taking me to St. Bart's yet, but we played miniature golf and went for a burger on Saturday. I had a blast."

"Wonderful," Bree said and giggled. "Have we ever been happy in our relationships at the same time?"

Jenna considered the question for a moment. "Hmm. I don't think so. Seems like one of us is usually comforting the other because things have fallen apart."

"I can't believe we're seeing guys who are, well, I guess they're not exactly friends. But co-workers."

"Kind of hard to be friends with your boss."

Bree smiled. "If you recall that's why we set up the vet clinic separate from the sanctuary even though they're both under the same umbrella."

"Do you think it would be awkward if we did something together? The four of us?"

Bree hesitated. "Look, Jenna, we both know you're not Griff's biggest fan."

"Agreed. But I'm *your* biggest fan. And you're crazy about him. Maybe if I get to know him better, I'll be a fan, too."

Although she'd love it if Griff and Jenna declared a truce, her skepticism must have shown, because Jenna rushed on. "Look, I'm not saying I'm not still suspicious of his motives or that I'll ever trust him a hundred percent. But, Bree, this is me trying, for your sake. Give me a chance. That's all I'm asking."

Conscious of that always ticking clock, Bree knew they wouldn't have many chances to get together with friends. She trusted Jenna would be on her best behavior for the sake of their friendship. "What were you thinking?"

"A cookout or something? You know I love to barbeque, and I hardly ever get to use my grill for anyone except you."

"Let me ask Griff. It might be something to cross off our bucket list. 'Dinner with friends.'"

"Bucket list? Bree, that is so depressing."

"It's more of a pack-as-much-living-as-you-can-into-the-time-you-have plan."

"Well, when you put it that way... it's only slightly less depressing."

Bree leaned toward Jenna. "You didn't tell Tyler, did you? About Griff?"

"No. But even if I had, Tyler wouldn't say anything."

"Jenna," Bree warned.

"I *didn't*, okay? I swear."

Griff and Bree were getting ready for their evening with Jenna and Tyler. Much to her surprise, he was on board with the idea. "Do you want to take the bike?"

"Sure, but I'm not sure how I can hang onto you and the wine at the same time." They'd been out for a short ride once and Bree had instantly understood the appeal of motorcycles. He'd insisted she wear a helmet, but she refused, since he never wore one. She loved the way the wind whipped past while she clung to Griff, the machine vibrating beneath them.

"That's what backpacks and saddlebags are for," Griff informed her. "So, what do you think?"

Bree had been rummaging in her jewelry box for a particular pair of earrings. She turned around. Her mouth dropped open in astonishment. "What are you wearing?"

Griff looked chagrined. "Too much?" He buttoned the cuff of the blue shirt and eyed her as if awaiting a verdict.

Everything else he wore was still black, and the shirt was a dark shade of blue, but it complemented his hair and eyes. Bree came toward him slowly. "Well, you know, color can be very distracting."

"It can?"

"Oh yes. For example, I think I'm going to be *very* distracted this evening because I'll be thinking about how much I can't wait to get you home and rip this shirt off and have my way with you."

"You hate it so much you can't wait to destroy it, huh?"

"I love it."

"Good," he said, as she stepped into the circle of his arms.

"And I love you."

"Good. But be gentle with my shirt. It's the only non-black one I have."

"I'll buy you some more."

Later, at Jenna's house, Griff relaxed in a chair on the back deck and watched as she and Tyler argued good-naturedly about who had better grilling techniques. Bree had gone inside to finish the salad and refill her wineglass.

The negative feelings he'd once had about Tyler and Jenna's happy relationship were gone. He wished them well. Everyone deserved to find someone that made them happy. He'd let himself find his. He'd let himself be happy. So what if he only had months left with Bree instead of years? He realized now, even if he'd only had one day with her, he could die a happy man.

Except for one thing. He did his best not to think about how his death would devastate Bree. There was nothing he could do about it. He could only live within the moments he had.

His thoughts drifted to Madeline and the double-edged sword nature of what it would take to break the curse. As he'd said to Bree, it wasn't a solution either of them would want.

"Not so much marinade! You're drowning them," Jenna scolded.

"I am not. They're going to be juicy and delicious," Tyler said.

Jenna raised a disbelieving eyebrow. "Oh, yeah?"

"Just like you." Tyler put an arm around her waist and tugged her close.

Griff wondered if they'd forgotten he was there. Bree came back out with her wine and another beer for Griff. She settled herself on his lap as if it was the most natural thing in the world. He let his fingers play through the ends of her hair and smelled the pleasant cool air scented by the smoke from the grill and the pine trees nearby. A thousand stars lit up the sky along with a half-moon.

"This is fun, huh?" Bree said. She took a sip of her wine, her gaze on Jenna and Tyler who were now engaged in an intimate conversation.

"I'm having the time of my life," Griff said. He wasn't looking at the other couple.

Bree looked at him. She smiled. "Me too."

Chapter Fifty-One

"What's so important that you had to see me after hours?" Bree asked as she reluctantly plopped into the chair next to Jenna's desk.

Hard as she tried, Bree couldn't let go of the annoyance and resentment she'd felt ever since Jenna had insisted on meeting in private. It wasn't Jenna's fault. Bree knew she'd resent anyone who took precious time that could be spent with Griff away from her.

"It didn't use to be an issue, did it? Hanging out after work or going to Dante's for a drink. But ever since the cookout, I hardly ever see you."

Bree's impatience softened. "I know. I'm sorry. It's just that—"

"I know. I know. He's supposedly dying, and you want to spend every waking moment with him. I never thought we'd be the kind of friends who'd let a man come between us."

Bree let Jenna's use of the word "supposedly" pass. "He hasn't come between us. Jenna, you're still my best friend. You always will be."

Jenna had a strange look in her eyes. "Maybe not after you hear what I have to say."

"Jenna, please, you're worrying me." Bree didn't think she could take any bad news. Every day her thoughts were filled with what her life would be like once Griff was no more. The only thing that held those thoughts at bay was the time when they were together.

"You know I was always skeptical of him," Jenna said.

"Skeptical? Overbearingly suspicious is more like it."

"With good reason, as it turns out."

"Jenna, if you've got something to say, spit it out. I want to get home. Griff is—"

"Griff is the one who attacked you."

Bree stared at Jenna. She'd certainly omitted plenty of things over the years, but she'd never outright lied to her best friend. She didn't want to start now. "What makes you say that?"

"I accidentally got one of Griff's hairs when you came for dinner."

Bree fixed Jenna with a displeased look. "Accidentally, huh? That's why you hugged him. You knew that damn bracelet you've always complained of snagging your sweaters would snag something else. Like his hair. That's pretty low, Jenna, even for you." She made as if to rise, but Jenna's hand on her arm and the worry she saw in her friend's eyes stopped her.

"I didn't do it on purpose, Bree, I swear. I hugged him because I was having some genuinely warm feelings about him after I saw the way you two were together. But yeah, when I took the bracelet off, one of his hairs was stuck in the links. I thought what the hell. Let me prove to myself that I've been wrong about him this whole time." She glanced away for a minute before she said, "I sent both samples to the lab. They're definitely from the same man. Or the same animal."

"What are you talking about?"

"His hair is like that of most humans, but with some anomalies. Characteristics that are only found in certain types of animals. Felines, actually."

Bree's gaze skittered away from the certainty in Jenna's eyes.

"You aren't denying it," Jenna pointed out.

Bree thought of how long it would take to explain the curse on Griff's family. How many questions Jenna would ask in her disbelieving prove-it-to-me way. Bree hadn't even plowed through all the research Griff had given her yet. Explaining everything now, even to her best friend, was not an option. "I want to explain everything to you. But not right now. I can tell you some things, but after Griff dies, you'll know everything. Everyone will."

"He really is dying?"

"Yes." Tears surged into Bree's eyes. "Jenna, please. Try to understand. Every minute with him is beyond valuable to me, and I don't have very many minutes left. Trust me, for once in your life, I need a hundred percent of your trust. What's going on in Griff's life is terrible. It's been happening for a long time, but when he dies, it will end. I promise you he isn't taking advantage of me. He and generations of his family have been the victims of something truly horrible, Jenna. Please keep what you've found between us. I swear I'll explain it all later."

"A rare hereditary disease? Is that it?"

"Not exactly. But it's something like that." Bree could tell Jenna wanted to ask a hundred questions. She wanted satisfactory answers. Bree couldn't blame her. It's what made Jenna such a good vet. She never gave up until she discovered the correct diagnosis, but finally she said, "Fine, Bree. If that's how you want it."

Bree jumped up and hugged her. Jenna sat stiffly and didn't return the embrace, even when Bree said, "I love you."

Instead, her friend sighed and said, "This isn't going to end up as a Netflix documentary, is it?"

Bree looked at her. "You know what? It might."

She ran to her car, breathless with anticipation at the thought of being with Griff again.

Chapter Fifty-Two

Griff had put it off as long as he could. He knew he had to tell her, but he didn't want to. Especially not now, after they'd made love and she was lying securely next to him, her head in the crook of his arm. He lifted the ends of her hair and let them fall.

"Tomorrow's the twenty-third," he said.

"Mmhmm," she agreed drowsily.

He picked up a lock of her hair and rubbed the silky strands between his fingers before he let them drop. "It's a new moon."

He could tell when the implication of his words registered. She tensed. The arm that lay across his chest, tightened, her fingers pressed into his side. She looked at him.

"You know what it means, right?"

"You'll transform?"

"Yes."

"You'll attack someone?"

"I have to."

She regarded him in silence. God, how he hated this. He was a prisoner in his own body, a captive of the curse. He couldn't stop the transformation, couldn't prevent himself from acting on what had become pure instinct.

Letting Bree into his life, loving her, knowing she loved him, had been a double-edged sword. He could never stop hurting her. And knowing he was hurting her made his own pain nearly intolerable.

Bree stacked her hands on his chest and rested her chin on them. Her gaze locked with his. "Attack me."

"No."

"Why not?"

He ran his fingertips through the hair at her temple. "I've hurt you enough already."

"This time I'll know what's coming."

He wished he could believe the confidence in her tone.

Griff looked away, the image of the woman lying dead in the street crowding his vision. The same thing could happen to Bree, couldn't it? What if he knocked her down, what if she hit her head hard enough to crack her skull? "I'll hurt you. I won't be able to stop myself."

If Bree inadvertently died at his hands, wouldn't that be somehow fitting? *We always hurt the ones we love.* He thought of his mother, how she'd pined for his father, how raising her sons became her only purpose after his death. And once she'd accomplished that, she'd checked out. That's how he thought of it. Her life was over. If Bree's life ended before his did, it was no less than he deserved.

"Griff, you know the harm you do these women isn't just physical. It's traumatizing. There's no reason for you to attack someone else when I'm right here. Yes, I'll have a few scratches and some of bruises, but I'll heal."

"It might be more than that."

"What do you mean?"

"I've never attacked someone I knew, much less someone I care about. I've never attacked the same person twice, either. What if it causes me to lose control?"

"I'd rather that than you attack some random woman."

He shoved the murky thoughts away and almost smiled at her. "I guess it's too much like cheating on you."

She swatted him. "Not funny."

"Sorry, I know you hate my bad jokes."

She pressed her lips to his throat. "I love you."

He turned and kissed her, searching for answers even though there were none. He pressed her down, covered her with his body, touched every inch of her skin, hoping, as always, that the pleasure he brought her would make up for the pain he caused.

All the next day, Griff asked himself why he'd given in to Bree's insistence that he attack her. Practically, he knew it made sense. Bree knew what to expect. He'd be there to comfort her afterward. And an innocent stranger wouldn't be scarred for life. Emotionally, though, it was killing him. He'd never loathed himself more.

They ate a simple meal and lay together on the sofa, watching the fire as darkness fell. Griff played with Bree's hair. He was glad she didn't seem to mind. Letting the strands fall through his fingers again and again soothed him somehow.

"We should go," he said, as the clock ticked toward nine.

"Okay." She kissed him long and lingeringly. She gave him a ghost of a smile. "Be gentle with me."

"If I had any control over it, I wouldn't hurt a hair on your head."

She left through the back entrance to access a path through the wooded hills behind the house where their privacy would be insured. After a few minutes, he followed her outside, just as the first prickles of the change began.

He didn't know if he needed to hunt for Bree or if she could simply wait for him at a predetermined location in the woods. But the hunt was part of the ritual and because he wanted it over as soon as possible, he'd told her to take the path.

He did his best to breathe, to calm himself as the transformation took root. He closed his eyes, not wanting to see the fur covering his skin, or the claws that replaced his fingernails. As always, once the unpleasant process was complete, he became a powerful animal on the hunt.

He sniffed the air, catching Bree's scent. She'd be easy to track. On all fours, nose to the ground, the animal took over, and started after her.

Once Bree's eyes adjusted to the darkness, she made her way through the forest easily. She kept the beam of her flashlight on the ground and walked slowly at first, but then sped up. The trail was well-traveled and only the occasional wayward branch slapped against her.

She was free, she thought. Adrenaline began to pump through her system, and she increased her speed. And maybe, just maybe, she could free Griff as well.

As soon as he'd mentioned the new moon, she'd caught a glimmer of an idea. What if *this* was the way to break the curse? What if he attacked *her*, and she wasn't afraid? What if she loved him? What if she told him she loved him while he was in his animal state?

It was the stuff of fairy tales, sure, but they were already dealing with witches and curses, so why not? But the truth was, she wasn't living in a fairy tale. Nor was she living in a romance novel where all it took was a declaration of love to make everything perfect.

But was it wrong to let herself believe, even for a little while, that she could save him? What if she had found a way to break the curse?

She sensed rather than heard the presence behind her. Not too close, not yet, but there was a disturbance in the air. The sensation beneath her feet of more feet following behind her. She raced on, anticipation and adrenaline and excitement all mixed together.

She risked a glance over her shoulder but saw nothing. Her hair tangled across her eyes as she kept running. The path narrowed and pressed close to the side of a steep hill.

Trees grew in thick profusion on the other side of the path.

She slowed her steps, sensing a steep drop to her right. The footsteps grew closer. She heard the snap of fallen twigs, the brush of foliage behind her. Even though she knew who, or rather *what*, was hunting her, a weird sense of panicked anticipation engulfed her.

Don't make it easy for him. She snapped the flashlight off and shoved it into her pocket. She put her hands out blindly. The darkness surrounded her now and her night vision was useless. She felt something cold and hard in front of her. She felt her way along carefully, her heart beating hard in her chest. The hill had turned into a wall of rock. She couldn't find the path.

She turned her back against the wall and stared at the darkness. She blinked and saw another pair of eyes staring back at her.

"Griff," she said, though she was out of breath. She wasn't even sure he could hear her. Perhaps his ears pricked up at the sound?

She could hear him panting in the almost silent forest. The eyes moved. He paced toward her, slowly. Her heartbeat sped up. This was like the dream she'd had repeatedly where something or someone chased her through the forest. She came up against the wall of rock and had nowhere to go. And just like in the dream what came for her was Griff.

He pounced and knocked her sideways, but somehow, she managed to break her fall. The air was knocked out of her lungs as he crouched atop her, and she struggled to take a breath. She wrapped her hands around his powerful front legs, her fingertips buried in his fur.

He fought her hold, pushing back away from her, his claws digging into her shoulders. She yelped and slapped at his paws to get them off her. He growled as his weight crushed her. She panicked, afraid she wasn't going to be able to breathe.

She bucked and rolled out from under him and sucked in a breath. She felt his nose, cold against her neck, then the tentative touch of a warm tongue as if he was trying to make it up to her.

A sob rose in her throat, and she wrapped her arms around his neck. She felt the power coursing through him, the lethal strength he held in check. Eventually she felt him relax and drop down to her side, his muzzle burrowed against her neck, alongside her ear, his nose in her hair.

She smoothed the fur between his ears and along the top of his broad head. She held him closer, the prickle of the scratches on her shoulders and his earlier crushing weight atop her forgotten. She could feel the fur begin to recede, and his body begin to shift.

"I'm not afraid, Griff. I love you." She whispered the words over and over again. "I love you."

Chapter Fifty-Three

G riff opened his eyes and waited for the disorientation he always felt at the end of a transformation to pass. He was lying out in the open, next to an unmoving Bree.

Worried, he crept closer to her and pressed his fingers to her throat to find her pulse beating steadily. Her chest rose and fell, her skin warm as it should be.

He breathed a sigh of relief, then shuddered at the memory of what had transpired between them. He'd attacked her. He'd hurt her. She'd tamed him. She knew his deepest, darkest secret. That she loved him anyway humbled him.

As soon as he felt like himself again, he found Bree's flashlight and turned it on to see her watching him. He helped her up and held her against him as they started back along the path. Fifteen minutes at the most, they'd be back in his house. He'd put Bree to bed and tend to her wounds.

He couldn't speak because he had no words. She'd stripped him naked. He had nowhere to hide. She'd seen into the depths of his soul, and she hadn't turned away. What other woman would have done that? She truly was his soul mate.

Bree crawled into bed while he retrieved warm water, a washcloth, and a tube of salve. He unbuttoned her torn shirt and saw the lacy black bra she wore underneath. Winced at the deep scratches his claws had left on her shoulders and lesser slashes on her chest and arms. He tugged her jeans off to find more of the same along her thighs below panties that matched the bra.

He pressed the warm cloth against her skin until the scratches were nothing more than narrow red lines. She watched him rub the salve along each one. .

When he finished, he pressed a kiss to her forehead and looked into her eyes. "Are you okay?"

"I'm always okay as long as you're with me."

He feathered his fingers through her tangled hair. "I heard what you said. You weren't even afraid."

"I love you."

She said it simply, the way a child would, as a statement of fact, as if it were an answer for everything. A tidal wave of desire rushed through him. He kissed her, rough and demanding, and she responded. He tore at her remaining clothes, and she did the same with his. They clashed with each other, competed with each other, but in the end, they both won. Like animals, they mated until they were both replete and satisfied.

They came awake just as dawn broke. Bree noticed a gray, murky light in the room and looked up to see four square patches of non-blackness. "What's that?" she whispered.

"Skylights."

"I didn't know those were there." Griff's house, like the man himself, always managed to surprise her.

"I usually keep them covered."

"Why?"

"I've always liked the dark."

"But?"

He picked up her hand and played with her fingers. "It's time I let some light in."

She wiggled closer to him, ran the tip of her finger down the wounds on his shoulder that mirrored the ones he'd left on her. She kissed him there. "I thought... maybe last night would break the curse."

He hated to kill the hope he saw in her eyes, heard in her voice. He hated that he was going to have to hurt her again. He'd lied to himself before. Bree knew all his secrets. All but one.

"I know."

"You don't think it will?" she asked in a voice filled with longing.

"This isn't a fairy tale, Bree." He said it as gently as he could, forcing her dreams to die.

Chapter Fifty-Four

I t took Bree weeks to wade through the research Griff had given her. She snatched minutes here and there when Griff came home later than she did or had an outside chore he couldn't put off. As he said, she didn't pick up on anything that indicated a way for the curse to be broken. But she found Madeline Stark's business card which gave her pause. She recalled the times she'd seen Griff and Madeline at Sanctuary. Obviously, Griff had dealings with her about his situation otherwise why would her card be in the file? After a careful search, Bree found nothing else associated with the woman.

When she asked Griff about it, he glanced at the card and back at Bree. "I thought she might be of some help, but it turned out to be another dead end."

There's something he's not telling me. Bree didn't know how she knew, but the same prickle of suspicion went through her as when he'd handed her the file and told her she wouldn't find anything. Maybe it was nothing, but Bree refused to leave any stone, no matter how small and insignificant, unturned. The next day she made an appointment to meet with Madeline.

Now, almost sick with nerves, Bree swiped the palm of her hand down her slacks before she came face to face with Madeline Stark's intimidating presence. At Sanctuary, Bree was in charge, and her interaction with Madeline limited. They were professionally polite, nodding whenever their paths crossed, but rarely talking.

In the back of Bree's mind was that embarrassing childhood memory when Madeline Stark caught her leaving a dead bird on her doorstep. Bree became that child again, humiliated and shamed by Madeline's anger, which Bree had thought at the time was out of proportion. Madeline hadn't given Bree a chance to explain before chasing her away.

Bree'd never forgotten it. She was certain Madeline hadn't either. Bree had also never apologized. Perhaps she should start with that.

She pressed the bell and waited. The porch on which she stood held wicker chairs clustered around a glass-topped table. An old-fashioned wood swing painted white hung by chains from the ceiling. Potted plants bloomed and trailed tendrils over the railings and from hooks above. A sense of peace fell over Bree as she stood there. Her nerves vanished.

The door opened and Madeline Stark regarded her for a moment from behind the screen before she said, "Hello," and held the door for Bree to step through.

"Thank you for seeing me."

Madeline nodded. She closed the door and strode down the hallway. Bree followed, her heels echoing on the wood floor.

They didn't make houses like this anymore, Bree thought, taking in the high ceilings and plasterwork and original crown molding. The rooms they passed looked cozy, furnished with antiques and gauzy lace curtains.

Madeline led her through the kitchen to a back porch, now converted to a sunroom. A door at one end opened onto a pergola-covered path which led to a greenhouse. Bree could see a couple of outbuildings at the back of the property. One was a potting shed, she decided, and the other probably stored lawn maintenance equipment. Madeline gestured to a rustic farmhouse table surrounded by matching cushioned chairs.

Bree set Griff's research file on the table in front of her.

From a sideboard, Madeline poured tea into two bone China mugs. She set one next to Bree, along with a napkin. She took the seat across from Bree and edged a delicate plate filled with small round cookies to the middle of the table.

Madeline seemed in no hurry to begin a conversation. She sipped her tea, her calm demeanor as unnerving as her silence. The sense of peace Bree felt earlier vanished. Now she felt what she'd been feeling the past several weeks: desperate.

"Thank you for seeing me." Bree repeated, unsure how else to begin.

"Of course." Madeline said.

Mrow.

A black cat leapt into Madeline's lap and stared suspiciously at Bree with golden eyes. Bree recognized the cat as one from Sanctuary. It had been hit by a car a few weeks ago. Jenna did what she could for it in the clinic and when it survived, she'd sent it to Madeline for recuperation. It appeared to be completely recovered.

"His injuries have healed," Bree said.

"He still has a limp, don't you James?" The cat turned its head to Madeline as if it understood what she'd said. Madeline returned her attention to Bree. "I call him that after James Bond. Golden Eye."

"That's perfect."

Madeline offered her a faint smile and sipped her tea.

"Mrs. Stark," Bree began, feeling she couldn't waste any more time.

"Madeline, please."

"Of course." Bree told herself to breathe, to find that place of peace she'd experienced before Madeline had answered the door. "First of all, I owe you an apology."

Madeline's eyebrows went up. "Do you?"

"It's long overdue, but yes. When I was a child, I did some very childish things. I've been ashamed of my behavior for a long time and, frankly, too embarrassed to say anything." Bree gazed at the file in front of her. Her eyes misted at the thought of losing Griff now that she'd found him. "I'm sorry," she said, forcing herself to meet Madeline's gaze. "For leaving those dead animals for you to find. I thought—I thought—"

"You thought what?" Madeline's tone was one of curiosity.

"I thought you could bring them back to life," Bree said in a rush. "There were all these rumors about you, that you had a gift for healing. You were so... mysterious and you kept to yourself. I didn't want those animals to die. I thought maybe the rumors were true and..."

"Ah," Madeline said.

"I'd seen an old Disney movie called *The Three Lives of Thomasina*. There was a woman in it who everyone thought was a witch—"

Laughter bubbled out of Madeline. "You thought I was a witch?"

Bree felt herself smile. "I was a kid. The woman in the movie takes in this little girl's cat. The girl thinks the cat is dead because it's badly injured, but it's alive. The woman nurses it back to health and when it's healed, the girl thinks it's because she's a witch."

"You must have been massively disappointed in me then," Madeline said with a touch of humor. "All I did was bury those poor creatures out past the garden. But now what you did makes a bit more sense."

"It must have been very hurtful to you, even though that's not what I intended. I hope you can forgive me."

"You meant no harm, and it was a long time ago. Of course, you're forgiven." She eyed the file on the table. "Is that why you wanted to see me? To apologize?"

"No." Bree hesitated. "I want to ask you about something, but I don't want anyone else to know about it."

Madeline gave her a slight smile. "I'm nothing if not discreet," she said, though not unkindly. "Your secrets are safe with me."

And so are half the county's, Bree thought. She knew Madeline's reputation. She knew she could be trusted. Mostly she was concerned about Griff's reaction if he were to discover what she'd done.

Chapter Fifty-Five

Madeline nodded at the file. "This is what you want to discuss?"

Bree hesitated. If she handed the file over to Madeline, there was no going back. She thought she'd prepared herself for an answer no matter what it was, but now she wasn't so sure. "Yes," she finally said.

"May I?" Madeline held out her hand.

As if the file weighed a ton, Bree slowly lifted it and handed it over.

Madeline slid the rubber band off and opened it. She barely looked at the top page before her gaze shot toward Bree in surprise. "This is Griffin Lancaster's file."

"How did—how do you know?"

"I've seen it before."

"But Griff said—he told me not to bother contacting you. That there was no point." Bree stared at Madeline.

Madeline's countenance didn't change, nor did her demeanor. "I'd like to clarify something before we go any further. Griff knows you're in possession of this file?"

"Yes. He gave it to me."

"Ah. You're here about the curse."

"Yes."

"You must be the one."

"The one?"

"The love of his life. The one he can't live without."

"Yes," Bree said, the word barely escaping her lips.

"You want to know how to break the curse."

"It's possible?" Bree barely dared to hope. "You mean there is a way?"

The corners of Madeline's mouth turned up in what almost passed for a smile. "Other than death, there are very few things in life that can't be fixed," she said. A shadow passed over her face. "Except perhaps a broken heart."

"Will you tell me how to end the curse?"

Madeline contemplated Bree for a long moment. "You must understand that knowledge is a powerful thing. Once you know, you can't give the knowledge back."

Bree could feel her impatience growing. "I'll do anything to save him," she declared.

Again, Madeline's eyebrows drew up. "Anything?"

"Yes."

"You love him that much?"

"I do."

"In that case, my dear, I'll tell you what I told him."

Madeline poured more tea though Bree had hardly touched hers. Madeline settled back into her chair, stroking her hand along James's back. He purred in contentment.

"You're familiar with the granny women of the Appalachians?"

"Yes. They were the healers when the villages there were first settled."

"Yes. Their gifts were thought to be hereditary, passed from generation to generation. Each grew wiser than the last in the healing arts as they gathered more and more knowledge about herbal remedies, poultices, and basic ways to treat routine illnesses and injuries. It was also said they could create potions to bring about certain desired outcomes and cast spells to chase away unwanted situations. Most granny women used their knowledge for good. But not all."

"You're talking about Emerald MacCallum."

Madeline paused and sipped her tea. "Wait here a moment." She retreated into the house. James wound his body against Bree's legs and purred loudly. Bree rubbed his head, trying not to anticipate what Madeline would tell her, but her sense of hope was strong, nonetheless.

Madeline returned with a file of her own and resumed her seat. She'd also brought a pair of reading glasses and she put them on when she opened the file. "With the help of a translator, I did a lot of research on this curse. Griff agreed to let me write it up as a case study for my book. But not until after ..."

"He dies?" Bree said.

"Yes." Madeline continued to look through the file. "Let me explain something. This curse is powerful. It's real. I went back through Griff's family, his genealogy, and mine. Emerald MacCallum was my great-grandmother."

"You and Griff are related?"

"Distantly, but yes. I tell you this, because when Griff came to me and I realized the connection, I had in my possession some material that proved extremely helpful in understanding his curse. Texts Emerald used which were eventually passed to me."

Bree didn't know what to say, so Madeline continued. "Only one man caught Emerald's eye. Colin Henry Lancaster, by all accounts a dark-eyed, black-haired charmer from a nearby town. He seduced young Emerald although he had already agreed to an advantageous marriage to another woman.

"It's unclear whether Emerald knew of his engagement. If she knew, maybe she believed he would break it. It's possible both women chose to look the other way. Colin, of course, married the other woman, leaving Emerald heartbroken and angry. She was now considered soiled goods, and, in that day, no other reputable man would have her as a wife.

"Colin gave her to understand that he loved only her, but he needed his new wife's money to make something of himself and Emerald had to understand. She wasn't the first young woman to fall for a charming liar.

"Colin wasn't faithful to his wife, nor was he faithful to Emerald as his mistress."

"He was a player," Bree said.

"Certainly, that's what he'd be called today. A gigolo in an earlier, era." Madeline smiled.

"Griff told me most of this," Bree said. "Not the details, but how Colin and Emerald's relationship led to the curse."

"And my research backs up the accounts that Griff had from previous generations of his family. As Emerald's bitterness and discontent grew, so did her powers of healing and mysticism. She came to hate Colin, but she couldn't give him up. She suffered greatly because of him. He'd ruined her, ruined her reputation, essentially stolen the life she thought she'd have with him, the life he'd probably promised her when he first seduced her.

"Her powers took a dark turn. She became known all through those mountains as a witch. People began to seek her out and she began to make quite a good living with her potions and spells and occasionally with her curses.

"Even though she knew the power of the darkness, from what I learned, she still used her powers mostly for good. When Colin's wife died, Emerald was certain Colin would come to her, that he would wed her as he'd promised her all along, for many years. And he did come to her. For nearly a year he strung her along, insisting that he had to observe the proper mourning period for his wife before he could wed again.

"And then he married someone else," Bree said.

"Exactly. Another monetarily advantageous marriage that he had arranged himself. After he'd seduced another young woman, her family had no choice but to agree to the marriage."

"I'd be furious," Bree said.

"Oh, yes. Emerald had fallen for Colin's lies not once but twice. I'm sure her fury was beyond all measure. She banished him from her presence forever, but not before she cursed him and every one of his male descendants.

"The curse of threes," Bree said.

"Yes. Griff explained it to you."

"And the only way to end it is for Griff's line to end. To die without having any children."

"He told you that was the only way to end the curse?" Madeline's gaze was intent even through the lenses of her reading glasses.

"Yes."

Madeline dropped her gaze back to the pages. "I think you should listen to him." She folded her glasses carefully and laid them aside.

"Please, tell me."

Twenty minutes later, Bree stumbled to her car. She locked Griff's file in the trunk because she didn't think she could bear to look at it ever again.

The curse *could* be broken, but the means were almost beyond contemplating. Now she understood why he'd tried to steer her away from Madeline.

Bree could feel her heart twist in her chest. Griff's words about finding a cure came back to haunt her.

If there is, I can guarantee you it won't be pleasant. It won't be something either of us wants.

He'd spoken the truth.

Chapter Fifty-Six

"**I**'ve been thinking about something," Griff said. They were making dinner together. While Bree made a salad, Griff sautéed chicken breasts.

"What's that?"

"My birthday."

Bree's stomach knotted. She knew the exact date of Griff's birthday. She couldn't believe they only had a matter of days left. There would only be a few more nights like this one, where they raced home from work to be with each other. After they put together a meal they talked while they ate. Bree wanted to know everything about Griff. What he'd done that day, the projects he'd put bids on, what he ate for lunch.

And he listened to her like she was the most fascinating orator who ever lived, even when she shared nothing more than the mundane day to day details about operating Sanctuary.

Every day she fell a little more in love with him and, as hard as she tried not to think about it, as much as she steeled herself to be upbeat, their remaining days together were slipping by faster and faster.

She tried to keep a jovial tone, pretending to herself and to Griff that his birthday would not be the last day she'd see him alive. "And what are we doing to celebrate?"

"There's a special place I want to take you. A family cabin that now belongs to me. It's a couple of hours from here."

"You never mentioned this cabin before. Tell me more."

"My grandparents built it. Though I should warn you, it's pretty rustic."

"Rustic as in no indoor plumbing?"

Griff laughed. God how she loved making him laugh. How she'd miss his deep rumble of amusement and the way his eyes crinkled at the corners. And to think she'd once thought the man incapable of laughter.

"Not quite *that* rustic. What's a better adjective? Basic. Livable."

"Livable is not a step up from rustic. In fact, I think I prefer rustic."

Griff grinned. "I'm just trying to prepare you. There's little in the way of insulation, but the tin roof doesn't leak and there's a wood stove for heat."

"Do we also have to cook on this wood burning stove?"

Griff jabbed her with a finger. "No, smarty pants. It's got electricity. There's a rudimentary kitchen."

"Rudimentary. So, like a college hot plate? This keeps sounding better and better."

"Trust me, it's beautiful up there. Like nowhere else on earth."

His tone changed drastically, and Bree looked up to see a faraway look in his eyes. He'd drifted away from her. And soon he really would drift away from her. Unless she did something drastic.

"The weather forecast predicts unseasonably high winds and thunderstorms on Sunday from a cold front, but we could still hike on Saturday. That's where I'd like to go," he said. "Just you and me."

"Just you and me. I like the sound of that."

The drive into the mountains allowed for stunning views of virgin forests, steep gorges, and the occasional water-fall. Then they got to the cabin.

Basic did indeed work as a description. Everything in it would fall into the vintage category, right down to the ancient farmhouse sink and the haphazard mint green tile in the bathroom.

But also, as promised, it was livable, especially if one were only planning a few days' stay and didn't mind doing without modern conveniences such as a dishwasher or microwave.

Griff plugged in the old refrigerator and the hot water heater when they arrived, assuring her that they'd both be ready for use later in the day. But first, they brought in the coolers, luggage, and supplies before they set out on the steep winding trail not far from the cabin.

She followed behind Griff while he chattered about what he referred to as "the chasm," which he was partic-ularly excited to show her.

"Geologically speaking, it's where the Blue Ridge mountains split off from the Appalachians. I can't wait for you to see it."

Bree smiled at Griff's enthusiasm. She'd never seen him so animated. He was this solid hunk of man, but right now he had a boyishness about him that charmed her. She wished she'd known him sooner. What had he been like as a child? His mother had probably doted on him. Maybe spoiled him and his brother since she'd known the life that awaited them.

That's what I'd do if I had a son like Griff.

Her heart squeezed painfully in her chest. By tomorrow night, she'd be a widow. Neither of them spoke of it. Every time Griff glanced back at her, she smiled at him. She promised herself she'd never regret one second of the time she'd spent with him. But losing him was likely going to kill her.

Unless she killed herself first.

That was the secret Madeline had shared, the thing Griff didn't want her to know. And as Madeline had warned, she couldn't give the knowledge back.

Her mind kept going there. She just didn't know if she had the guts to do it. She knew she'd want to die once Griff was gone, and maybe, after he was gone, she would.

But if she was going to do that, why not do it now, and save a life in the process?

Because she was afraid. She could save him, but then he'd be the one going on and living his life without her. But would he feel the same way she did? That a life without her wouldn't be worth living?

She'd gone round and round with this circular argument ever since she'd left Madeline's house. She couldn't discuss it with him. He would forbid her from even considering sacrificing herself for him. He was already filled with remorse for involving her in his life and his secrets. She couldn't add to his pain.

And yet, she couldn't imagine any kind of life she'd want to live without him in it. No matter who died, whoever was left behind wouldn't want to go on living.

"We're almost there," he called over his shoulder. "How you doing?"

"Great," she called back. Indeed, her quads, calves, and glutes were tight from exertion. They wouldn't mind a rest. The trail grew increasingly rocky the higher they climbed, and if their arms were long enough, they could have touched some of the treetops on either side.

When Griff reached the summit, he reached for her hand. She joined him and saw a huge, rounded mound of granite. Treetops surrounded them on either side, but nothing grew on the bald rock. Bree turned around, taking it all in. To the west, the high Appalachians rose above this not as impressive elevation. To the east, the Blue Ridge range seemed endless and glorious. Bree became aware of a whooshing whistle nearby, which seemed odd, as although there was nothing to block the wind, the day was otherwise calm and sunny.

"Come here," Griff said in a reverent whisper. He led her across the slight rise in the roundish rock. It was bigger than she'd realized, almost like a giant human head, but higher in the middle before it sloped back down on the other side. Down its center was an enormous jagged crack in the rock at least three feet wide at its narrowest and maybe four and a half or five at its widest.

"Be careful," Griff warned. He held her hand tight as they approached the chasm. "It's easier to see if we lie down and look," he said. "Plus, there's no danger of falling in."

Chapter Fifty-Seven

They lay on their stomachs and looked over the edge. Bree felt an odd sense of vertigo, as if what she was looking down at she was really looking up at. Although the first several feet of the chasm were nothing but solid walls of rock, further down the chasm it appeared to widen. At the bottom she thought she saw a gurgling stream, maybe even some trees growing inside the space.

"They've looked for the source of that stream," Griff told her. "They've also looked for the end of it, but it's never been found. They think it feeds an underground spring."

"It looks like its own little world down there," Bree said in awe.

"It is. A chasm like this has its own ecosystem, although no one's ever been down there as far as I know. But I think scientists have lowered cameras down to take a look."

"It seems like it's wide enough for someone to rappel down," Bree pointed out.

"It's too dangerous. Hear that noise?"

The whooshing, whistling noise was even more pronounced than before. Wind suddenly gusted upward right at them. She nodded.

"The surrounding rock has fissures in it all the way around this big split down the middle. Apparently, the air currents are something else once you get beyond the first fifteen or twenty feet. The space opens up, but it's like a mini hurricane, depending on the weather conditions. On a really windy day? The air churns and spins and blows back up the opening, like a tornado."

He sat up and looked around, then dug into his pocket. He held up a penny. "Watch this." He dropped the penny into the chasm. Bree watched it drop straight down the wall of rock before it seemed to stop in midair. It turned and spun and flipped, caught on the air currents, until finally she could see it no longer. "Cool, huh?" Griff grinned at her. "Sometimes it will spit a penny right back out. That happened the last time I was up here. In fact, there were a whole bunch of pennies along the edges that day. There's a local legend that if it spits your penny back out, you'll have good luck for a year."

"How long has it been since you were here?"

Griff's smile faded a little. "About a year ago."

They looked down into the chasm, but Griff's penny never reappeared.

Eventually, Bree sat up, hugging her knees to her. "Thank you for sharing this with me."

Griff regarded her. "I've never brought anyone up here with me."

"You haven't?"

"Never got close to anyone before." He crawled toward her. "There are a couple of other things I've never done up here, either."

Bree grinned. "You're kidding, right? Rug burn's one thing, but—"

"Hard as a rock burn's not your thing?"

She laughed and groaned at the same time. "No way."

"Come on baby. You know you want it," he teased.

She scrambled away from him and stood up. "I'll tell you what. You hang onto that hard as a rock burn—"

"Literally? Or figuratively?"

She swatted him. "*Until* we get back to the cabin."

He stalked toward her. "And then what?"

"And then... I'm going to rock your world."

He laughed. Bree grinned, happy to know she was responsible for his glee. Her smile faded though, as she followed him back down the trail, thinking it might be the last time she ever heard him laugh.

They put together a simple meal when they got back and as they were clearing up, Griff said, "There's something I've been curious about."

Bree turned to him, an eyebrow lifted in silent inquiry.

"The photograph on your desk at Sanctuary. It looks like it's from high school."

Bree focused on stowing food in the cooler. "It is."

"Who's the guy?

She closed the lid and faced him. "His name was Jeremy."

"Was?"

"He died that day." Griff listened intently while she told him what had happened.

"Oh." For some reason Bree couldn't fathom he seemed disappointed. "I thought maybe...after I'm gone...forget it."

Evidently, he'd been trying to look out for her. Did he think someone from her past could take his place? She slid her arms around his waist. "You were always my destiny. There's no one else."

He didn't look happy to hear those words. "But why do you keep that picture where you can see it every day? It seems kind of morbid."

"It's a reminder. I've always asked myself could I have saved Jeremy if I'd been braver? Stronger? When I'm faced with difficulty, remembering that day makes me try harder. Makes me push myself a little further. Even when I'm afraid."

"You're amazing, you know that?" He kissed her. "Amazing."

Some time later she said, "I guess we can cross making love in front of a fireplace in a rustic cabin off our list now." Bree's head was on his shoulder, her hand on his chest. She watched the fascinating combination of candlelight and firelight play across his skin.

Griff linked his fingers through hers and turned on his side so he could look at her. "And hiking to the chasm. Roughing it."

Bree grinned. The cabin was simple, sure, but it they weren't exactly roughing it. "Our list is getting shorter." *And so is our time.*

Griff's fingers combed through her hair. "Do you know how much it's meant to me to have you in my life? To have you for my wife?"

Tears surged into her eyes, and she wasn't entirely successful at holding them back. "I do."

She locked her arms around Griff's neck, and he held her tight. "I'm sorry," he said softly, stroking her hair. "I'm sorry for hurting you."

She shook her head as best she could, denying his words. She wouldn't have traded one moment of her present, past, or future pain for the time she'd had with him. "I love you."

Chapter Fifty-Eight

Bree woke before dawn. For once she'd slept dreamlessly and as soon as her eyes opened, she knew exactly what she was going to do. The answer that had eluded her these past few weeks became crystal clear to her last night after Griff had asked about Jeremy. All she'd needed was that reminder to push herself. Even when she was afraid. She lay quietly, listening to the wind whip the tree branches against the side of the cabin.

If Griff woke up, she knew he'd stop her, even if he had to use brute strength to do it. She eased out of bed and tiptoed around the room, gathering her clothes and shoes. She went into the living area and got dressed.

As she passed through the kitchen, she spied the contents of Griff's pockets on the kitchen counter.

She picked up a lone penny and looked at it for a long time. It seemed like an omen, a sign that she was doing the right thing. A sense of peace settled over her. Griff would wake up tomorrow. Without her. But he would wake up. The sense of doom that hung over his life would be gone. She'd take it with her. The curse would be lifted. She kissed the penny and put it back down face up on the corner of the counter. She found a dull pencil and a weathered pad of paper and quickly scrawled a note. *It's your turn to live. I love you.*

Maybe, when Griff woke up, when he realized what she'd done and why, he'd keep that penny as a memory of their last day together.

She slipped out the door and started up the trail.

Griff didn't know what woke him. One minute he'd been dead to the world, so to speak. The next, he was wide awake. He knew the moment he opened his eyes he was alone in the cabin. Bree was gone.

He jackknifed off the bed and got dressed. Shirt. Jeans. Socks. Boots. He hopped on one foot to get his boot on and looked out the living room window. The sun wasn't out. The light outside was an ugly yellowish gray. He saw his truck still parked where he'd left it.

The wind had picked up during the night. The trees were swaying with the strength of it, leaves, twigs, and pine needles dropping to the ground and blowing across the gravel driveway with each gust.

Where would Bree go? Why would she leave? If she wanted to take an early morning hike, watch the sunrise from the top of the mountain, why hadn't she woken him? Not like there'd be any sun today. It looked like the predicted storm was headed right for them.

Out of habit, he picked up his keys, wallet, and cell phone. He glanced at the penny all alone at the corner of the counter.

He picked it up and rolled it over and over his fingers feeling as if it was trying to tell him something. It was a clue to Bree's whereabouts.

Then he saw the words written on the notepad. His mind went back to the file he'd given Bree, the moment she'd asked about Madeline's business card, which he'd foolishly left for her to find.

He'd told her it was a dead end and thought no more about it. But he knew Bree's persistent nature wouldn't let her leave any stone unturned if she thought there was even the slightest chance of saving him. Damn Madeline, she should have warned him.

It occurred to him that she might have tried. He'd let a lot of things slide, intent on spending every minute he could with his wife.

The penny meant the chasm. Had to be. Bree planned to save him.

He had no idea what kind of head start she had on him, but he had to stop her. He took off at a run toward the trail.

"Bree!" he called as he started up. His voice got caught in the trees and the wind before it echoed back to him. Perhaps he shouldn't call her. It might only panic her, maybe push her into a decision she might still be contemplating.

The wind gusted against him, determined to slow him down. Dark gray clouds obliterated any chance of the sun peeking through now. The scent of rain blew through the air. Thunder rumbled in the distance.

His mind refused to contemplate a world without Bree in it. Even though as he thought it, he knew he'd never experience such a world. Except maybe for the rest of today.

He urged himself up the trail, breaking out in a cold sweat as he thought of the meaning of Bree's note. He understood. She wanted him to live. What she didn't know was these past few months were enough. In some ways, he felt like he'd lived a lifetime with her. She loved him and now he knew the depth of her love. Being with her had always been enough.

His strides ate up the trail, every muscle in his legs screaming at him to ease up. But he couldn't. The thought of Bree sacrificing herself so he could live without her killed him. *No pun intended*. Who else was going to groan at his bad jokes? Who else was going to make him laugh like he hadn't laughed in a very long time? Who else could make living his life worthwhile, fill up that empty space inside of him? If Bree died to save him, he wouldn't want to go on living. The irony of it nearly overwhelmed him.

Almost before he realized it, he had reached the top of the bald mountain, stumbling across the rough granite surface. The sun struggled to find its way through the storm clouds, sending tendrils of amber light through the trees.

With nothing to stop it, the strong wind blew unencumbered, causing a high-pitched whistling. The tops of the trees bent and swayed against the rock. "Bree!" His voice was hoarse, his breathing labored.

She stood with her back to the edge of the chasm, the wind causing her to teeter at the edge. He started toward her. She held up a hand. "Don't."

He stopped. "Please don't do this."

"I want to. It's the only way."

He shook his head. "You don't understand."

"Yes. I do."

Her calm unnerved him. "Madeline told you."

She lifted her chin. "Yes."

"You're going to give up your life for me."

"You deserve a chance to live. Really live."

"My life won't be worth living without you."

"Please." Her voice faltered. "Let me give you this chance."

He edged closer. "Bree. Please." Tears filled his eyes. He couldn't breathe. "Don't do this."

"I love you."

"I know."

She stepped back, teetering again, caught in a rising tornado-like gust. Griff rushed at her. He got there in time to grab her wrist. Her weight and momentum floored him.

He hit the ground, nearly getting the wind knocked out of him.

Super-charged air roared through and around the chasm, above and below them, knocking Bree against the rock face as if she weighed nothing.

"Griff! Let me go!"

"I can't," he screamed, desperate to make her understand. "I can't let you do this."

She reached up with her other hand, but it wasn't to grab onto his. She pushed at his fingers, trying to get him to release her. "*Please*. Please let me go."

"I can't!" He shouted again. "I can't live without you. I *won't* live without you."

He stared into her eyes. Her calm countenance. He saw his whole life there. Past. Present. Future. She understood.

So did he.

Thunder sounded and lightening cracked above them. The rock beneath him trembled. Stinging rain started to pour, whipped by the wind.

The muscles in his arm and shoulder must be screaming in protest. Still, Griff didn't let go. Bree knew he couldn't hold her forever, even though he now grabbed on with both hands. He could only keep her weight suspended for so long. The wind forced her dangling body into the rock and the rain made his hold slip further. She looked into his eyes, willing him to believe it had to be this way.

Then everything clicked into place for him the same way it did for her. This was the only way they could be together.

The bond she'd had with Griff from the first became fluid, tensile, unbreakable. His love filled her and hers flowed into him until it became such a huge presence between them that's all she could feel. The certainty that death was preferable to a life lived without the other. Somehow, she knew everything she felt, he felt. He *knew*. He was inside her and she was inside him. And maybe this wasn't the answer, but at the same time it was the only answer.

When she fell, she knew a moment of panic. She opened her mouth to scream as the chasm's granite walls sheared past. But Griff hadn't let go. He still held her hand.

They were connected. They always would be. Emerald's curse would end, but not their love. She'd brought them together and allowed them to experience everything she'd felt for Colin. But where she'd allowed evil to flourish, they'd embraced each other and let love triumph.

No regrets. When Bree made that promise to Griff, she didn't know what it would ultimately mean. *Knowledge is a powerful thing.* Bree acknowledged the truth of Madeline's words and embraced the power knowledge had given her. The most powerful gift of all: her life.

The whooshing, whistling noise grew stronger the further they fell. The wind tangled her hair and tugged at her clothes. A sudden gust pushed her sideways. Rain slashed against her. She floated for a moment, and she wondered if this is how birds felt when they found an air current they could ride effortlessly with their wings outstretched spinning in a lazy circle.

She let the novel sense of weightlessness take over making her think of astronauts in space doing somersaults in the air. Bree wasn't afraid. She wasn't alone. Griff held her hand and kept his eyes locked on hers. She wanted to laugh as joy shot through her. That happily ever after romance novel ending she'd fantasized about had been granted to her. She and Griff together. Forever.

The crazy strong wind pulled her and Griff apart and sent her into a dizzying somersault, until she couldn't see him anymore. Still, peace enveloped her because she knew, in this life or the next, she'd see him again.

Chapter Fifty-Nine

Griff woke up to find himself soaked to the skin. Cold, stinging rain continued to pelt him. He lay face down in a tangle of brush and mud near the top of the trail. He used his hands to push himself off the ground and gasped as the pain caused him to buckle. He rolled over and sat up, cradling his arm. Wincing, he ran his fingers over it gingerly. He'd broken this same arm as a ten-year-old Little Leaguer when he slid into home base and the other team's chunk of a catcher fell on him.

He got to his feet, trying to orient himself. A solid wall of rain hammered him from all sides as he made his way up the muddy trail to the bald rock.

He'd held on to Bree as long as he could, but it hadn't been enough.

The crazy wind from the storm had tossed him around, banging him into the side of the flat granite face. He thought he was dead, but he must have lost consciousness before the tornado-like gust had apparently spit him back out.

Griff surveyed the mountaintop, the downpour obscuring his vision. Everything swam before his eyes for a minute. He put a hand out for balance, but lurched sideways anyway, before he landed hard on his ass on the unforgiving rock.

His brain swam back to the first night he'd met Bree. When he attacked her. Their head wounds. Her unsteadiness. The rain. If he was still alive...did that mean she was too? Would he be able to see Bree's body, if it lay twisted and broken at the bottom of the chasm?

He crawled to the crack in the rock carefully and peered down. Sadness welled inside him. If he lived but lost her? What would be the point? Better if he had died with her. If she was down there...God, did he have the kind of guts she did? Could he throw himself into the chasm again *now*? Just to avoid facing the rest of his life without her?

It seemed wrong somehow, to kill himself when she'd sacrificed her life for his. What he should do, what he'd *have* to do, is honor the gift she'd given him. The sacrifice she'd made so he could *live*.

Damn that black cloud that had followed him since the day of his birth, hovering over him, keeping him from ever having the things he truly wanted. *Normal things.* Love. A family. A long life.

One out of three ain't bad. He cursed Emerald and her diabolical mind. Cursed her ability to intertwine life and death and love into a sick, twisted vine that bore only paralyzing heartache and devastating pain for so many generations of his family.

He followed along the edge of the chasm, trying to see the bottom, but the pounding rain made it hard for him to know exactly what he saw. He tried to remember what Bree had been wearing. Jeans. Hiking boots. A green hoodie, he thought. And a white T-shirt. He didn't see anything that looked like her crumpled body.

He moved back from the edge and looked around. If the chasm had spit him out, it could have spit out Bree's much lighter body as well, right? Maybe she had landed somewhere nearby, just as he had? Hope surged through him as what ifs ran through his brain. What if she survived? Would he still be cursed? What if it was still broken and they could be together again?

There! What was that? On the other side of the chasm?

Griff cupped his hand over his eyes to shield them from the downpour. Was that the sole of Bree's hiking boot? Griff scrambled back along the edge to the narrowest gap in the chasm. Three feet was nothing, he told himself, except he was soaking wet, the rock slippery, and his arm was most likely broken. The dizziness hadn't completely subsided, and he probably wasn't going to be too steady once he got to his feet.

But if Bree *was* there on the other side, if she was alive...

He crawled back several feet, then stood. He shook his uninjured arm and hand out the way competitive runners did before they lined up on the starting blocks. His balance seemed okay. Now or never.

Head down, he took a couple of deep breaths before he took a running start and leapt across the gap, his sodden boots slipping and sliding as he landed on the other side. He lost his balance and slammed down hard, automatically bracing for the impact with his arms out to break his fall. The impact jarred his injured arm further before he cradled it close to his chest. If it wasn't broken before, it sure was now. He cursed to distract himself from the pain and picked himself up, carefully stepping toward what he could now tell for sure was Bree.

She'd landed at an awkward angle at the edge of the granite face. One more foot and she'd have rolled down the side.

If her neck was broken at least death would have been instantaneous and she wouldn't have suffered. Griff was barely aware of the tears on his wet skin. There'd be a funeral, of course. At least he'd be able to properly bury her body. A headstone he could visit and leave flowers. He'd plant a Christmas cactus on her grave, he decided, grimly smiling at the thought. And asters like the ones she'd uprooted.

Assuming he lived, that is. If Bree's death saved him. But maybe by tomorrow he'd be dead, too. Because he didn't trust the cure to Emerald's curse. Nothing was guaranteed.

Resigned, Griff gently pressed his fingertips to Bree's throat, checking her pulse. Her skin was cold and wet, but her pulse beat strong and steady. His heart soared.

"Bree!" he shouted. She did not respond. He bent close to her ear. "Bree!"

Griff looked her over. He ran his hand along her arms and legs, checking for anything broken or dislocated. She seemed okay. With his good arm, he pulled her away from the edge. Only when he slid his arm beneath her shoulders and cradled her close to him, did he see the egg-sized bump swelling above her ear.

"Bree. Sweetheart." Her clothes and hair were soaked, her skin chilled, but she was alive. *Alive.* He pushed the wet strands of her hair back from her face and pressed his lips to her temple, to her cheek, to her lips.

She remained unresponsive. He looked around. Even as the rain began to let up, he realized his options were not great. He pulled his phone from his pocket only to find the screen had shattered. He must have landed on it. The display still lit up but showed no reception.

He couldn't imagine EMTs hiking up the trail with a gurney or a stretcher, anyway. A Medivac wouldn't fly in this weather. Somehow, he was going to have to get himself and Bree back across the chasm and down the trail to the truck. The nearest hospital was at least thirty miles away.

First things first. He eased himself away from Bree and laid her head gently back down. "I'll be right back, baby." He kissed her lips once more. He got to his feet, pressed his injured arm tight to his chest and held it there with his other one, took a run at the chasm and leapt across, managing to keep his feet under him when he landed this time. He hurried along the trail, slowed somewhat by the mud and wet leaves. It'd be a hell of a feat to carry Bree all the way down a steep trail in these conditions. Even if she woke up, he wasn't sure she'd be steady enough to hike down on her own. He wasn't even sure *he* was steady enough to make it.

But he told himself he'd do it. Somehow. He found a couple of saplings that looked like they'd work for what he had in mind. In his haste to find Bree, he'd ignored one of the first rules of hiking, to be prepared for an emergency. He had no knife. No emergency medical supplies. No water. Nothing except his useless cell phone and his bare hands, well, hand.

Using his feet and his good hand, he wrestled with the saplings, finally managing to break them and tear them away from their roots.

He went back to the top of the mountain. The rain continued to dissipate, and the wind finally began to die down. Bree hadn't moved. Griff sat and undressed awkwardly, sucking in a breath as he drew off first his saturated flannel shirt and then his T-shirt. He wrung the flannel out as best he could and hung it on a nearby branch then wondered why he'd bothered since it was still raining.

He went to work with his hand and his teeth, tearing his tee shirt into uneven strips. By the time he was done he was sweating, and the rain had nearly stopped. He maneuvered one of the saplings into position on top of the strips of cloth, laid his arm on it and placed the other sapling on top of his arm.

His broken arm objected to every bit of movement or pressure. He used his teeth and his hand to create the makeshift splint but kept losing the ends of the strips or not tying them tightly enough and having to start over. It took him much longer than he felt it should have before he was able to make a reasonable facsimile of a splint. By the time he was done, the sun reluctantly peeked through the clouds, but the air remained moist and chilly. He looked at his flannel shirt hanging forlornly on the tree branch. He'd forgotten to put it back on before he'd tied the splint on. The flannel would have shielded his upper body from the branches along the trail on the way down. But it was going to stay here.

He leapt back across the chasm. Getting Bree to a hospital was his number one priority.

He knelt beside her. "Bree?" He touched her forehead and her cheek with the back of his fingers. Gently, he patted her cheek. "Bree? Wake up."

Nothing happened. Griff swallowed the lump in his throat. What if she never woke up?

No. He wouldn't allow himself to think that way. She might only have a concussion. She got knocked out when she landed. She'd be okay. She had to be.

But getting her up from this prone position, getting back across the chasm with her, and down the trail? Not a problem, Griff assured himself. The woman had died for him. This was nothing.

He bent over and slid his good arm under her. All he had to do was get her up, get her over his shoulder in a fireman's carry. From there, it would be a piece of cake. That's what he told himself.

He did it somehow, although there was a difficult moment where he'd instinctively put out his injured arm for support. The pain nearly brought him to his knees where Bree would have been in danger of another bump on the head. He swayed, dizzy with the pain, as he got to his feet and waited for his vision to clear.

God, she was heavy. Her wet clothes dribbled water down his back and chest as he adjusted his hold on her. The sooner he got back to the cabin, the better. He did a one-two-three count and raced as best he could back toward the chasm. He leapt, stumbled under the added weight as he landed on the other side, but managed to stick the landing by adding a few running steps. Bree had taken a bounce when he'd let up on his hold to use his arm for balance, but he hadn't lost her.

"So far, so good," he muttered as he started down the trail. He had to go slowly because the mud alternately sucked at his soles or sent him sliding when he wasn't expecting it. Sunlight filtered through the trees now and then, and every insect inhabiting the wooded mountainside this late in the season came alive.

Griff gritted his teeth and kept putting one foot in front of the other. He blocked out the pain, his fears about Bree, and the protesting muscles of his legs and feet. He'd be blistered and sore and beat up and bitten by the time he got to the bottom, but he didn't care. He and Bree were both alive.

Chapter Sixty

F ueled by fantasies of the future, Griff made it to the bottom of the trail. He'd never been so happy to see his truck in his life. Every muscle in his body screamed for relief. His upper body had gone numb from the pressure of Bree's weight and his legs were ready to buckle.

He laid Bree gently across the back seat. He couldn't believe she was still out. "Bree!" He leaned over her, willing her to open her eyes. "Bree! Can you hear me?" He patted her face. "Bree!"

Her eyelids fluttered when he called her name again. She opened her eyes, briefly, looked directly into his, then closed them again. "Bree?" When she didn't respond further Griff gave up.

In the cabin he stripped off his wet clothes and exchanged them for dry ones, dressing as quickly as he could with the use of only one arm. He draped a button-down shirt over his shoulders and put his good arm through the sleeve. He wished he could dress Bree in dry clothes, but he didn't see how he could with his injuries. He grabbed a bottle of water and raced to the truck with only one thought in his head. Get Bree to a hospital.

He covered Bree with a blanket and flipped the truck's heater to high. He cast glances to the back seat as he drove, encouraged that nothing had changed. He adjusted the vent and noticed his wrist for the first time. The mark he'd lived with forever wasn't there. His skin looked smooth, like nothing had ever marred it. He slowed to a stop and twisted around to check Bree's wrist. Her mark was also non-existent.

He didn't know what this new development meant for sure, but it seemed like a good omen. Might it mean the curse was at an end? He'd know for sure if he survived past midnight tonight. Feeling cautiously optimistic, he began to hum Happy Birthday to himself over and over as hope took hold. If this wasn't the last time he'd hear that tune, he planned to have elaborate celebrations every year. Big birthday parties with DJ's and tons of food. Dancing. Fireworks.

Another idea sparked. Do the birthday party as a fundraiser bash for Sanctuary and the botanical garden. Do a silent auction on donated items like cruises and spa and golf vacations. Every year it would get bigger and better and more successful. He and Bree would flourish. Together. He found any alternative unthinkable.

Bree hurt in every part of her body. She knew she was awake but didn't open her eyes. A steady beep sounded above her head somewhere and bright light pressing against her eyelids made her wince.

Hospital? She must be lying on a bed under covers. She raised her hand and dragged whatever was attached to it up to her chest, where she felt the flimsy, thin material of whatever she wore.

Reluctantly, she blinked her eyes open and confirmed her suspicions. She was in a hospital room. Tears filled her eyes as her memory came flooding back. Somehow, she was alive. Which meant Griff was dead.

She moaned. How had she gotten here? How had she survived the fall? Who found her?

She looked frantically around for a call button. She had to know what was going on. Had Griff's body been located as well?

"Hey."

That one word took away her breath. It was what she wanted to hear more than anything, but it was also impossible.

Griff, looking like he'd been in a fight, appeared in front of her. His face was bruised and scraped. His hair was a disaster. Instead of his tee shirt and flannel, he wore the top of a set of scrubs over his jeans. There was a foam cast on one of his arms. Tears filled her eyes. It was the same day then. By midnight tonight, he'd be dead. Because she'd failed.

She looked away from him. The tears slid into her hair.

He bent close to her and gently smoothed the tears with one finger. "Don't be sad."

She swung her gaze back to his. "I screwed up. I was going to save you." She didn't even try to stop the flow of tears. "I'm sorry."

He gave her one of those almost smiles. "Oh, sweetheart." He dabbed at her tears with a corner of the sheet. "You did save me. You saved us both."

She held back a sob. "How?"

"I don't know how."

She hiccupped and tried to concentrate. She had the mother of all headaches. And she noticed now one of her arms was in a sling. "You went over the edge with me."

"I did." He sat beside her.

"We should be dead."

"We should."

He played with the ends of her hair, gazing at her thoughtfully.

"But..."

"I can't explain it. I held onto you as long as I could, but the wind pulled you away. I don't know if we were riding an air current or what, but we got spun around and banged up pretty good.

"The next thing I knew, I woke up flat on my face at the top of the trail. Beaten to a pulp, but still alive. You weren't so lucky."

"I was dead?"

He chuckled. "No. You, my love, landed on the surface of the mountain on the other side of the chasm."

"Love on the rocks."

He laughed. Bree smiled at the sound of his laughter.

She was afraid to ask, but she had to know. "What time is it? What day is it?"

Griff held up his cell phone and squinted at the shattered screen. He turned it around so she could see the numbers. "Just after midnight. Technically, it's Monday."

Griff pressed his lips gently against her temple and looked into her eyes. "You saved me," he whispered.

"But could you still die?"

"I don't think so."

"How do you know?"

He held up his wrist. Then he held up hers. She sucked in a breath. Their matching imprints were gone. Not even the faintest of outlines remained.

Hope surged through her. "The curse?"

"Broken."

"Are you sure?"

"As sure as I can be. I called Madeline and told her what happened. She feels certain the curse is gone."

"But—but how?"

"You broke it. You loved me enough to give up your life for mine."

"But I'm still alive."

He grinned. "A for effort, though. Apparently, that's what counts."

"Then I didn't screw up?"

"You've got a concussion. A broken collar bone. Bruises and scrapes. You're going to be sore as hell for a couple of weeks. But you definitely did not screw up."

Bree beamed at him. Because every dream she'd had, everything she'd ever wanted sat right in front of her. And he wasn't going anywhere.

"Now I have a question for you," Griff said with mock sternness. "Why didn't you tell me you were pregnant?"

Bree stared at him in shock. "Wait, what? How? I can't be. We were so careful."

"Then we're looking at another miracle because the hospital ran tests before they treated you and confirmed it. Unfortunately, they won't risk giving you much in the way of pain relief."

"I don't mind."

Griff kissed her. "Can I tell you what I've been thinking ever since they told me?"

"What?"

"I hope it's a boy."

For my editor, Noah J.D. Chinn
Without Noah, this book would not exist.
I wrote the original draft in 2015, but never completed it.
I revisited the manuscript several times over the years,
but I couldn't pinpoint what was missing nor could
others who read it.
Nothing became clear until Noah beta read it in 2022
and identified the
weaknesses in the story and suggested several avenues to
make my idea workable.
I then did a lot of rewriting before Noah did a first pass
edit.
Without his help, I would still be floundering. I am forever grateful.

Acknowledgements

Thank you to all the members of Lakeland Writers who read and critiqued numerous pages of Animal over many months. Their encouragement was invaluable.

Thank you to Sandy Carmouche for her friendship, patience, feedback and cheerleading. She read an early draft and offered many helpful suggestions.

Thank you to editor Noah Chinn for beta reading, editing and more editing, and for pointing me in the direction this story needed to go.

Thank you to cover artist Stephen Novak.

Thank you to Bill for his never-ending support and for his patience with cover consultations.

Thank you to beta readers Jessica Cash and Cristy Spangler for their enthusiasm and feedback.

As always, I thank God for every bit of writing talent, direction, and inspiration He gives me.

Thank you everyone who took the time to read and review Animal, especially Joz via Book Sirens.

Dear Readers,

Paranormal romance is a new genre for me, and I know *Animal* doesn't follow the typical path of a paranormal romance. If it wasn't what you were expecting, I hope you were pleasantly surprised.

Whatever you felt about it after reading it, I kindly ask that you review it. Reviews are extremely important to authors, and you are doing a great service by leaving one and I will truly appreciate it.

Although this is in no way a Christian book, as I edged closer to finishing this book, two Biblical-related themes emerged for me.

The first is about generational sin, which mirrored in a way, the generational curse put on Griff's family and comes from Exodus 21:5:

"And when I punish people for their sins, the punishment continues upon the children, grandchildren, and great-grandchildren of those who hate me;"

The second is from John 15:13:

"Greater love hath no man than this, that a man lay down his life for his friends."

For more about me, my writing journey, and my books, please sign up for my newsletter and follow me on social media via my website: http://barbarameyers.com

I wish you much enjoyable reading in your future.

Sincerely,

Barbara Meyers

About the Author

Since I am unable to concentrate on one genre, I write an eclectic mix of contemporary romance and women's fiction stories which often feature a displaced child.

Who knew I'd still be married to my first husband, have two fantastic children and adopt Winner, a rescue who looks like a black lab but isn't.

Originally I'm from Southwest Missouri, (I blame my roots in the Show Me state for my somewhat skeptical nature) but I currently reside in Central Florida.

When I'm not writing or doing writing-related things, I'm reading, taking Winner for walks, or bicycling around my neighborhood.

Come visit me at www.barbarameyers.com

Look for these titles

Cleo's Web

White Roses in Winter

Training Tommy

A Family for St. Nick (Christmas Novella)

Coming Soon:

Those Who Can, Date

Barbara Meyers writing comedic fantasy as AJ Tillock:

The Grinding Reality Series:

The Forbidden Bean (Book One)

Cool Beans (Book Two)

www.ingramcontent.com/pod-product-compliance
Lightning Source LLC
Chambersburg PA
CBHW050947210726
48287CB00004B/1165